THE DARKNESS OF

STARS

THE DARKNESS OF

STARS

A Dustpunk Faerytale

Sydney Cobb

For Madison,
I promised the first one to you.

PROLOGUE

"You must carry a chaos inside you to give birth to a dancing star."

—Friedrich Nietzsche

Thirteen years later, the little star wouldn't remember quite what had happened. He wouldn't remember who he had been with, how he gotten there, where he had come from. He would only remember the chaos. Everywhere, there had been chaos. At five years old, he couldn't understand all of what was happening, but he knew enough. He knew he couldn't find his parents.

He had let go of his mother's dress, the mass of scattering people had pushed him away from her, and now he couldn't see her or his father anywhere.

Through the bodies of fleeing Seelie and the mass of attackers, he caught a glimpse of the queen, saw her place her granddaughter into the arms of a man he knew was her husband, and she pointed off toward something. The boy wondered where the little girl's own parents were, but the queen ran off in another direction and out of sight, and he forgot about why it seemed so important.

He kept searching, looking for someone, anyone he might know, in the midst of the crowd. He had only just met the queen, and she still seemed foreign to him. He wouldn't go after her. Someone called out to him.

He whipped around and looked up. The man was tall, with light brown hair, and his smile didn't quite reach his grey eyes, though the boy wasn't quite old enough to realize a false smile yet. He would become far more familiar with it later on.

The man crouched down so that they were at each other's eye level. "You're Jiri and Erran's little boy, aren't you?"

The boy couldn't find his voice to answer. He nodded.

The man's smile grew, and it glinted off his eyes this time. "I know where they are. Do you want to come with me?" He stood and held out a hand.

The boy nodded again. His unruly red hair fell into his eyes, and he brushed it away from a face full of freckles, letting the man take his hand and lead him away.

ONE

"I wonder what is out there in the quiet of the sky..."

—Ellis Felker

For whatever reasons, Ainsley Harper was simply not allowed outside at night, not once the stars came out. Her grandfather had, in fact, expressly forbidden it. Townsley Harper was not a bad man, far from it actually; he just believed in protecting Ainsley from...

Well, Ainsley had yet to discover what it was he was protecting her from.

At any rate, if she could not go outside, then she would let the out in. She would open her window as wide as it would go and would turn off all the lights in her room to let in the ink of the night sky. This night, it was well past midnight and well past the time her grandfather had wanted her to be in bed and asleep.

At the moment, she didn't care what he wanted. The two of them had had an argument over her parents, earlier during dinner, and she hadn't talked to him the rest of the night.

Ainsley had lost both of her parents when she was two. She couldn't remember much about them. She had asked her grandfather more than once what had happened to them, but every time, she would only get half-answers, and even those answers occasionally changed. She didn't ask about them often, but when the stars were especially bright, she found herself wondering. She had asked questions, he had given no answers, neither had been willing to bend, and everything had quickly gone downhill. She didn't feel guilty about yelling at him. What had made her feel guilty was the way he had gone quiet when she pushed too far, the way his expression looked hurt.

She didn't want to feel guilty. She wanted to stay angry.

The night was cool, and there was a slight breeze drifting into the window, stirring her white-blonde hair softly. The stars were out brighter than Ainsley had ever seen them, it seemed. Ainsley's mind drifted back to a lullaby of her mother's, a song that she remembered mostly from her grandfather singing to her on starry nights.

She leaned over on the windowsill, dark eyes half-lidded, and sang the lullaby to herself.

"There once was a star, fell in love with the moon,

5

But the moon was a jealous thing.
Said the star to the moon, 'I'd do anything
To prove my love to you.'
The moon desired the star's magic wand,
And so she thought of a plan.
Said the moon to the star, 'You need only do this,
And then my love shall be yours.
Go down to the sea and bring back for me
My reflection bright on the waves.'
And so the star, blinded by love,
Knew not he would go to his grave.
The star flew down to bring back his gift.
A hand came up from the sea.
The star sank down beneath the waves,
And the moon, she smiled with glee.
The wand was lost to the care of the Maids,
To belong to the stars no more.
So trust not shadows made in the night,
Lest they lead you astray."

She had just started to drift to sleep when something crashed into the closed section of window. Ainsley started, thinking the sound had been her grandfather still awake. Then she realized that whatever had flown into the window was sitting dazed on the windowsill.

She rubbed her eyes and looked again.

"What kind of bug…?" she asked.

The thing on the sill blinked at her with unnaturally large eyes and cooed.

"What…are you?"

It looked like a tiny person fitted with dragonfly wings. It had a brown face and wild hair and was clothed in what might have been leaves.

"Star," the creature said, pointing at her. Ainsley was standing now, staring and wondering if she'd need something bigger than a flyswatter. "Star," it said again. Ainsley didn't move.

The creature made a frustrated, raspberry sound and pulled a wad of paper from its belt. It handed it up to Ainsley, shaking it impatiently when she hesitated.

The creature put off enough light to read by, and Ainsley unrolled the note, reading the intricate handwriting slowly.

Ainsley,

It's time for you to come back to Seelie Court. Your grandmother needs you. Follow the pixie. Answers when you arrive.

-Indigo

PS: Bring the gear.

"Okay then," Ainsley said, bemused. "'Follow the pixie'. That's not weird." A sudden thought, a memory, came to her. "No way." She looked down at the creature, who was attempting to untie the string around its waist. "Wickertwig?" she asked it.

The pixie looked up at her in response, and then there was no denying anything. "Wickertwig," she said again. "My old imaginary friend, from when I was little. You were real all along."

The pixie cooed with delight, gnawing on the string. No one else Ainsley knew had ever believed her when she'd said he was real. They couldn't see him. After a while, he'd disappeared off somewhere, and Ainsley hadn't seen him again. Eventually, she'd convinced herself that she *had* imagined him.

To discover she *hadn't* made him up—

She wasn't yet sure what to think, but part of her seemed to accept the idea.

"Alright, then, Twig," she said, slipping into the use of his old nickname. "What is this gear?"

Wickertwig shook the piece of copper on the string.

"Easy enough," Ainsley said, untying the string and regarding the gear in her hand. It looked like a piece of a clock. She shook her head. "This is crazy. My grandmother's dead."

Her grandfather had never told Ainsley how she'd died. The same as with her parents, he was always skirting the subject. If this person had answers…

Wickertwig had taken to exploring Ainsley's bedroom and was presently examining his reflection in the television screen.

"My granddad knows these people?" she asked him.

He shrugged, shaking his head.

"You don't know?" He shook his head. She thought for a moment. "What is a Seelie Court? And this Pixie Tree and...a hill?"

"Through hollow tree," he answered, as if it was all very simple. "Not far. We go?"

The thought crossed her mind to ask her grandfather about the note, but it was quickly stamped out. He would never allow her to even go outside at night, much less go traipsing about, looking for a tree. She remembered how angry she was with him and decided she just wouldn't ask. Forgiveness could come later.

The thought also crossed her mind that this could be a very bad idea, meeting up with someone she didn't even know, in the middle of the woods at night. But the possibility that she could learn something about her grandmother, maybe even her parents, far outweighed logical reasoning.

"Yes," she said. "We go."

She changed out of her pajamas and into a long-sleeved shirt and jeans, running her fingers through her pale blonde waves to smooth them out. She turned her backpack upside down and dumped out the pencils and school books and started filling it with other things: her cellphone, a few candy bars she'd stashed in her desk drawer, a flashlight, and a notebook and pen in case she needed to take notes. Then she fished a silver chain out of her jewelry box, threaded the gear onto it, and fastened it around her neck.

As an afterthought, she fished her pocketknife out of her closet and tucked it into an outer pocket of her backpack. Just in case. Surely, she could be both reasonable and reckless at the same time.

She took a last look around to see if she had forgotten something before turning to Wickertwig. "Alright," she said, partially to herself. "Let's go."

He flitted out the window and hovered, waiting. She tossed the backpack out first, belatedly realizing she should be quieter. Then she went out the window backwards, thankful for living in a single-story house. She closed the window behind her, slung the backpack over a shoulder, and motioned for the pixie to lead the way.

The pair of them had barely made it to the line of woods in the backyard when a voice stopped them.

"Where are you going?"

Ainsley turned around, but the voice didn't belong to her grandfather.

Khade lived next door to Ainsley and her grandfather and was Ainsley's best friend. He was of average height, a few inches taller than Ainsley, with dark brown hair and blue eyes and skin tanned from the sun. He was sixteen, not quite a full year older than Ainsley, but he still usually let her tell him what to do.

"Nowhere," she said.

Khade snorted a laugh. "If your granddad catches you, you're dead. You know that, right?"

"'If' is rather open to interpretation, don't you think?" she said.

"Hm." He arched an eyebrow at her. "What *are* you doing? You and I both know you're not supposed to be out here." He eyed the backpack. "Running away?"

She shook her head, though she supposed she was, in a sense. "Wickertwig, my imaginary friend, the pixie—you remember him, right?"

Khade nodded. "Yeah. I thought you'd never give that thing up when we were younger."

Ainsley pointed to Wickertwig. "Well, turns out, he's not so imaginary. And he brought me this note that said my grandmother needed me, and—"

"Whoa, whoa, wait," Khade said, holding up his hands. "I thought your grandma was dead. And what are you pointing at?"

"Well, I've always believed she was dead too, but then I got this letter, and I have to go see for myself. It's kind of complicated, and I don't really understand it either. I'll explain when I get back." She stopped to take a breath. "And I was pointing at Wickertwig. My pixie."

Khade gave her an incredulous look. "Your pixie?"

Ainsley sighed. "Yes. My pixie. Apparently, I'm the only one who can see him, or else everyone would've believed me when I used to say he was real. Just trust me on this."

Khade rolled his eyes, shrugging. "I think you're hallucinating, but okay. Whatever. And hey, wait a minute. What do you mean 'when you get back'?"

"I already told you. I'm going to find the person who wrote me that letter and sent Wickertwig to find me."

11

"Are you serious?" he asked, like he was sure that she wasn't.

Ainsley answered him with a flat stare.

He sighed. "Fine then. I'm coming with you. Someone's got to make sure you don't fall in a hole and die."

"What? No, you're not coming. You're going back to your house, and you're not telling anyone about this," she said, poking him in sharply in the shoulder.

He crossed his arms. "Or I could tell your granddad. So either you let me come with you, or you spend the rest of high school grounded."

He smirked when she deflated. "Fine. You can come," she agreed and turned to start off into the woods. "And you'd better be glad you're not in your pajamas, 'cause I wouldn't have waited for you to change."

"Yeah, I fell asleep in my clothes," he said, shrugging. "I woke up and was going to change, and I saw the light outside. Figured I'd check it out."

Ainsley gripped her flashlight sullenly and continued as if she hadn't heard him. Khade just smiled and followed her into the woods.

The trees were thin enough to make maneuvering through them fairly easy, but Khade still kept tripping over unearthed roots and vines as he read the letter Ainsley had handed him.

"This is insane, Ainsley," he said, eyes on the note as he stumbled along behind her and Wickertwig. "This Indigo person is totally crazy. What the heck is he talking about, anyway? I mean, seriously?"

Ainsley rolled her eyes. "I already told you, Khade. I only know what's in the letter. Meaning, I know what you know."

"Yeah, I guess," he conceded. "How far is—whoa!"

He almost ran into Ainsley when she stopped, pointing ahead of where she was standing. Wickertwig was hovering in front of a large tree with twisted bark and a wide hollow that extended up from the ground. Mushrooms grew in a little ring around its base, popping up through the grass between winding, uncovered roots.

"I think that might be it," Ainsley said.

Khade didn't look impressed. "That didn't take too long. So now what?"

Wickertwig waved his hand in a beckoning motion and flitted into the hollow. Ainsley headed after him. Khade grabbed her by the shoulder as she got down on her knees.

"Hold on a minute," he said, pulling her back up to her feet. "I'll go first."

Ainsley brushed his hand off. "If it makes you happy," she said, watching him crawl through the hollow. "Not like it's going to eat me or anything."

She waited a moment for him to come back out and announce that it was okay for her to take a look as well, but he didn't come. "Khade?" She tapped her foot impatiently, making a show for when he reappeared. He didn't. "Khade," she repeated, sticking her head into the hollow. She couldn't see anything and crawled a little further inside—

—And fell right through the other side, rolling down a rather sizable hill and landing on something soft that moved.

Khade started mumbling, purposely making himself just loud enough to be heard, but Ainsley wasn't listening, instead training her attention on keeping up with the pixie in front of her, who was flying jerkily from one side to the other in a sort of haphazard waltz. She only hoped that she hadn't made a very large mistake.

TWO

"You and I are flesh and blood, but we are also stardust."

—Helena Curtis, *Biology*

    Rowan stood in front of Lord Zake with a carefully neutral expression. The man lounging behind the desk looked as he had thirteen years ago, when they had first met and Zake had taken over rule. He had the same cold eyes that seldom smiled, even when his mouth did, and pale brown hair that had not greyed even slightly. Nor would it any time soon. Stars took centuries to show signs of age, and Zake had several more yet to go.

Rowan pushed stray red hair out of his face and stole a glance to his right from beneath his hand. The man standing there had a much rougher appearance. His dirty-blond hair was long and tangled at the ends. He was large and muscled, and his eyes were glimmering with a malicious grin. He was half river troll and half star, meaning he was both terrifying and powerful. His name was Fince, and he seemed to make it his personal goal in life to be as vicious to Rowan as possible.

A hand came up to rest on Rowan's left shoulder, and he turned to look the other person in the eye. This third man was tall as well, taller than Zake but shorter than Fince. He had black skin and dreadlocks that were currently pulled back from his face and tied with a ribbon. His ears curved into short, pointed tips. Joel was the closest person Rowan had to a parent. He never had found his real parents again after getting separated all those years ago. Zake had made sure of that.

Joel gave Rowan a look that he understood to mean he shouldn't press his luck at the moment.

Rowan turned back to watch Zake as the latter began to speak, and the hand dropped from his shoulder.

"So this morning, I had placed something in my room, on the desk," Zake said, twirling a pen in his hand. "And then tonight, when I returned, it was gone." He looked up at Rowan pointedly. "Strange, isn't that?"

Rowan's expression moved into one of cautious curiosity. "Maybe one of the maids misplaced it when they were cleaning. Have you asked around in the servants' quarters?"

It was a dangerous game they were playing, seemingly harmless words tossed back and forth, but Zake seemed to be enjoying himself. "I quite imagined it might have sprouted legs and walked off," he said. "Or wings maybe, tiny wings, and it flew straight out the window."

Rowan could feel the panic start to stir inside him. Surely the mention of wings was a coincidence. "I'm sorry, sir. I'm not actually certain what this object is that we're talking about."

Zake stood and came around to lean against the front of his desk. "Have you ever seen the inside of a clock? They're so meticulous and orderly, clocks. I like things that are orderly, people that are orderly."

Zake was messing with his head, Rowan knew that, but still he asked in a confused voice, "Sir?"

"It's a small copper gear, came out of one my clocks. My favorite clock actually. I had been repairing a broken piece earlier and accidently left out a gear on my desk. My only request is that you keep your eyes open for it and tell me if someone happens to find it." Zake smiled, eyes blank and mirthless.

Rowan forced a smile onto his own face and inclined his head in a sort of semi-bow. "Of course, sir."

Zake didn't remove his gaze from Rowan as he continued. "Joel, if you wouldn't mind staying a bit longer, there are some things I need to discuss privately with you. Fince, if you would escort Rowan back to his room, please."

19

Rowan hoped his expression hadn't broken into one of terror as he turned and left the room with Fince following closely behind him. He could feel Joel watching him as he walked away.

They had arrived in front of the door to his quarters, and Rowan was just beginning to think, beyond hope, that he had escaped with luck on his side today when Fince wrapped a hand around his arm and spun him around. Rowan winced, slightly in pain but mostly in expectation of what was coming.

"You know what I think?" Fince hissed in Rowan's face. Rowan didn't much care what he thought, only that Fince needed to brush the scent of pond water from his teeth, but Fince didn't give him time to say that. "I think you got your little friend to take that gear. He's known for having sticky fingers, the little sneak."

Rowan tried to free his arm. "What would I want with a piece of a clock?" he asked.

"Maybe your girlfriend took it then." Fince gave an unpleasant smile. "She's a pretty little thing, isn't she? Wonder if she'd tell me where it was if I asked nice enough."

Rowan jerked his arm away angrily. "You leave Indigo alone, or I swear—"

"What?" Fince asked, shoving Rowan against the door and bracing a firm hand against his chest. "You'll what?"

Rowan couldn't answer. The familiar burn started over his skin as tiny specks of golden dust hung around Fince's hand. His breath started coming in rapid spurts of panic. He knew what was happening, knew from experience what a Dusting felt like, and there was nothing he could do about it except pointlessly hope Joel would come down the hall. If he fought back, Fince would only beat him senseless and then Dust him anyway. He suspected Zake had kept Joel behind for this reason.

"Go on," Fince whispered, far too close and smelling like algae. "Tell me what you'd do."

Rowan's knees were starting to feel weak. His left hand groped for the door handle, but his brain wouldn't cooperate and he couldn't get the handle to turn. His vision began to fade into a whorl of bright, blurred colors.

He heard Fince snicker. "That's right. You can't do anything."

The knob turned in Rowan's hand. The door swung open from the weight against it, and he fell backwards as Fince stumbled forward. Rowan kicked the door shut, slamming Fince in the face. He scrambled up and turned the lock as Fince started swearing in the hall.

Unsteady on his feet, still in disoriented panic, he staggered blindly into the dresser and blacked out.

***

Humming. Someone was humming softly.

Rowan opened his eyes, slowly, to see where it was coming from, but all he could see was black, and a faint light lingering around the edges. He blinked a few times, but it looked the same. Belatedly, he realized there was something cool and damp draped over his forehead, and he pushed it up out of his eyes.

21

He was in his room, on his bed, and someone had removed his jacket and hung it over the back of his desk chair. A few lit candles were on top of the dresser, and a pixie-dust lantern was glowing on the desk. The window was open, letting in a light breeze and a stream of moonlight.

Across the room, he could see Indigo's half-shadowed figure. Her dark brown hair was almost black in the dim light, except for the stripe that grew white down one side of her face. Rowan watched her bustle quietly around, picking up shirts that had found their way onto the floor and straightening stacks of charts and maps, humming to herself all the while. Rowan smiled. He thought she had a pretty voice, but he figured he was slightly biased in his opinion.

Rowan pushed himself up to sitting position as silently as possible so as not to disturb her. Now she was picking at a stain on the desk, made from when he had overturned a bottle of ink. Her face was scrunched up in concentration.

"That's kinda creepy, man."

Rowan and Indigo both jumped and turned to look toward the door. Indigo's twin brother, Dekk, was leaning against the frame, arms crossed. His mismatched eyes, one blue and the other green, shimmered in amusement. His white hair gleamed in the candlelight. "You left this in my room," he said, and tossed Rowan's sketchbook across to him. Rowan caught it with an annoyed look at him.

Dekk came into the room and closed the door behind him with a dirty bare foot. "Thought you might want it at some point," he said, jumping up on the dresser to sit dangerously close to one of the lit candles. "Unless you want to go back to staring at my sister. Then, of course, I don't mind."

Indigo marched up to him and punched him in the arm. "You could've let me know you were standing there. You startled me." Then she turned to Rowan, who was giving Dekk a dirty look. "And you could've let me know you were awake," she said, embarrassed anger overtaking the concern she might have otherwise shown. She had mismatched eyes like her brother, though hers were blue and brown.

Rowan did his best to appear contrite. "Sorry."

Indigo huffed, but her face softened quickly enough and she shook her head and went back to scraping at the ink stain.

Rowan nodded his head at Dekk. "How long have you been standing there?"

Dekk grinned. "Long enough to wish I hadn't been."

Indigo flung a wadded-up shirt at his head.

Rowan arched an eyebrow at him. "And you say I'm creepy."

Dekk's grin only widened.

Indigo gave up on the ink stain and came over and sat on the edge of the bed. Her face was serious. "So what happened?"

Rowan's first instinct was to play dumb, the same game he played with Zake and Fince, and the words tumbled out from habit, "What happened when?" and he could've slapped himself for thinking she would accept that as an answer.

Indigo only said, "You know what I mean."

23

Rowan sighed. "Fince said something, and it set me off. I knew he was doing it on purpose, and I walked into it anyway."

"What did he say?"

"He said… He mentioned you." His voice sounded dangerous. "I didn't like his tone."

Indigo blinked and looked at Dekk. His eyes were dark. She placed her hand on Rowan's knee. "Come on, guys. You know I can take care of myself." It was truthful, but she'd also meant to be hintingly humorous. No one laughed.

"Either way," Dekk said, "Next chance I get, Fince is going to find something slimy in his bed."

"Other than himself?" Rowan asked doubtfully.

Indigo and Dekk both gave a muffled laugh, and the atmosphere lightened somewhat. At least until Rowan asked, "How long was I out?" He wasn't even sure he wanted to know.

Dekk glanced at the clock on the wall. "A little over an hour, I think."

"I think you scared a few years off Joel," Indigo said. "He tried to get in, but Dekk had to come and pick the lock. He was here until a few minutes ago. Zake called him back for something."

"He knows we took it," Rowan said. "Zake does, I mean."

"Was he angry?"

Rowan shook his head, confused. "I don't think so. He seemed almost, I don't know, amused. Like it was a game."

"He's only going to think it's a game as long as he's winning."

"So we keep him thinking he is," Dekk remarked, and yawned. He looked like a cat.

Rowan fingered the corner of his sketchbook. "It's late. You two should go to bed."

Dekk nodded, sliding down from the dresser and yawning again. "Yeah, that sounds good. Good night." He slipped out the door and across the hall to his own room.

"You too," Rowan added when he noticed that Indigo hadn't moved.

She pushed him down and crawled up beside him. "Nope. I don't want to leave you. You scared me."

"Sorry," he said, letting her take the sketchbook from his hands and place it on the bedside table.

"Not your fault." Part of him wanted to argue with that, but she went on. "I talked to Merdi earlier. She said she'd let me know when the Harper girl shows up."

"*If* she shows up," Rowan corrected.

Indigo sighed into his shoulder. "I'm too tired to think about ifs right now."

"Okay," he said and fell silent, staring at the ceiling, but his thoughts chased one another around in his head, refusing to be quieted so easily.

***

Rowan was awakened by something vibrating in his pocket. Indigo was still asleep beside him, and his right arm was asleep beneath

25

her. He eased it out from under her, managing not to disturb her, and shook his hand in an attempt to stop the tingling. The candles on the dresser had burned out, but the pixie-dust lantern was still glowing.

He slid a round compact mirror out of his pocket and eased it open with his thumb. Joel's face immediately stared back at him.

"Sorry to wake you," said his voice from the mirror. "Feel any better?"

"A little," Rowan shrugged sleepily.

Joel nodded without seeming terribly convinced. "I tried to call Dekk and Indie first. Neither of them answered."

"Dekk's asleep in his room, as far as I know." He looked over at Indigo. "I guess Indigo left her talking-glass in her room."

"Left it in her room? Where is she now?"

"She's with me."

"Oh." Joel smiled knowingly. "In your room, then."

Rowan's face broke out into a furious blush. "Shut up. Why did you call me?"

"Partly because your friends were otherwise occupied." He had to stifle a laugh at the look Rowan gave him. "Mostly though, I needed to tell you something." He sighed heavily. "Zake is sending us out tonight. The starshooters have hit another one. It's somewhere close to Merdi's Pixie Tree. Fince'll be gone too, so you won't have to worry about him for a little while."

Rowan's heart sank. "Did you tell Merdi you'd be near her house?"

"No, she'll likely be asleep, and we have no reason to bother her anyway." Joel looked hard at him, studied his face. "Rowan, are you okay? You look really pale."

Rowan forced a laugh. "I'm always pale."

"More so than usual then," Joel said and then paused, thinking. "Have you done something I don't know about?"

Leave it to Joel to get straight to the truth in a matter of moments.

"If I have, I'm sure you'll find out soon enough."

"That's not funny, Rowan."

"It wasn't supposed to be."

Joel sighed again. "Get some rest. You look terrible."

"Appreciate your honesty, as always," Rowan said, and he flipped the talking-glass shut without saying good bye.

He knew that he shouldn't be angry with Joel, but he had to have someone to take it out on. Joel had been the one to tell him about the gear, what Zake had said it was, what it was for. Joel hadn't been the one to tell Dekk and Indigo, though. He hadn't been there while the three of them planned out what to do. He hadn't written the note. Indigo had, because her handwriting was neatest. And Dekk had been the one to steal the gear. Rowan hadn't done anything but get them into trouble.

He felt lightheaded and sick, and he wasn't sure whether it was from apprehension or from the lack of stardust in his system. He lay back down on the bed. He hadn't planned on starshooters finding the girl as soon as she arrived.

If she arrived tonight, he reminded himself. He smiled, just slightly. Thank goodness for pessimism.

He closed his eyes. He was exhausted. He only hoped that, if the girl showed up, Merdi would have the good sense to keep her hidden.

THREE

"Come away, O human child!
To the waters and the wild
With a faery, hand in hand,
For the world's more full of weeping than you can understand."

—W.B. Yeats, *The Stolen Child*

They had been walking for a little over an hour, at least according to Khade's sense of time, and Ainsley was beginning to wonder if they were going the wrong direction entirely. She didn't say anything. She would never hear the end of it.

She turned to glance at Khade behind her. He had settled into a sleepy sullen silence and there were scratch marks across his face from where he'd run into a tree branch. He looked incredibly displeased. Ainsley opened her mouth to break the quiet. Khade spoke first.

"What's that smell?"

Ainsley started to say she didn't smell anything. Then it reached her, a gagging combination of over-ripe cheese and dirty socks. Wickertwig was scenting the air like a dog and then went still, his wings moving only enough to keep him in the air.

"Goblins," he whispered.

"Goblins?" Ainsley repeated.

Khade looked at her. "What?"

"He said it was goblins," she said, glancing around.

"The pixie said," Khade said doubtfully.

Ainsley ignored him. "Are goblins bad?" she asked Twig.

"They eat pixies," Wickertwig said.

"What about people?" she asked, but the little faery only darted into her backpack, leaving them in shadow beneath the canopy of trees.

"It just got darker," Khade said.

Ainsley turned to look at him. Something moved in the dark next to him. "Khade, there's something in the bushes beside you," she said, pointing.

The thing shifted, and Khade jerked his hand away with a cry of pain. Blood dripped from a jagged bite mark.

He whipped around to see what had bitten him, backing toward Ainsley as he stared at it. The thing in front of him was about three, maybe four feet tall, with greenish brown mottled skin and black eyes. Its serrated teeth were bared and stained with Khade's blood.

"What the heck is that?" he cried.

"There are more of them," Ainsley whimpered, looking around. Three more had come out of the underbrush and were gazing at her with hungry beetle-like eyes.

A loud wailing sound came tearing from between the trees. Something with a disfigured appearance ran out at them, waving a large branch over what looked like its two heads. Ainsley and Khade dove instinctually out of the way, but the creature wasn't headed for either of them. It shook the branch at the goblins, growling something in a strange language that neither Khade nor Ainsley could understand. The goblins growled something back and inched closer. The two-headed creature wailed again, branch held high, and the goblins scattered back into the brush.

The creature turned to Ainsley and Khade, and they saw that it wasn't disfigured after all. It was an older-looking lady, no more than five feet tall and pleasantly plump, with short curly black hair and violet eyes. Her ears jutted out through her hair and ended in sharp, slender tips. Her second head was not actually a head, but rather—

"Goblin!" Ainsley cried. "There's a goblin on you!"

"Oh easy, deary," the lady said in a heavy accent that sounded vaguely Scottish. "That's only Hobbs. He wouldn't hurt a thing. Scared of everything, he is."

"Hobbs?" Ainsley said, at the same time that Khade said, "You named it?"

"Don't be stupid, boy. I didn't name him. Every creature comes into this world with a name. All fey have a true name to set them apart," the lady said, tossing the branch down and patting the goblin on the head. One of his cat-like ears had a bite taken out of it, making it shorter than the other. He looked a bit like a puppy that had been genetically crossed with a toad. "And his name — at least part of it — is really Hobblewiggen, but that's a bit long, so we call him Hobbs."

She took in Ainsley and Khade's astonished faces and laughed. "But there I go, chattering away like someone senile. The name's Merdi, dears. But I have to say, I was only expecting one of you." Their expressions only increased in alarm. "Oh, I'm going to take you to the Pixie Tree, don't worry. I know all about that note you were sent. And where's little Wickertwig, I wonder?"

Wickertwig flew out of Ainsley's backpack and snuggled against Merdi's cheek affectionately. "Oh, there you are, dear. Now go on ahead. We'll be along soon." He darted off in the direction they had been headed previously.

Khade's eyes widened. "Was that the pixie?" he asked in awe, watching the glowing ball disappear between the leaves.

Ainsley turned to him. "You can see him now?"

"Hmm, probably because of that bite," Merdi remarked, sounding thoughtful. "You've acquired the Sight, dearest. You can see everything now. That looks a bit nasty though. We'll want to clean that up in a minute."

Khade stared at her as if she was crazy, and Ainsley was starting to think she might be.

"I don't mean to frighten you, believe me," the lady said with a kind smile. "You must be Ainsley. So then, young man. Who are you?"

Khade stammered for a confused moment before answering. "Uh, Khade."

"Well, aren't you both adorable." Merdi patted his face lovingly. "Come along now, you both can get some rest, and I'll explain that note a little better than Indigo did."

"Why?" Ainsley asked. "Why should we follow you?" went unspoken but implied.

"Dear, if I wanted to do you harm, I'd have left you to the goblins."

Ainsley and Khade exchanged a glance, but they couldn't argue with the logic. And Ainsley had a desperate desire to find out more.

Merdi seemed to know they would follow her and turned to walk off in the same direction Wickertwig had gone. Trailing behind her, Ainsley noticed immediately that she had a long tail, tipped with a tuft of black at the end.

"What are you?" she blurted before she could stop herself.

Merdi didn't seem offended in the least. "I'm a forest troll, dear." Hobbs still clung to her back like a baby monkey. He hadn't made a sound so far.

Merdi pushed aside a few branches, and then they were all in a clearing. A large tree house was built among the limbs of several enormous trees and a small fire burned on the ground, lined by a circle of stones. The glow of pixie-dust seemed to be everywhere.

"Wow," Ainsley breathed. "It's so pretty."

"Glad you like it, dear," Merdi said.

"Why are there so many pixies here?"

"Pixie-dust is quite useful for a lot of things around here. The dust falls off their wings, and then it's collected and used." She waved a hand at the clearing. "This is one of the places used to house pixies. They're allowed to come and go as they please, and they have a safe haven to stay. It's all very nice at both ends of the bargain. We also happen to have our own guard-goblin. Even if he is terrified of everything."

Hobbs apparently saw his chance at escape from these strange people and climbed down from Merdi's back and skittered away up one of the trees. Merdi shook her head at him. "Don't worry, he's always like that. He'll talk to you soon enough."

Ainsley didn't see why his not-talking would worry her.

Khade asked, "He can talk? Like, he can speak normally, or he'll sound like the monsters that just tried to eat us?"

"Well of course he can speak normally. I'm the one who taught him."

Khade looked as if he might pursue the subject, but Ainsley had only one question on her mind. She pulled the note from her pocket. "So what was the point of this?" she asked, holding it out for Merdi to take.

"You keep it, dear," Merdi said, pushing it back to Ainsley. "Make yourself comfortable by the fire, and I'll get some tea and something to clean that bite with."

Ainsley and Khade sat down, far from comfortable, as Merdi clambered into the tree house.

"This is insane," Khade muttered.

"Mysterious notes don't get sent every day, Khade," Ainsley said, shedding her backpack and setting it down beside her. "I have to know what it means."

Khade gave her a look that was far from amused. "Maybe there's a reason they don't get sent every day," he muttered.

"All right then," Merdi said, returning and settling down beside Khade. "Let's see that, and I can fill you in, Ainsley." Khade reluctantly extended his hand to her. "How much do you know about your parents, then?"

Ainsley felt suddenly very ignorant. "Not really that much. My grandfather never tells me about them."

Merdi stared at her. "But surely you know what you are, at least?" she asked. Ainsley only stared at her.

"Oh, Townsley, I swear," Merdi said, shaking her head in annoyance. "That man is something else. *What*, I'm not sure, but something."

"Wait, you know my grandfather?" Ainsley said.

"Yes, dear, and it seems he hasn't changed much since the last time I saw him, before your grandmother and parents disappeared."

"He told me they were dead," Ainsley clarified. "Not disappeared. Of course, he didn't tell me he was friends with a troll either," she added bitterly.

Merdi's eyebrows went up, but she continued wrapping Khade's hand without comment on that particular statement. "I suppose I'd better start at the beginning then." She sighed. "Wherever that is. There you are, dear."

Khade retracted his hand, turning it over and then looking at her. "Thanks."

"Never tell a faery 'thank you', dear. It's such an empty statement, and it's sure to get you into more trouble than you're likely to get out of."

Khade didn't ask why that was. He didn't look like he wanted to know.

Merdi settled cross-legged on the ground, her skirts pooling around her. Ainsley noticed that she'd forgotten about the tea, but Ainsley didn't really like it much anyway so she said nothing.

"Now then, Ainsley. Your grandmother — Saydie, most people called her Say — was a star."

36

"A star?" Ainsley asked.

"Oh dear, I'm going to have some kind of words with Townsley," Merdi said, turning her eyes upward for a moment. "The stars in the sky, dear. They're not all that ball-of-flaming-gas gibberish that gets put into books where you live. They're people. Say was one of them. She was also the Seelie Queen of Avyn."

"Seelie Queen of Avyn?"

"Yes, you're in Avyn right now, in Seelie territory. You're her heir."

Khade glanced at Ainsley, unfazed. "Princess Ainsley. Has a nice ring to it." But she was listening intently to Merdi.

"Now dear, save your questions till I'm finished, and I might answer some along the way."

Ainsley nodded.

"Say married Townsley, who is fully human, and he became Seelie King through marriage. Your father was born to the two of them. He married your mother, who was a full-blooded star, and then you came along. That makes you three-quarters star. Your father was the heir to Say's kingdom, a right which would have been passed on to you. And then Zake stepped in.

"Zake is a star too, Say's older brother actually. He was jealous of the fact that Say had been handed the throne from their parents, even though he was firstborn, and he was power-hungry. If he were to get Say and her family out of the way, the Seelie throne would fall to him. He took over the Unseelie throne first, ruled for a few good decades, and most of the Unseelie didn't mind his cruelty. They tend to possess a bit of a dark streak themselves. Having acquired a kingdom of his own, Say didn't think he would become too much of a problem — at least, no more than the Unseelie usually are — but he gained enough support to lead an Unseelie army against her. Their kind is almost always out for a fight, just for the pure thrill of bloodshed. Zake left Lady Morag, a favorite subject of his and just as cruel, as his regent to rule the Unseelie territories in his place while he ruled the Seelie lands personally. He rules both Seelie and Unseelie lands now, king of all Avyn, but Townsley escaped with you, and Say and your parents weren't found. He's still looking for them. He thinks they fled to Skyline, the land of the stars, high in the sky. That piece of copper around your neck—" she pointed to the metal disk "—is what we think will open the gate to Skyline, a supposedly missing piece, to allow us to gain the upper hand after all this time. It was taken from Zake's room, and he seems rather keen to find it again.

"So Rowan, Dekk, and Indigo — you'll meet them soon enough — created a plan to get you back into Avyn. We need your help, and the help of the other stars in Skyline. Aside from you, Zake and Rowan are the only known stars alive in Avyn right now, and Rowan's only going to stay that way as long as he's useful to Zake. Zake is the only person we know of who knows where the gate to Skyline is." Merdi sighed. "And it seems you might not know where it is either. It certainly seems your grandfather never told, if even he knew, the old fart."

"I'm sorry," Ainsley said. "I don't know. Are you sure there are only two other stars besides me?"

"Well, Fince is half star, but he's also half river troll. He works for Zake. He's a nasty bit of work. And there are stars shot down all the time, but they never last long."

"What do you mean, shot down?" Khade interjected.

"Shooting stars, dear," Merdi said sadly. "That's where the name comes from. They're shot down out of the sky and their stardust is stolen. It was illegal and nearly unheard of when Say was Seelie Queen. Now Zake hires starshooters to bring him the stars they acquire. Stars can't survive without dust. When they lose a certain amount, they turn into Shades, ghostly versions of their former selves, black shadows with hollow, white eyes. If they lose more than that, they die. Zake uses what dust he steals to make himself more powerful. It's a rather unnerving thought, actually."

"How do you steal dust from a star?" Ainsley asked.

"It's called Dusting. One star can Dust another by touching them and channeling their own dust to steal from the other. It's not very pleasant for the star being Dusted. It can also work in reverse, but these days, that hardly ever happens. Dusting isn't always fatal though. As long as the star doesn't lose too much, they can gain it back. But it takes a little while. Like blood loss, in a way."

Ainsley wasn't sure what to do with all the information she'd been presented with. It made her head spin to think about it. Merdi appeared to realize this and patted Ainsley's knee comfortingly.

"Don't worry, dearest. We'll do our best to find your family. In the meantime, the two of you can get some rest, and if you'd like, in the morning, we can get you back through Harper's tree and on your way home. Of course, you're more than welcome to stay here, but you don't have to decide right now." She stood up and brushed her skirts off. "I'm going to go make up some beds and make a glass call. I'll be back in just a minute."

Ainsley and Khade watched her climb up one of the trees to the tree house, equally and completely bemused by the account Merdi had given. Khade's addled mind could only come up with one thing to ask.

"What's a glass call?"

FOUR

"We come spinning out of nothingness, scattering stars like dust."

—Rumi

It was a dream. Even as it happened, he tried to tell himself that, that it wasn't real, wasn't true. It just couldn't be true, because if it was, then they'd worked at freedom all those years for nothing.

But it felt so very real.

He didn't know what the girl looked like anymore. She'd had pale blonde hair when she was little, and dark eyes. She could have changed — probably *had* changed — in thirteen years. But the girl in the dream was an exact replica of her younger self. She must have been around fifteen or sixteen now, tall and thin with very pale skin. But she was no longer sweet-looking and angelic.

True, her fair hair, that was so long it dragged behind her, gave her a glowing appearance, but her dark eyes burned like hollows in her face. Her white gown trailed the ground, and it was ripped and stained with blood from the knees down. A bloodied spot covered the bodice over her heart. Her mouth was open but motionless, even as she spoke to him.

"It is your fault," she said. Her voice was harsh and whispery, as if she had a sore throat. "It is you who are to blame for my death. You are responsible for bringing me here, for luring me into danger."

She pointed a long white finger at him. "You have brought ruin upon all who dwell in Seelie lands. And so, you must suffer for this. As all stars do."

And then she was gone, and he was falling, tumbling through the sky. The stars he passed at first were tiny lights, wheeling past him as he dropped through space, and then they turned into faces. They jeered at him, hissed, laughed, called things out to him. He tried to call back, but his voice was broken. Something grabbed him by the shoulder, and he tried to throw it off.

"Ouch! Rowan."

His eyes snapped open. Indigo was looking down at him.

"Are you okay?" she asked.

Rowan glanced around. He was still in his room. He rubbed at his eyes. "Yeah. Fine."

Indigo didn't look quite convinced, but she let it pass. She held up Rowan's talking-glass. "Merdi wants to speak to you."

"Brilliant." He sat up and took the glass. "I hope she has good news. I could really use some of that."

He opened the glass to see Merdi looking anything but pleased. When she saw him, however, her expression quickly changed.

"Rowan, dear, you look terribly pale. Are you alright?"

Rowan sighed. He was getting really tired of that question. "I'm fine."

"No, you're not. What happened?"

He wasn't up to refusing her an answer. She always won anyway. "Fince," he said simply.

Merdi's nose wrinkled at the name. "Oh, he's a right horrid creature. One of these days—"

He had to stop her before she really got going and forgot what she'd called him for. "What exactly did you need to tell me, Merdi? I'm really tired."

Merdi stopped mid-rant. "Oh, I'm sorry, dear. Ainsley's here. She brought a human boy with her — a friend, I'm guessing," she said. "But she doesn't know anything."

"What do you mean she doesn't know anything?" Rowan asked.

"The girl has no idea what she is," Merdi clarified. "For goodness' sake, she didn't even know what a star *was*. I'm telling you, Townsley is going to hear from me about—"

"Are you serious?" Rowan asked. "What the heck has he been telling her? That the stork dropped her off?"

"If it did, then it hit him right hard upside the head in the process," she said. "I had to explain everything to her. From the beginning."

"So she doesn't—"

"No." Merdi shook her head. "She doesn't know where the gate is."

Indigo had been listening to the conversation as she sat next to Rowan. "Then we've put her in danger for nothing," she said.

"No," Rowan said. "I did. I put everyone in danger, and Zake isn't an idiot. If he finds out..." He trailed off as a thought came to him. "Oh no," he breathed. "Merdi, where is she now?"

"She and her friend are sitting out by the fire," Merdi said, looking a bit confused at the sudden change in tone. "Why?"

"Joel called me earlier. I don't know what time it was. I was half-asleep when I talked to him. The starshooters were going to be near the Tree. He said they'd gotten another star. They could be looking for it now."

"Oh dear," she muttered. The picture on the glass turned sideways and leafy shadows shifted across it as she climbed down from the tree house and hurried over to the fire. The view made Rowan dizzy, and he had to resist the urge to shut his eyes.

Merdi's face came back into focus. She looked blank. "She's gone."

Rowan's head spun. "What?"

"Both of them."

"Maybe they went to look at some stray pixies," Indigo said hopefully.

"I'll go look for her," Merdi said. "I'll call you if I find her." She closed the glass on her end, and the surface of Rowan's went blank.

If. She'd said *if.*

Rowan and Indigo sat in silence for a moment, lost in thought, before Indigo spoke up.

"We'd better go wake Dekk. We can leave while it's still dark, and maybe no one will notice we're gone until we're far enough away."

"No." Rowan grabbed her arm to keep her from leaving. "I messed this up. I'm going to fix it."

"What are you going to do?" She looked hard at him. "No. You're not going to Blink."

"You can't really stop me," he said, then instantly regretted it. She looked hurt. "I'm sorry. I just... We can't leave tonight. Zake will *know* we're in on this then." He reached over and picked up his sketchbook and pencil, turning it so the pixie-dust lantern illuminated the pages. "Give me some time. I'll come up with some kind of plan."

"I know. You usually do," she said.

Just hope it works this time, he thought. His pencil had taken off with a mind of its own, and he noticed morbidly that the picture was starting to bear a distinct resemblance to the girl in the dream.

Indigo leaned over to look at the page. "Who is that?" she asked.

45

"Her," he said, and shut the book.

FIVE

"a shooting star
streaks the sky
making it real

clear night —
in the space of a smile
the meteor is gone"

—Giovanni Malito

"Do you believe her?" Khade asked when he was relatively sure
Merdi would be gone for a little while.

Ainsley stared into the fire. The flames were bright enough to make her eyes sting, but she didn't look away. "I honestly don't know what to believe right now." She shrugged. "Why wouldn't he have told me?"

"Maybe to keep you away from your grandma's psycho brother, the dude that goes around sucking the life out of people for the sake of his own personal gains?"

Ainsley gave him a look. "Do you think I should leave then? Go back home?"

Khade put his hands up. "Hey, I'm just saying."

She sighed. "It would have been easier to decide if he hadn't given me reason to wonder. If he'd just told me something. Anything."

"Well, I don't know. Maybe he had his reasons." He paused. "Did you hear that?"

Ainsley turned her head to the side, listening. "Sounded like a voice. Merdi said she was making a call of some kind."

"No. That sounded like a guy's voice," Khade said.

Both of them were silent for a moment.

"It can't have fallen far from here."

The voice was muffled slightly but undoubtedly male. Ainsley and Khade exchanged a glance.

A second voice chimed in, sounding slightly aggravated. "You've got ten minutes, or I'm going back to the castle. I've got better things to do."

"Oh, I know exactly what you want to do," the first voice said, an unrecognizable accent evident in his tone. "You can't wait to get back to check on your little ginger puppy."

"He's not a puppy, Fince, and it's your fault he's in the state he's in, anyway. I'd appreciate it if you just left him alone. Don't be so belittling."

"I meant it affectionately, Joel. Really."

The conversation was getting close. Khade whispered into Ainsley's ear, "We've got to move. Now."

He grabbed her by the arm and herded her out of the clearing and into the trees. Unfortunately, Khade was not a master of direction, and the owners of the voices walked right by them, followed by about seven other men, all strange and foreign looking with their sharp ears and unusual features. Khade and Ainsley crouched down in the brush and sank back as far as they could without moving their feet. None of the men seemed to notice either of them.

"Fince. You don't know the meaning of *affection*. Leave him alone." The owner of the second voice, Joel apparently, was tall and dark-skinned and blended almost seamlessly with the shadows of the trees. He was lean but muscular, and he looked incredibly annoyed by his companion.

"Alright, alright. Let's just find that blasted star then." The owner of the first voice was borderline terrifying. He was big and hulking, with long, tangled hair and a sharp, crooked grin. Ainsley remembered his name from the story Merdi had told her. She held her breath, waiting for him to pass by.

Instead, he stopped and sniffed at the air. "I smell it," he said.

Joel glanced back at him with an expression somewhere between annoyance and disgust. "Really."

"The star's close." Fince took a step closer to Joel before quickly turning, approaching Ainsley and Khade's hiding spot, and parting the shrubbery.

Khade and Ainsley tumbled backward away from him.

Fince looked surprised. Then his face spilt into a grin. "Well, well. Two for one." He bent down into Khade's face and sniffed him. Khade started to scramble backward. "Or maybe not." He grabbed Khade by the shirt, pulled him off the ground, and shoved him toward one of the men. "Human," he said with a feral gleam.

Fince turned back to Ainsley. "Must mean you're the star then." He smiled wider for a moment before a look of confusion crossed his face. "What's this here?"

He reached down to lift the copper gear around Ainsley's neck. "So you're the one," he said, and the grin intensified into something maliciously satisfied. He grabbed her by the arm and pulled her up. "They're both comin' back with us, boys. This is far better than any regular old fallen star."

Ainsley was handed off to another of the men, and she and Khade were pushed along after Fince and Joel. The two of them were speaking up ahead, but Ainsley could only catch snippets of what they were saying. What she could understand was that the one called Joel was clearly unhappy. Fince, however, looked like he had just received the greatest gift of his life. He kept looking at Joel, grinning and laughing, as though he was pleased with the other's discontent.

Ainsley tried to turn back to make eye contact with Khade, but the man holding her by the arm only jerked her forward and made her walk faster.

"Where are we going?" she heard Khade ask. No one answered him.

Sometime later, the group came out of the woods and into view of what seemed to be a small sailing ship. Ainsley looked around but saw no water. She figured asking would get her nowhere, so she simply allowed herself to be directed onto the ship.

Walking up the boarding plank, Ainsley noticed the ship had no sails. In their place were strange panels that appeared to be solar powered. What had seemed to be mere wooden boards and railing was a combination of both wood and metal. Unusual dials and knobs were littered across digital-looking charts and table tops. Ainsley would have liked to have kept admiring the ship, but she and Khade were led away to a doorway.

Before they could be shut inside, Ainsley heard Joel call out, "No, no, no. I want them in my cabin, not yours."

There was a momentary hesitation where nothing happened and no one was pushed anywhere. Ainsley turned her head to see Fince looking decidedly less pleased than he had earlier. Joel was wearing a challenging expression.

Fince made a sound that resembled a growl. "Fine then."

Ainsley and Khade found themselves redirected to a different door. The man who held Ainsley shoved her inside roughly.

Khade bristled. "Hey! You don't push a lady."

The man chuckled. "Terribly sorry." He gave a mocking bow and extended a hand toward the door. "Go right ahead then."

Khade glared at the man as he and his companion laughed. After a moment, he huffed and went inside the room. The sound of the door being locked behind him had a striking sense of finality.

Khade stared at the door in silence for a second. He turned to Ainsley, who had taken a seat on top of the large desk in the room. She seemed like she was waiting for something. "What?" Khade asked.

"Just waiting for the I-told-you-so," she replied.

"Hey," he said, "It wasn't my stupid pixie thing we went running through the woods after."

"Yeah. That's what I was waiting for, actually." Ainsley crossed her arms, appearing suddenly very tiny and insecure.

Khade went over to sit next to her on the desk. He put an arm around her shoulders. "We'll find a way out of this."

"That's what they always say."

"Well, must be true if everyone says it."

Ainsley shook her head, but the smallest of grins forced its way onto her face. "What are you going to say next? At least we get to die together?"

Khade shrugged. "If it'd make you feel better." He paused for a minute. "Hey, that's cool."

"What?" Ainsley turned to him, but he was looking up at the ceiling. She followed his gaze.

Above them, painted on the curved ceiling, was a multitude of stars. Each was painted in a varying shade of red, yellow, orange, white, and blue. The moon and sun came clashing together in a show of sparks.

Khade lay back on the desk and crossed his arms behind his head. "On the bright side, the view's nice."

Ainsley turned one leg sideways on the desk and kicked him, but she lay down beside him anyway. "I just hope we don't get eaten."

Whatever Khade might have said in response was cut off by the ship suddenly vibrating violently. Ainsley and Khade immediately sat up.

Ainsley jumped off the desk and ran to one of the paneled windows. Khade followed quickly after her. They both looked out the window, then down.

"We're rising off the ground," Ainsley said.

Khade gave a nervous laugh. "At least it explains the lack of water."

"I wonder where we're going."

Khade sighed. He had no answer for that one.

SIX

"Faerie is a perilous land, and in it are pitfalls for the unwary, and dungeons for the overbold."

—J.R.R. Tolkien, *On Fairy Stories*

When Rowan woke next, the sun had risen enough to light up the room. Indigo was still asleep and had apparently pulled a blanket over both of them at some time in the night. Rowan slipped out from beneath the blanket and out of bed while managing not to wake her. He still felt like he had been hit by an airship.

He started to stretch before a wave of dizziness hit him, and he abandoned the motion. He stepped into the closet to change clothes, just in case Indigo were to wake up. Last night had been awkward enough as it was.

He traded his old jeans for another pair and pulled his boots on. Next, he put on a couple layers beneath a loose white button-down. Thanks to Fince, he was consistently running low on dust, effectively keeping his body temperature lower than it should have been, and he was cold more often than not.

Indigo was still asleep, turned over on her side now, when Rowan stepped back out of the closet. He grabbed his jacket from his desk chair and his flight goggles from his dresser, looped the goggles around his neck, and left his room in search of something to eat.

He had gone maybe five steps into the hallway when someone jerked him by the shoulder and shoved him against the wall.

"Hey, what the hell?" Rowan demanded, because his first thought was of Fince. His second thought was that he *really* didn't want to do this again.

For a brief moment, he was happy to see that it was Joel standing in front of him. Then he saw the look on his face, and the moment was gone.

"What have you done?" Joel whispered angrily into Rowan's face.

Rowan pulled away. "What are you talking about?"

Joel pointed an accusing finger. "Explain to me why there are two kids down in the prisons, why one of them is wearing Zake's clock gear, and why the other one is human."

Rowan's face went white. "What?" he asked. "She was supposed to be at the Tree. Merdi was supposed to be looking for her."

"You dragged Merdi into this?" Joel whispered, in a voice more accusing than the last. "Who else is in on your scheme?"

Rowan didn't meet Joel's eyes. "Indigo and Dekk."

Joel gave a deep sigh and closed his eyes, looking very much as if it were taking all his self-control not to strangle Rowan on the spot. "What did you tell them?"

"What you told me."

Joel sighed again. "I told you that I needed to find out more, and I expected you to keep everything between the two of us until I did." He looked both ways down the hall. "Zake had me stay in his office last night so he could tell me that gear doesn't go to the gate. He's trying to weed out the disloyal. He asked me if I told anyone about it."

"What did you tell him?" Rowan asked.

Joel raised an eyebrow. "I warped my words as best I could, but you know I can't lie to him like you can."

Rowan shook his head. Faeries were incapable of lying, but that didn't mean most of them weren't masters of deception. "You shouldn't have. He knows it's me anyway. He wouldn't think it was anyone else. Especially after what Fince said."

"What did he say?"

"He said he thought that Dekk took the gear." He added in an undertone, "He also mentioned Indigo."

56

Joel's expression softened. "You've really got to let those comments go, Rowan. You're going to get into serious trouble one day." When Rowan didn't say anything in response, Joel continued on a different track. "Do you have a plan on how to fix this now? You've brought a lot of people into this."

"I know," Rowan snapped. "Just...I'll fix it, okay?"

Joel didn't back down. "Look, just because I told you about the gear doesn't make this my fault. I accept part of the blame, but don't go shoving it entirely on me."

"I know," Rowan admitted again. "And I will fix it."

Joel didn't seem completely convinced. "Well, fixing will have to wait. Your unintended victims have a court date right now."

"*Right* now?" Rowan repeated. "That didn't take very long."

"Well, we both know he doesn't like to wait," Joel said, attempting to straighten out Rowan's hair. Only slight improvements were made, and Joel sighed in acceptance. "That'll have to do. Put on your jacket. Let's go."

Rowan followed him, managing to get one arm tangled in his sleeve. "What about Indie? She's still asleep."

"I've already talked to Dekk," Joel said. "He'll get the message to her. I'd feel better if she weren't present anyway."

Rowan nodded in absolute agreement.

***

The Court was full when Rowan entered. The room was long and open but felt threatening and gloomy, despite the rows of flickering lamps that lined the walls. The sound of hundreds of voices mingled as one continuous drone, falling just short of deafening. An empty strip of carpeted floor separated the two sides of the room. The rest of the space was filled with scores of Unseelie fey, shrieking for a spectacle and the possibility of bloodshed. All around, creatures were adorned with jagged wings, spiraling horns, shaggy faces, and bloodied claws. Several spriggans snatched out with spindly brown arms as Rowan passed, and a spider-woman took a break from slurping the juices out of an unfortunate carcass to leer hungrily at him.

Rowan kept his head down and his eyes forward as he walked over to stand beside the dais where Zake was seated in a throne made of branches and vines grown up from the ground. The throne looked as though it was slowly dying, with ash-colored bark and withering leaves. Zake was talking to someone on his left — Rowan didn't look to see who — and he seemed not to notice Rowan's presence on his other side. The rest of the Court, however—

Rowan knew they were watching him. He could feel their stares, hear the way their whispered conversations seemed to have shifted subject.

Rowan's tentative standing with Zake was no secret among the Court. Neither was anytime Fince beat the living starlight out of him. River trolls were not much for subtlety, and Fince was far more troll than star. It was almost more than Rowan's dignity could stand against. The only thing the Court didn't know was why Zake kept Rowan around instead of treating him like all the other stars unlucky enough to cross the path of the Seelie King. Truthfully, Rowan didn't know either. He could only assume it was his favoritism with Joel that had allowed him this much time.

Joel came to stand next to Rowan, but Rowan didn't look at him either, not even when Joel placed a hand, that was meant to be comforting but only felt condescending, on Rowan's shoulder.

Rowan did look up when Fince brought out the "prisoners", dragging one by the arm and shoving the other ahead, and made them stand on a platform set up in the center of the room. Fince took a stance behind them, like some hulking bodyguard, and flashed a glance and a smile in Rowan's direction. It was all Rowan could do to quell the instinct to run.

One of the prisoners was a boy, around sixteen or so, with dark brown hair and a wary expression that bordered on terror. Rowan could tell he was definitely human, and he looked as though he had never seen anything remotely fey in his life.

The other was a girl, with pale blonde hair and very dark eyes. Rowan knew exactly who she was. She looked just like her grandmother. She was being half shielded by the boy, and she looked very small as he stood protectively in front of her.

Rowan thought he should be standing behind her instead, in order to shield her from Fince.

Rowan dropped his eyes again when Zake began to speak.

"So I trust you both know why you're here," he said, addressing the two on the platform. Neither of them answered, so he turned to the crowd instead.

"Does anyone know what happens to thieves around here?" The crowd of Unseelie erupted into raucous laughter. "Now tell me, thieves, what are your names?"

Make something up, Rowan thought wildly. *Please make something up. Don't give away your names.* His fingernails dug into the palms of his hands, and he forced himself to relax his shoulders.

"We're not thieves," the boy answered boldly, though Rowan could see him shaking and knew everyone else could too.

"Answer the question, boy," Zake said, strangely patient.

"I'm Khade," he said with narrowed eyes.

"And your friend, *Khade*," Zake continued, making the words sound patronizing, "What is her name?"

Khade hesitated for a second, no doubt seeing the leers and sharp teeth that smiled at him from a crowd in anticipation. "Lily," he answered.

Rowan stole a glance at Zake. *He doesn't believe it.* He knew from all the head games they had played over the years. Zake would be enjoying this as it all went downhill.

"Really?" Zake asked. "A lovely name for such a fair lady. Her beauty could rival that of the stars above."

Khade and the girl exchanged a look.

They think he believes them.

"Of course, that's hardly surprising," Zake went on. "Do you know who your grandmother is…Ainsley?"

"What…what did you say?" the girl asked in a small voice. She was so quiet that Rowan could barely hear her. His mind descended further into panic mode.

"I know your name is Ainsley," Zake clarified. "And I know you have the clock gear that went missing from my room recently. You see, I may have let it slip to certain people that that gear went to the gate to Skyline, the land of the stars. Without that gear, the missing piece, the gate could not be opened, and so no help could come to aid those who would have me overthrown. But it was all a lie, you see."

Rowan thought he could feel Zake's eyes stare down at him, for a fraction of a moment, and then the feeling was gone.

"The thing is that gear truly does go to one of my clocks. It's actually rather useless to me. Unless I want to check the time, of course." The crowd gave another round of laughter, shrill and scream-like. "What I really want is the Blue Wand, and I'd prefer you give it or its location to me with as little resistance as possible."

"The what?" Ainsley asked.

"Oh, come now, don't play dumb," Zake said. "Give it up, and I'll let you go."

What he really means is he'll make your deaths a little less painful, Rowan thought.

"I don't have any kind of magic wand," Ainsley said.

"Then tell me who does have it or where it is."

61

"I don't know."

"Think a bit harder then."

She only shook her head in answer, her expression lost.

"You're whittling my patience very thin," Zake said. Rowan could hear the veiled anger beneath his voice. "Tell me where it is."

"I really don't know," Ainsley said, shaking her head again.

Zake stood abruptly from his seat. "I'm warning you, little girl–"

"She said she doesn't know!" Khade shouted, stepping forward.

Zake stared at him for a moment. His expression became deathly calm. "Well then. I suppose you're not any use to me at all then." He nodded his head in a silent command. "Put them back in the prisons. We'll have a little show for the stars tonight. Something flashy to accommodate the princess. Let's show her how the Unseelie do things."

The mocking laughter started up again, louder than ever and soaked with excitement, and Fince led Ainsley and Khade away. Zake walked down from his dais and towards Rowan.

"I have to thank you," Zake whispered in Rowan's ear in passing. "I may not have everything I want, but I am one step closer."

***

Rowan's first stop was Indigo's room. It was impeccably clean, everything in its place. The bed was made up in dark ruffles and lace. The vanity was well-stocked with perfumes and powders. He knew the wardrobe housed an array of clothing and a fair assortment of shoes.

But the desk was covered in potion-making materials and notes, and he was aware of a box under the bed containing several sharp and well-polished daggers. He was also aware that she knew very well how to use them all.

The only thing missing from the room was Indigo.

Rowan's next stop was Dekk's room. The handle didn't turn when he tried it, so he started banging on the door instead.

"Dekk, let me in! It's Rowan!"

He could hear the lock being turned from the other side. Dekk opened the door with an irritated expression and opened his mouth to use a few choice words. Rowan shoved him back inside and looked into the room.

Dekk's room was very much the opposite of Indie's. The bed was unmade, the wardrobe door was open and crammed full of random things, and half of Dekk's clothes were on the floor or thrown across furniture. Leaning against the wall in the cleanest corner of the room was a pair of matching swords.

Sitting on the bed, looking highly out of place, was Indigo.

Rowan breathed a sigh of relief.

"Shut up," he said to the still-rambling Dekk, and closed and locked the door behind him.

"What pixie flew up your butt?" Dekk asked. An expression of annoyance was on his face.

Rowan chose to ignore him. "Zake knows what we did."

"What did he say?" Indigo asked, sliding off the bed and coming closer.

"He thanked me. That gear we sent off is worthless. He's really looking for some kind of wand. The Blue Wand, he called it." He turned a hopeful look in Indie's direction. "Have you heard of it?"

She shook her head. "No, but we might can find someone else who knows about it. Maybe Merdi does."

"I really don't want to involve Merdi anymore than we have to," Rowan said. "I'll check the library for any books that might mention a wand."

"Good luck with that," Dekk said. "If there *are* any books on the subject, then Zake's probably hidden them away for his own use."

"Still, it's a start. And we've got to get Ainsley and Khade out of the prisons and out of *here*."

"Khade?" Indigo asked.

"Ainsley's friend," Rowan clarified. "The one Merdi mentioned. Zake's planning to off them both tonight. 'A show,' he said. 'Something flashy'. I don't know what it'll be, but it didn't sound nice."

Dekk turned toward Rowan with a thoughtful look on his face, never a good sign as far as Rowan was concerned. "You said they're in the prisons?"

"Yeah, that's what Zake told Fince."

Dekk held out a hand. "Give me your talking-glasses."

Rowan and Indigo regarded him with a strange look. "Why?" Rowan asked.

"Just trust me," Dekk said, and the other two handed over the glasses. He promptly turned and lobbed both of the devices against the wall. Broken glass and dented metal rained to the floor. Dekk pulled his own out of his pocket and threw it after the other two.

"What was that for?" Indigo asked indignantly, her shocked expression mirrored by Rowan's.

"We don't want anyone tracing us. Besides—" A wolfish grin plastered itself across Dekk's face. "I think I've got a plan."

SEVEN

"Fairy roses, fairy rings, turn out sometimes troublesome things."

—W.M. Thackeray

Townsley Harper woke in the morning feeling like he usually did after an argument with his granddaughter—apologetic. He got out of bed and dressed, in his usual attire of pinstripe trousers and a matching vest, apparel that reminded him of the styles of his wife's strange society. Then he made his way to Ainsley's bedroom, trying to think of something to say that would appease her while still allowing him to keep his secrets.

Townsley came to the closed door and cleared his throat. Still unsure of what to say, he knocked.

No answer came.

He knocked again, thinking she might still be asleep.

Still no answer.

"Ains?" Townsley called, pushing the door open slowly. He peeked around the door and glanced toward the bed. The covers were pulled back but free of wrinkles. The bed was empty. Townsley stepped into the room. A pile of school supplies had been dumped onto the floor. A set of pajamas was thrown against the closet doors.

The window was open.

Townsley ran to the window, placing his hands on the sill and looking out. One of his hands brushed against something soft yet gritty. He lifted his hand and looked down at the windowsill. Some kind of glittery, powdery substance covered part of the wooded surface. He recognized it immediately.

"Pixie dust," he whispered, feeling his heart drop. "No, no, no."

She was gone.

The phone rang in the other room. Townsley rushed to answer it, hoping it would be Ainsley on the other end. She had run away, and now she was lost and sorry and needed to be picked up.

"Ainsley?"

Khade's mother answered instead, her voice filled with barely contained tears. "Townsley? Have you seen Khade? He's not here. I've looked all over the house and outside."

Townsley swallowed the nervous lump that rose in his throat. "I haven't seen him. Ainsley's gone too."

A strangled sob escaped the phone speaker.

Townsley quickly continued before things could have a chance to get even worse. "It's okay. Don't call the police. I know where they are."

"You do?" Her voice sounded hopeful. "Where?"

Townsley sighed. "I'll be over in a few minutes. I'd rather tell you in person."

"Oh. Okay." Complete confusion, with a dash of worry. Just as he had expected.

This would be an interesting conversation.

EIGHT

"If you're betwixt and between, trust the one with red hair."

—O.R. Melling, *The Hunter's Moon*

Ainsley and Khade sat in their cell, both silent and curled in on themselves. They had run out of things to talk about long ago, and now they could think of nothing more than how much they would rather be almost anywhere else than where they currently found themselves. Ainsley was tired, but she didn't want to sleep. She didn't want to risk missing something. If they planned to kill her, she figured she would have plenty of time to rest later.

She could hear the guard talking a little ways off. "How you doing tonight, Miss Indigo?"

A smooth, feminine voice answered back, "Very well, thank you." And then the sound of glass breaking and a thud, and the smell of something sweet drifted through the air.

A girl with brown and white hair came around the corner, a couple of years older than Ainsley and wearing a purple jumpsuit with some sort of white bustle attached to the back. A small dagger was tucked into the belt around her hips. Her heeled sandals clicked lightly on the stone floor.

"Alright, guys," she said, motioning forward with her hand.

Two boys came in after her, both appearing somewhere around the same age. The shorter one was lean and wiry, with wild white hair and bright two-tone eyes. He wore a red button-down shirt and holey pants with a black jacket tied around his waist. Belted under the jacket, Ainsley could make out two sheathed swords. He was completely barefoot.

The taller boy was long-limbed and very thin, with a pale face and freckles across his nose and cheeks. He was wearing a bomber jacket and jeans and boots. A pair of goggles was pushed up on his head, half hidden by red hair. There was a strange-looking pistol holstered in a belt around his hips. Some part of Ainsley registered that it seemed to be on the wrong side.

The white-haired boy came forward and started picking at the lock on the cell. He had the door open in a matter of seconds.

70

"Come on," he said. "Come with us."

Ainsley followed after him, but Khade grabbed her wrist.

"Hold on a minute," he said. "We don't know who you people are."

"Oh, sorry," the girl said. "I'm Indigo. This is my twin Dekk, and this is Rowan." She motioned to each of them. "And you're Ainsley and Khade, right?"

"You're Indigo?" Ainsley asked. "You're the one who wrote that note that Wickertwig brought me."

Indigo seemed hesitant to acknowledge the fact. "Yeah, that was me. Where is Twig, anyway?"

"Back at the Pixie Tree. He wandered off somewhere."

"Whoa, whoa, whoa," Khade said, at the same time that Rowan whispered, "Guys, we don't have time for this."

Rowan's remark caused Khade to round on him first. "I saw you earlier, standing next to the guy on the chair, or throne, or whatever it's called. You're working for him." He addressed the other two next. "And you two are probably in on this too. I'm not going anywhere with you people. For all we know, you could be leading us out so we can get caught trying to escape."

A dangerous look crossed Rowan's face. "So you think you have a chance without us?" he asked.

"It was your stupid letter that got us here in the first place," Khade snapped. "So yes, I think I can handle it better."

71

"Handle what you will," Rowan said. "But handle it alone, because the princess is coming with us. You can rot in this cell by yourself." He reached toward Ainsley as if he was prepared to drag her out physically.

Khade let go of Ainsley's wrist and took a step toward Rowan. Indigo and Ainsley instantly stepped between them, and Dekk grabbed the back of Rowan's jacket.

"You two can have it out later," Indigo said firmly. "Right now, we need to get out of here, or else we're all dead."

That was enough to make Rowan back down, but Khade didn't seem as willing.

"Khade, really," Ainsley said. "Even if they do lead us into a trap, what chance do we have by staying here?"

Khade stared at Rowan. "Fine," he said.

"Great," Dekk said, letting go of Rowan's jacket. "Follow me then."

Dekk led them all up into the upper hallway and down several turns. There were a few flights of stairs and more turns, and soon enough, Ainsley felt completely lost.

"Does anyone find it strange that we haven't run into anybody else?" she asked.

"I noticed," Rowan answered. "But we can't turn back now."

"So *you* say," Khade whispered.

Ainsley decided to drop the matter to avoid further conflict.

They went up a stairwell and through a door and came out onto some sort of deck. Tethered to large posts were several floating ships.

"That's what they brought us here on," Ainsley said.

"Airships," Rowan said, leading them all toward one of the smaller vessels.

"See?" Khade remarked. "This is the part where they take us out and kill us."

Rowan rounded on him. "Please shut up. I'm asking you nicely."

Khade gave him a dirty look but didn't say anything else.

They boarded the ship, and Dekk cut the line that tied the ship to the dock.

Rowan got behind the wheel and the control panel. "Hold on, everybody. Time to leave this place behind."

Everything began humming to life. Ainsley took this second chance to admire everything that she hadn't been able to last time. The ship was wood and metal like the last one had been. She noticed it was all brass and copper and silver. There was no iron or steel anywhere. The sail-like panels lit in rows from the bottom upward, as they gradually powered up. A few long pipes pumped out what appeared to be glitter-filled smoke. The charts and knobs surrounding Rowan lit up in different shades of shimmery red and blue and green. He flicked and pushed switches and buttons like it was something he had been doing his entire life.

He probably has *done this his whole life,* Ainsley thought. *This isn't the world you grew up in.*

73

Another voice quietly added, *But it's the world you belong in...right?*

The ship began vibrating roughly and rose up higher into the air. Rowan turned the wheel hard, and the ship rotated around to face the other direction. He pulled a lever, and the ship took off.

Ainsley was certain it was the most wonderful feeling she had ever felt. The ship was traveling fast enough to make her feel exhilarated, slow enough to allow her to see everything they passed. She leaned over the railing, pushing her hair back from the wind, watching far away trees whip beneath them. Little villages stood apart from each other in huddles. Most of the houses looked just as she had imagined them, like fairytale hutches where gnomes and elves lived in stories. She didn't remind herself of all the dark creatures she had seen in the short time she had been in Avyn.

An earlier thought occurred to her. "Hey, Rowan," she called. When he looked down at her from behind the wheel on the upper deck, she went on. "Does iron really burn faeries, or is that part of the made-up stuff?"

Dekk answered her instead. "Yes, it really burns. Hurts like crazy. Why? Are you planning to use it against us?" He sounded suspicious, but he was smiling.

She gave a slight smile in return. "Not unless I have to. Is that why there's no iron on the ship?"

Dekk and Rowan looked a little surprised. "Yeah," Rowan said. "Well noted. Can you sense it or something?"

"I used to hang out a lot with Wickertwig," she replied. "I had read somewhere that faeries didn't like iron, so I would always look for it, to make sure it never hurt him."

Rowan and Dekk exchanged a glance that Ainsley couldn't quite decipher.

"This is sweet and all," Khade spoke up. "But where are you taking us?"

"We'll head in this direction for a while to get them to follow us," Rowan explained. "Then I'll Blink everyone back to Merdi's. That should throw them off and give us enough time to get you guys back through the tree and back home."

Ainsley couldn't argue with the fact that the plan sounded good. Evidently, Khade still had something to say.

"Blink? You mean like—" and he blinked his eyes twice in an overly exaggerated manner.

Rowan closed his eyes as if he were trying to resist the urge to kill Khade on the spot. Then he opened his eyes, looked down at Khade, and said, "The more you talk, the less I like you."

"Feeling's mutual," Khade said.

"Oh, sweet mother of—" Rowan cut himself off and sighed. "Blinking is like…teleporting or something. Some stars can do it over short distances. I can take all of you from here, back to Merdi's house, just by focusing a little. Ainsley should probably be able to do it too, with a bit of practice. Just don't jump into it all at once. Start small."

Ainsley nodded. She had no idea what he was talking about.

Indigo came up from below deck, bearing a rather large wicker basket. "Hey, you two," she called to Khade and Ainsley. "Any chance you might be hungry?"

Ainsley nodded. Even Khade had to admit to it. Indie waved them over, and Dekk followed after them. Inside the basket was an assortment of cheeses and fruit and some sort of sweet bread that was loaded throughout with berries.

While the others helped themselves to the contents of the basket, Indie wandered up to the upper deck to where Rowan seemed to be deep in thought.

"What are you thinking about?" she asked.

"Everything," he answered.

"You don't have to, you know."

He looked over at her. "I know."

She handed him some sort of strange-looking fruit. "Here."

He took it with a smile.

Ainsley watched Indigo take a bite of her own fruit and lean into Rowan. He put an arm around her as if it were the most natural thing in the world.

Ainsley turned to Dekk. "Are they...?" and she pointed between Rowan and Indie.

Dekk swallowed the bite in his mouth. "Hot for each other?" he asked. "Very much."

Ainsley blushed. "Yeah. Something like that."

"She could do better," Khade said.

Ainsley punched him in the arm.

"What, do *you* want him?" Dekk asked. "If that's the way you swing, I could—"

"Dekk!" Rowan cut in, sending the sidhe a pointed glare.

Dekk grinned knowingly, while Khade did his absolute best to try to disappear on the spot.

NINE

"I like too many things and get all confused and hung-up running from one falling star to another till I drop. This is the night, what it does to you. I had nothing to offer anybody except my own confusion."

—Jack Kerouac, *On the Road*

Lord Zake was sitting behind his desk, feet propped up, a glass of faery wine in one hand, and a satisfied smile on his face. The gear Fince had taken back from the girl lay in front of him across some papers.

A knock came at the door. Zake didn't look up, just announced for the visitor to come in.

Fince swaggered into the room, looking one shade off from infuriated. "They're gone," he snarled. "All of them. I checked the prisons, and the girl and her human friend are gone." His green eyes shimmered venomously. "So are Rowan and the sidhe twins."

"I figured as much," Zake said, rolling the stem of his glass between his fingers.

A look of confusion crossed Fince's face. "You expected this?"

Zake smiled at him. "Fetch Joel for me, please."

Joel stood before Zake a few minutes later. Zake told Fince to leave the two of them in private, and Fince left the room, glancing back smugly at Joel before closing the door.

"Well, then," Zake said. "How did you think the trial went?"

Joel shrugged. "Other than the fact that it didn't seem like much of a trial, I think it went well."

Zake tilted his head. "You don't believe I was fair?"

"I didn't say that. I only meant that, with the girl wearing what was stolen, it didn't seem like a trial. More like a confession of guilt."

"Well reiterated," Zake said. "Tell me, have you noticed anything else missing lately?" He twirled his glass idly.

Joel seemed a bit confused. "No. What's missing?"

"More like *who*, I should say." Zake looked Joel straight in the eye. "Someone under your supervision?"

Joel's countenance didn't slip. "He's not in the castle?"

"No. And neither are his friends."

"They may have gone out for a little while. I'm sure they'll return sooner or later."

"No," Zake said, standing. He held up the gear on the chain. "And I think you know that."

"What do you want me to do then?" Joel asked. "I can't control everything he does."

"I don't want you to. I want you to keep an eye on him." Zake paused to take a sip of wine. "You and Fince. Let me know when one of them gives away the location of the Blue Wand."

Joel nodded. Zake smiled evenly as he watched him leave the room. Now all that was left was to wait.

TEN

"We need to learn to set our course by the stars, not by the lights of every passing ship."

—Omar Bradley

Around an hour had passed on the ship when Rowan decided they had been waiting around long enough. He had changed direction twice in order to make it appear though they were actually going somewhere, just in case anyone was following them. He hadn't seen anyone, but that didn't mean no one was there. He wished he could call Merdi to make sure it was safe at the Tree, but Dekk had already seen to that. It was just as well. Stars forbid they get a call and open the glass to discover Fince's face looking back at them.

Ainsley lay on the floor by the railing, her head and one hand between the bars, watching the world fly by beneath the ship. Indigo and Dekk had gotten out Dekk's pair of swords and were having an impromptu sparring match, which involved more laughing than actual fighting. Khade was sitting at the front of the ship, leaning back with his arms crossed, staring at Rowan. He had been doing that for nearly the entire hour. Rowan rolled his eyes. He really wasn't sure why the two of them had taken an instant dislike to each other. Conflict of interests, perhaps. Or maybe humans dealt with stress by lashing out at people who were trying to help. Whatever the case, the boy was clearly out of his element, but if he thought he could take on the fey, Rowan had no objections to being his first opponent.

"Alright, guys," he called, coming down from the upper deck. "Time to go. Everybody, come over here."

Everyone except Khade gathered around him. "Are you sure you're not leading us to our deaths?" Khade asked.

Rowan narrowed his eyes at him. "Get over here, or I swear I'm leaving you on the damn ship."

"Fine," Khade huffed. "I'm not leaving Ainsley with you."

"Everyone, grab hold of each other," Rowan said, pulling Indie close and holding Ainsley by the arm. Ainsley grabbed Rowan by the jacket. Dekk took hold of Rowan's shoulder with one hand and Indie's arm with the other. Khade wrapped both arms around Ainsley. "Hold on then."

Rowan closed his eyes.

All at once, a tingle spread over him, and he felt his breath stop. He felt as though he was being pulled apart and compressed at the same time. He focused hard on where he wanted to land. And then he gasped, and his concentration snapped.

Unfortunately, they were all still a few feet off the ground.

There were surprised shrieks all around as they tumbled down and landed in a tangled heap. A chorus of groans followed.

Rowan got to his feet and helped Indie up.

Indigo looked him over. "Are you okay?"

"Yeah, I'm fine." He nodded, stuffing his hands into his pockets so she wouldn't see that they were shaking.

"Nice landing. Really." Rowan turned around to see Khade helping Ainsley up from the ground.

"Sorry," Rowan said sincerely. "That's never happened before."

"You probably did it on purpose."

"I don't like you."

"I don't trust *you*."

"I'm trying to help," Rowan said.

Khade looked incredulous. "By dropping us out of the sky?"

Rowan's hands came out of his pockets, and he took a step toward Khade. Indigo reached for his arm.

"Stop." She looked intently at him. His breath was coming in hard, shaky gasps, and his eyes seemed a little unfocused.

"Listen to your girlfriend then," Khade snickered.

Rowan didn't have to reply this time. Ainsley wound back a fist and punched Khade hard in the arm. "Knock it off," she said firmly. She glanced back at Rowan, looking like she was concerned for him.

So he looked that bad then.

Rowan allowed Indie to lead him over to the fire Merdi had burning, but only after making sure Khade had seen the choice hand gesture Rowan had given him.

"Very mature," he heard Khade mutter.

Thankfully, Merdi came scrambling down from the tree house and toward the fire.

"Oh goodness me!" she cried, running over and hitching up her skirts, revealing bare feet with nails made for climbing. "I was so worried about you all!"

She grabbed Ainsley in a rough hug, squeezing hard and then letting go just as quickly. She seized them all in turns, though Dekk tried unsuccessfully to worm away from her. She was stronger than she looked. She came to Rowan last. She was a full foot shorter than he was, but she still managed to grip him by the jacket and pull him down to the ground. She placed a hand on either side of his face and proceeded to turn his head from left to right and look into his eyes. Whether or not she found whatever she was searching for, Rowan didn't know, as she turned around suddenly to everyone else and asked, "Is anyone hungry?"

As they had eaten on the ship, no one was. Merdi wasn't deterred. She was always determined to feed people whether they wanted it or not. "I'll make some warm drinks then," she announced. "Would you like to come into the tree house or sit by the fire?"

"Tree house," Indigo answered. "In case anyone wanders by."

"Good point," Dekk agreed. "It always smells like berry pastries up there."

Merdi scurried back up the tree, leaving everyone else to follow. Dekk climbed up first, making it look effortless. Rowan was reminded vaguely of a squirrel. Indigo went next, far more gracefully than her twin but with just as much ease. Ainsley stepped up next, but she only stared up at the tree as though she wasn't quite sure what to do with it. She turned around to Rowan, who stood waiting behind her.

"How am I supposed to get up?" she asked. "There's not a ladder or anything."

Some part of Rowan felt slightly annoyed that the girl couldn't even climb a tree properly. Still, he linked his fingers together and crouched down. "Put your foot here, I'll help you up."

"I'll help," Khade offered.

"First time I've actually seen you be nice," Rowan commented offhandedly.

"I don't trust you not to drop her," Khade returned.

Rowan gave a strangled sounding laugh. "And we're back where we started."

Together, he and Khade helped Ainsley up into the tree house. When she was safely up, Rowan stepped aside for Khade to climb up next.

"Would you like some help too?" Rowan asked.

Khade grinned back. "No, but I'd be willing to help you if you need it."

Rowan's face fell. He hadn't expected a comeback. "I'm good," he deadpanned.

Khade raised a satisfied eyebrow and climbed, somewhat clumsily, up the tree. Rowan grinned at the lack of grace and followed after him.

He thought his arms would give out before he got to the top, but he made it without falling and then Indigo was there to take his hand and pull him through the doorway. Rowan stumbled to his feet, and then turned and lowered the door over the opening to the tree house, pushing the lock into place.

The door led into the main room. Merdi had decorated her home in different shades of lavender and had used the natural form and bend of the tree to create furniture from the branches, each of which was covered with a mass of cushions.

Indigo made her way through to the kitchen to help Merdi with drinks. Dekk trailed after her, looking hopeful. The scent of berry cocoa drifted out into the main room, followed by the sound of a wooden spoon against flesh and Merdi's indignant voice. Dekk skittered back out of the kitchen.

Ainsley and Khade were, meanwhile, looking somewhat out of place and very uncertain, standing in the middle of the room as if they were afraid to touch anything.

"You can sit down, you know," Rowan commented, taking his own advice and sinking into the nearest chair. It was far more comfortable than it appeared, though he couldn't have cared less at that point. He lowered his head into hands that refused to stop shaking.

"Yeah," Dekk said, perching himself on the arm of a sofa. "The furniture only bites a little. More of a nibble, really." He grinned widely.

Ainsley and Khade exchanged a glance. Rowan shook his head. "He's kidding."

Ainsley edged over to the sofa Dekk was sitting on and sat down carefully. When nothing unordinary happened, she relaxed further into it. Khade joined her as Merdi and Indigo came back into the room bearing trays with silver mugs.

"Here you are, loves," Merdi said, handing a mug each to Ainsley and Khade. "It's hot now, so take care."

Indigo handed a mug to Dekk then handed one to Rowan and sat down next to him.

"Appreciated," Rowan said, but he didn't take a drink. He just held the mug tightly, letting the warmth of the cocoa heat both hands.

Indie sighed and scooted closer to him, pulling her legs up to her chest. Rowan put an arm around her and leaned his forehead against the top of her head. The scent of her hair was incredibly pleasant.

"Are you sniffing me?" she asked quietly, so only Rowan heard.

"Mm-hmm," he murmured against her hair. She gave an amused giggle in response.

"Oh, and this is yours as well," Merdi was saying. "You left it here when you— Well, when you left."

"Oh thanks!" Ainsley said. "I'd forgotten all about it." Rowan looked up to see her going through a backpack in her lap. "Look, Khade, the flower you found hasn't wilted yet." She pulled out a pale blue dandelion, twirling it appreciatively between her fingers.

"Really?" Khade asked. "Some flower…"

Rowan's eyes widened. "Some flower, indeed," he said in amazement. "Do you have any idea what that is?"

Ainsley and Khade stared back at him, looking clueless.

Everyone else had taken notice as well. "Is that a starbud?" Dekk asked.

"Goodness me," Merdi cried. "I believe it is. Those are rare, they are."

"It's a what?" Khade asked.

"A starbud," Indigo answered. "Whenever someone makes a wish on a falling star, wherever the star lands, a single starbud will grow there. Make a wish and focus it into the flower, and the wish will come true." Indie shrugged. "It's how the whole wish-on-a-dandelion thing got started. They just look similar."

"So we could just fix everything now, right?" Ainsley reasoned. "Everything that's wrong here: Zake, the falling stars, my grandmother."

"Whoa, whoa, whoa," Rowan interrupted. "It doesn't work like that. Wishes are fickle, just like the rest of Faerie. You have to word things just right, or else you get something entirely different from what you wanted. Ever heard the phrase, 'careful what you wish for'?"

"What if we were careful though?" she asked. "Then we—"

Rowan shook his head. "No. Too risky. Besides, I thought you wanted to go back home."

Ainsley's face fell. "Yeah. I guess you're right." She carefully replaced the flower in the backpack.

"Seemed like a good idea to me," Khade muttered. He cast a sideways glance at Rowan and took a sip of the drink in his hands. "This stuff is delicious, by the way."

"You think this is good, you should try the food," Dekk remarked.

"Oh, you boys are just being too sweet," Merdi said, waving a hand, though she had obviously enjoyed the compliments.

Rowan leaned his mouth close to Indigo's ear. "That's funny. I didn't think either of them had the capability to be sweet."

Indigo took a drink to hide her smile. The ghost of it was still on her face when she lowered her mug.

"Rowan, can I ask you something?" Ainsley said.

Rowan almost responded that she already *had* asked him something, but she looked so deadly intent that he changed his mind. "Sure."

"What else can stars do?" she asked. "Other than Blinking and Dusting, I know about those."

"Well, I don't confess to know everything about it," Rowan started. "But I do know about Novas and Supernovas."

Ainsley leaned forward in her seat.

"Okay, how can I put this? A Nova is like a firework, and a Supernova is like an explosion. A Nova is a small burst of stardust that's usually used in a defensive way, to knock someone back maybe. A Supernova is much larger and much more powerful. One big enough could probably take out a few buildings or more, depending on the power of the star at least. The downside is that, while a Nova generally doesn't take too much dust, a Supernova will pretty much wipe out a star's dust entirely. Which doesn't end well for the star."

"Yeah," Ainsley said. "Merdi told me about dust."

"Very true," Merdi said. "I've never heard of a star that pulled a Supernova and lived to tell about it."

Ainsley nodded. "Can I ask something else?"

Rowan shrugged. "Might as well, while we're at it."

"What was it—" She took a deep breath and started again. "What was it like before? I mean, before Zake, when my grandmother was still queen?"

Rowan looked down at the drink in his hands and thought for a moment. "I don't know, really. I only remember a little. Or maybe I've just made up a memory. I don't know." He glanced up at her and shrugged. "Sorry. I wasn't very old. None of us were." He motioned to Dekk and Indie.

"You weren't very old?" Ainsley repeated. "But I figured stars and faeries would live a really long time."

Rowan and the twins laughed. "We do," Indigo said. "But everyone has to start somewhere."

"We're probably just a few years older than you guys," Rowan said.

"Besides, faeries are one thing," Dekk added. "Depending on the race, there are fey born every day. Stars are different. As far as we know, only three stars have been born in the last hundred years: you, Rowan, and your mother."

"Wow, really?" Ainsley said.

"Yeah. The birth of a star is kind of a big deal."

"So let's throw a baby shower then," Khade said. "I feel like the major point is seriously being missed here. How are we supposed to get home?"

Rowan stared at him. "Taking selfish ass to a new level, are we?"

"Selfish? Oh no, I'm planning on taking Ainsley with me," Khade replied. "Besides, why didn't anyone fight back when this first happened, huh? Why let it go this far? Seems like your queen lacked a bit a foresight."

"Seems like you're just scared," Dekk said. "The attack came during the May Day festival, when both Courts come together for a time of peace. Zake broke the code and set up for the attack to happen while he and the other Unseelie Gentry were inside at the ball. The queen wouldn't have had any way of knowing that would happen. Tradition states that any conflicts are put on hold during the festival, so normal security wouldn't have been in place."

"Okay, fair enough," Khade admitted. "Next question: aren't you two supposed to be on the bad guy's side? Being his kind and all?"

Dekk's eyes narrowed. "You're walking a fine line, human boy."

Merdi was absolutely flustered. "Now come, come, boys, knock it off."

"Apologies," Khade deadpanned. "I've only been lost in an alternate realm, kidnapped by some World of Warcraft characters, locked in a castle dungeon, and faced with the threat of execution. I'm not sure why I'm on the verge of a nervous breakdown."

Ainsley gave him an indecipherable look. "I've been right alongside you for all of that too. And, come on. World of Warcraft? Really? I'm from this world too. What does that make me?"

"But you're not like them."

"Would it be a bad thing if I was?"

Khade looked at her, blinking. "I'm sorry," he said. "I didn't mean that the way it sounded."

"Sorry?" Rowan repeated, putting his mug on the floor and standing. "Sorry? You owe everyone here a lot more than 'sorry'. If you'd open your eyes and ears more and your mouth less, you might actually learn something. Ever think that maybe Ainsley doesn't really need you? Maybe you're the one that needs her? You have no idea what this world is like. I bet you haven't grown up without your parents, wondering if they're even alive. If you have, then my sincerest apologies. But for some of us, Ainsley included, that's a reality." Rowan shook his head. "We've got enough problems without you blindly interjecting your opinions. So stop apologizing, and either grow a pair or go home."

Rowan turned and retreated to the nearest bedroom, slamming the door and siting down against it. Angry tears pricked at his eyes. The room was dark and felt incredibly inviting at the moment. He could hear Merdi talking.

"No, no, dear. Leave him be." He knew she must be talking to Indigo. Good. He didn't want anyone following him. "Come on, now. I've got spare rooms enough for each of you. Indie, would you show Ainsley to one? Dekk, show Khade, please. And don't kill him along the way."

"Wouldn't dream of it…" Dekk said, a grin obvious in his voice.

There was a pause, and Rowan thought for a moment that they had all left the room.

"Oh, and for what it's worth, dear," Merdi said, sounding wistful, "Before Zake came along, things were much, much better than this."

Rowan tugged off his boots and jacket and crawled into bed with the rest of his clothes still on. He pulled the covers over his head. He couldn't decide what sounded worse: knowing better times and having them taken away, or never having known what better times were like to begin with.

ELEVEN

"Her eyes the glow-worm lend thee,

The shooting stars attend thee;

And the elves also,

Whose little eyes glow,

Like the sparks of fire, befriend thee."

—Robert Herrick

After lying awake for what felt like hours, Ainsley conceded to the fact that she wasn't going to be able to fall asleep any time soon. She slid out of bed and put her shoes on. Then she opened the bedroom door and stepped out into the hallway to find Khade's room. She had seen him with Dekk earlier, looking dejected. She had a feeling he would be awake too.

The hallway was darkened, but the moon was bright and had found a way to cast itself through the holes in the branches above. The floor was dotted with little spots of white light.

Ainsley came to the door she thought was Khade's and, hoping she was right, gave a soft rap on the wood with her knuckles.

Khade's whispered voice came from the other side. "Ainsley?"

She took that as an invitation and pushed the door open. Khade was sitting on the bed, knees pulled up to his chest.

"Can't sleep?" he asked.

She shook her head. "You either, I guess. What are you doing?"

He shrugged. "Wallowing, mostly." He laughed dryly. "I was kind of a jerk earlier."

Ainsley sat down across from him. "It's okay. Well, it's not *okay*, but I'm not mad. We have had an interesting time here."

"You think the others hate me yet?" he asked, meeting her eyes.

"No, I don't think they hate you. Not yet," Ainsley replied. She smiled wryly. "Well, maybe Rowan. He doesn't seem too fond of you."

"Yeah, well, I'm not too fond of him either," Khade said.

"Everyone noticed," Ainsley said. "Why though? What's the deal between you two?"

Khade looked at her as though it was obvious. "I don't trust him. There's more to him than we're seeing," he said. "And I think he just wants me out of the picture."

"I think he just wants his life turned right-side up. To keep his friends safe. Doesn't sound like he's asking for much."

"Maybe not," Khade said. "But I want to keep my friends safe too. That's why I came here in the first place, to look after you and make sure you make it back home in one piece. And I intend follow through with that." He looked at her. "If that's okay with you, I mean."

Ainsley looked away, both touched and embarrassed. "What if I didn't want to go home?" she said softly.

"What?"

"Not right away, at least," she added.

"What on earth do you want to stay for?" Khade asked, incredulously. "It's a mess here. Your family's missing, your great uncle's a psycho, and people want to kill us."

"That's just it, though," Ainsley said. "What if I can change that? This can't have been an accident. My granddad always told me that sometimes bad things happen in order to make room for better things. Maybe I'm... Maybe we *are* the better things."

"Ainsley..."

"You don't have to stay. I won't hold it against you."

He sighed, looking resigned. "Have you really thought about this?"

She nodded. "Yes."

"Alright then," he said. "I'm in too. I told you I'd come with you. All the rash things you do, someone needs to look after you. And I don't trust Rowan to do it."

"I'm sure Rowan doesn't trust you to look after me either," Ainsley laughed. "Thanks."

"No problem." Khade smiled. "Thanks to you too, for not turning me down."

Ainsley returned the smile. "No problem."

***

Ainsley was awakened the next morning when Merdi flung open the bedroom door, looking panicked and out of breath.

"Goodness me, child," she huffed. "There you are. You weren't in your room."

Ainsley realized she and Khade had fallen asleep while they were talking last night. "Oh, sorry," she said. "I couldn't sleep last night, so Khade was keeping me company." A split second later, she realized just how wrong that statement had sounded. "Wait, I didn't mean—"

Merdi shook her head, smiling. "Don't worry, dear. Now, both of you come into the kitchen for some breakfast."

Ainsley and Khade exchanged an embarrassed glance before their faces simultaneously split into wide grins. They followed Merdi out of the room and into the kitchen. The sidhe twins were already there. Indigo was toasting bread while Dekk sliced strawberries.

"See?" Indie said to Dekk when Ainsley and Khade came into the room. "I told you she didn't get eaten last night."

"Yeah, yeah," Dekk said, putting the strawberries into a bowl and placing the bowl on the table. "She was probably in *Khade's* room last night. I don't blame her. He's easy on the eyes, to be human." He wiggled his eyebrows at Ainsley. She felt her cheeks heat up and sat down at the table without saying anything. Khade made a strange face and joined her at the table.

"Shut up," Indigo said, shoving Dekk aside and setting a large plate of toast and a jar of honey next to the strawberries. "You're making people uncomfortable."

"I'm glad you noticed," Dekk returned, bowing and passing plates around the table to Ainsley and Khade. He set an extra four down for Indigo, Rowan, Merdi, and himself.

"Indie, dear, would you fetch Rowan for me?" Merdi asked. She was bustling busily around the kitchen, making what seemed like coffee and some kind of milkshake mix.

"Of course," Indie said, leaving the room.

Dekk took a seat on the other side of Khade. "Sleep well?" he asked, looking positively wicked.

"Like the dead," Khade said with a malicious grin. "Do you know how the dead sleep?"

Dekk pulled back, eyebrows raised. "I could ask you the same thing."

"Here you go then," Merdi said. She handed Khade and Ainsley each a glass of the milkshake-like drink, then handed Dekk a mug of coffee.

"Do you really need that?" Khade asked doubtfully, glancing at the coffee.

Dekk gave him a mischievous smile and took a long drink.

Ainsley took a tentative sip of her own drink. It tasted of strawberries and chocolate and vaguely of orange peel, along with something else she couldn't quite place. It was delicious, but then, she had expected it to be.

Dekk began helping himself to a few pieces of toast and honey, so Ainsley followed suit. Khade watched her for a moment.

"Go ahead, dear," Merdi urged him. "Before it gets cold."

Khade slid a piece of toast onto his plate and drizzled it with honey and took a bite. "The food at home will never taste the same after this," he told Ainsley.

"Tell me about it," she said, licking honey from her fingers before popping a strawberry into her mouth.

Indigo reappeared into the kitchen, followed by a sleepy-looking Rowan, who had apparently bothered to put on neither shoes nor jacket and his shirt tails were wrinkled and untucked. He fell into a chair at the table, folded his arms, and laid his head down.

Merdi set a mug of coffee in front of him. "Morning, love."

He answered her with a muffled, "I hate mornings."

"I'd expect nothing less from a nocturnal creature," Merdi said.

Rowan raised his head and gave her a look of amusement. "What do I look like, a raccoon?"

"You don't want me to answer that," Merdi said. "Now have some breakfast."

Rowan sighed. "I'm not hungry."

Merdi turned to stare at him, one hand on her hip. "Eat something or be force-fed, dear. It's your choice."

"Okay, that's terrifying," Rowan answered and reached for a piece of toast.

"That's better," Merdi said, and she turned back to bustle busily around in various cabinets and drawers.

Ainsley had just reached for another piece of toast when it happened. She was watching the way Indigo put her hand on Rowan's knee under the table, the way he gave a slight smile and started to lean toward her. The piece of toast in Ainsley's hand hovered over the space between her and the table as Indigo leaned in as well.

Then Ainsley let out a high, startled shriek. A set of sticky green fingers had come from under the table and snatched her toast right out of her hand.

Indie and Rowan, and everyone else, whipped round to look at her. "What's the matter?" Merdi asked.

Ainsley turned wide eyes on her and pointed beneath the table. "There's something under there," she whispered, barely resisting the urge to pull her feet up into her chair.

Merdi sighed. "Hobbs," she said firmly. "Come on out from there."

A mottled green face, followed by a short, plump green body dressed only in tatty trousers, slowly emerged from under the table. Hobbs looked up at Ainsley in a way that was half apologetic and half entreating. Bread crumbs hung around his mouth, glued in place by honey.

Dekk burst into laughter. "You just got scared witless by *Hobbs!*" he cried. "Of all things! Hobbs!"

Ainsley huffed and gave him a look. "Funny," she said.

Khade rubbed absently at his injured hand. "He *is* a goblin." He glanced at Dekk. "Maybe he's just waiting for the right time to spring."

"Yeah, sure he is. *Dun dun dun,*" Dekk sang in a low voice.

Rowan snorted. "You guys obviously haven't spent much time around Hobbs. He's scared of everything. One time, a squirrel ran past him, and he nearly broke down in tears."

"Seriously," Dekk said. "It was pathetic."

Ainsley watched as Rowan stealthily picked up his previously untouched piece of toast, slid it off his plate, and held it beneath the table. He pulled his hand, now minus the toast, back up to the table and pretended not to hear the smacking noises that followed.

Merdi was quick to whack him on the head with a spoon. "I saw that."

Rowan twisted around in his seat. "I told you I didn't want it," he pointed out.

Merdi placed one hand on her hip, using the other to point the spoon in Rowan's face. She opened her mouth to start what would likely be a long and unpleasant lecture.

So Ainsley seized the moment to ask, "What's the Blue Wand?"

Merdi stopped and turned to her. Rowan stayed facing backward in the chair, but Ainsley noticed that his shoulders became tense.

"Where did you hear about that?" Merdi asked. She sat down at the table, all thoughts of badgering Rowan seemingly gone.

Ainsley was acutely aware that everyone except Rowan was watching her. She cleared her throat. "Zake said something about it," she continued. "He said the gear was a fake and that what he really wanted was the Blue Wand. He wanted me to tell him where it was. But I've never heard of it before."

"The gear is a fake?" Merdi repeated, glancing over to Rowan. He had his head against the back of the chair though and didn't see her looking at him.

Merdi sighed, turning back to Ainsley. "There's a legend, a very old one, about a blue star who fell deeply in love with the moon. The moon, however, did not return his love. The star had in his possession a very powerful magic wand, one that could only be wielded by blue stars. The power of stars is designated by color: red, orange, yellow, white, and blue. Blue stars burn the brightest, followed by white, then yellow, and so on.

"Now the moon was incredibly jealous of the star's light. She disliked having to rely on the sun's light to make her shine at night. So she proposed a quest for the star to complete. If he were to be successful, he would win the moon's affection. The quest she gave was this: go down to the sea and bring back her reflection from its surface.

Well, the star was in love, so of course he agreed." Merdi shook her head.

"So the star made the journey down to the sea. He reached out to scoop up the moon's shining reflection, and a hand shot up from the waves, wrapped itself around the star's wrist, and pulled him under the water. The star's wand, the magnificent Blue Wand, was lost to those who dwelled in the sea, the merfolk and kelpies and whatnot. What the star was unaware of was that the sea creatures are under the jurisdiction of the moon. She is the Queen of the Tides. They delivered the Blue Wand to her, and she was dismayed to find that the wand would not work for her. And so, disgusted by both the wand and herself, she cast it away into some obscure corner of her domain, to be forgotten. And for the most part, she has succeeded in that endeavor."

Merdi sat back in her seat, leaving her rapt audience to finish absorbing her tale. "It's only a legend, of course," she added.

"I know a song about that story," Ainsley said.

"Oh, yes," Merdi said. "Townsley would teach you that, would he? But nothing else, of course." She rolled her eyes.

"He didn't teach it to me," Ainsley said. "I just sort of…remembered it, I guess."

Merdi gave her a strange look but didn't comment.

"If it's only a legend," Rowan began — he had turned around in his chair at some point during the story — "Why would Zake be after it?"

"And if it's not a legend, he'd have to be a blue star in order to use it," Indigo pointed out. She looked at Merdi. "Is he a blue star?"

Merdi shook her head. "Not that I know of. I believe Saydie mentioned some time ago that her brother was a yellow star. Blue stars are a bit rare. They don't come round too often."

"Are you sure he said Blue Wand, Rowan?" Dekk asked. "Not...puce or vermillion or something?" He spread his hands with a grin.

"You're not cute, and Ainsley and I both heard it," Rowan said pointedly. His eyes narrowed in thought. "The legend's got to be true. He's not stupid. He wouldn't go off chasing something unless he was sure it existed."

"Well," Merdi mused out loud. All eyes turned in her direction. "If there's anyone who can answer that question, then I might know of who it would be. His name is Neverens'il. Supposedly, he's part of the Unseelie Royal Family, the last one left from when Zake had them all done off with. He's got a strange familiarity with legends and tales of older days, at least the darker ones. Knowledge hidden away and passed down from past generations from the old ruling family. He might be able to answer your questions."

"Where is he?" Rowan asked.

"The village of Phoenixdown. It's about forty miles or so east of here."

"I don't want to walk that far," Dekk said, glancing at Indigo. She shrugged at him.

"It's okay," Rowan said. "We can ride."

"We want to go too," Ainsley said.

Rowan and Dekk both gave her skeptical glances. Indigo smiled. Merdi looked worried. "I thought you wanted to go home," Rowan said.

"I did," Ainsley said. "But then I realized: I might be able to help. You keep talking about how I should have taken over the Seelie Court after my grandmother. I want to take back what should have been mine. And Zake has been making everyone's lives miserable. If these are my people, shouldn't I have to take responsibility for them?"

"Dear, you're merely fifteen," Merdi said. "You needn't take responsibility for anything yet."

"I think she should come," Indie said. "It's just as much her place as it is ours, maybe more so."

Everyone turned to Rowan, as if they had all agreed that he held the deciding factor.

"Please," Ainsley said, trying to catch Rowan's eyes. "I've dreamed of adventure all my life. Please, just let me come."

Rowan looked up at her, studied her hard. Then he smiled softly and nodded. "You can come. You both can."

Ainsley squealed and bit her lip in excitement. She shared a look with Khade, who smiled back at her and shook his head. She clasped her hands together, attempting to stifle the sudden buzz that filled her.

"But he has to play nice," Rowan added, pointing at Khade, "Or else I'll be highly tempted to kill him, and that may put a slight damper on things."

Khade put his hands up in a surrendering gesture. "I can't promise to be nice, but I will be civil."

"Fair enough," Rowan conceded, standing. "But forewarning to you both: adventure is nothing more than bad luck with good media coverage."

TWELVE

"Stars, hide your fires;
Let not light see my black and deep desires."

—William Shakespeare, *Macbeth*

Joel and Fince stood within Zake's office once again, but this time, they had news for him. Rather, Fince had news for him. Joel would have preferred not to have even been present.

"They're planning to head southeast to the village of Phoenixdown," Fince announced smugly. "They don't even know what they're doing."

Joel doubted that the spunky little group was going into anything entirely clueless. Three out of five of them had grown up in Avyn, and growing up in Avyn wasn't easy for everyone. They had learned to be smart and watch their backs and each other's backs. Each had something different to offer: Dekk's craft, Indigo's level head, and Rowan's fire. Three things of which Joel felt Fince had not the slightest possession.

"Did they say why they were going to Phoenixdown?" Zake asked, skimming an old book of Avyn legends and myths. The pages were thin and worn.

"According to the pixies we wrangled, the forest troll said there was someone in the village that knew a lot about legends and things," Fince explained. "She said he was kin to the last Unseelie rulers."

Zake looked up at Fince with an intense gleam in his eye. "What?" He jumped up from his seat. "I got rid of them. All of them. Except..."

"That blond kid," Joel offered. "He got away. Remember?"

Judging by how red Zake's face was becoming, Joel figured he did remember.

"What do you want us to do?" Fince asked.

Typical Fince, Joel thought, *Always asking for orders. Can't think for himself.*

Zake didn't say anything for a moment, just stood behind the desk, hands splayed against the wood surface, head down.

"Do you want us to get the troll?" Fince asked. Joel's heart sank at those words.

Zake's grey eyes were dark, calculating. "No," he answered at last. "The troll is worthless. I can't use her. She's not worth my time." He looked up, smiling. "Send out the Shades. I want them all dead. Don't worry about the troll. Kill the others. The girl and her human friend, the sidhe twins. Kill them all... Except Rowan."

Joel almost felt sick with relief, until Zake added, "I want him brought to me."

The words came out before he had even thought them through. "What do you want him for?"

Zake gave him a look that bordered on pity. "You care too much for him, Joel. Would you prefer he were dead?"

That depends, Joel thought but said nothing. He stared the other in the eye for just a moment before looking away.

"I'll take that as a *no*, then. Anyway," Zake continued. "I want you two to pay a visit to Phoenixdown. Talk to our little escaped royal. I might have a proposition for him." He shrugged. "Never hurts to have a backup plan."

THIRTEEN

"You can't stand up to the night until you understand what's hiding in its shadows."

—Charles de Lint, *The Onion Girl*

Rowan was already beginning to regret the fact that he had agreed to travel with Ainsley and Khade. Merdi, as soon as it was finalized that the princess and her friend were tagging along, had begun fussing in earnest over Ainsley and Khade's dirty clothes. Rowan figured that they *had* been traipsing through the woods and had spent the night before last in a cell, so of course their jeans might have a few smudges on dirt on the knees. They surely weren't planning on staying clean on the way to Phoenixdown, were they?

But Merdi would have her way. She usually did. So while Dekk lay sprawled on the floor in the main room, hands resting under his head, and Rowan lounged in an armchair, sketching on the back of a map, Merdi set to work.

She started with Ainsley. She dug through piles of dresses and gowns in her bedroom wardrobe. She'd had most of them for several years — the old pack rat — and had outgrown several of them (in the chest and hips, she said with a wink, much to the boys' chagrin).

As Ainsley was much thinner and about six inches taller than Merdi, there was a fair bit of trying on that ensued. Indigo helped to make sure that Merdi stayed on track, for the most part at least. Otherwise everyone feared they would spend the entire day playing dress up.

Ainsley eventually came into the main room dressed in a sleeveless pink gown that came down to her knees. The edges were tied with black ribbons that held up the outer layer, revealing a silver underskirt, and the waist was belted and cinched to account for Ainsley's smaller frame. She was wearing black and white striped stockings and she still had on her black sneakers. Indigo had done up Ainsley's pale blonde waves in a messy twist, and whitish locks fell around her dark eyes. She had a black jacket in one hand.

"How does it look?" Ainsley said, doing a little half turn.

Dekk whistled. "Very nice, Miss Harper. Not quite what I'm into, but still."

"Shut up," Khade said, glaring at Dekk. He turned back to Ainsley. "You look pretty."

Ainsley's cheeks flushed a little, though Rowan couldn't be sure whether that was because of Dekk's comment or Khade's. "Thanks," she said, giving a small grin and biting at her lower lip.

Merdi bustled into the room then, saving Ainsley from further embarrassment. "All right now, Khade, dear," she said. She waved him over. "Your turn."

Rowan grinned, feeling a hint of maliciousness drift in. "Go get pretty, Khade," he said. "I'm sure she has something that'll really bring out your eyes. Lots of ruffles."

Dekk snorted and giggled from his position on the floor, clapping his hands over his face to hide his amusement and doing a rather terrible job of it.

Khade's face reddened. "I thought we had an agreement to be nice to each other," he said.

"I am being nice," Rowan said, eyebrows raised, mouth twisted into a smirk. "I just don't think it's fair for Ainsley to be prettier than you."

Dekk giggled harder.

Merdi stepped in, putting her hands on Khade's back and gently pushing him out of the room. "Come on, deary. You're a right mess, now."

Khade cast a final glare at Rowan and Dekk and allowed himself to be led away.

Indigo swatted at Rowan's shoulder. "You shouldn't egg him on so," she chided. "It really doesn't help."

"I'm not sure anything would help those two," Ainsley remarked with a resigned smile.

"He started it," Rowan said. "I'm only paying it forward."

"I'm sure he'd say the same thing," Ainsley said.

Indigo chuckled softly. Rowan didn't look amused any longer.

Khade took a considerably shorter time getting changed than Ainsley had, a fact which Rowan was rather glad of. They had wasted enough time as it was. Khade came back into the main room wearing one of the shirts Dekk had left at the tree house at some point — Merdi had hopefully since washed it — and a brown jacket with embroidered cuffs. He was still wearing his own jeans and sneakers, though the knees of his jeans had been cleaned up.

Merdi pinched his cheek affectionately. "Cleans up nicely, doesn't he?" she said.

Rowan and Dekk snickered quietly, which Khade answered with only a blush and an annoyed look.

"So are we ready to go then?" Indigo asked.

"Yes," Rowan said, then quietly, "Finally."

Rowan and Dekk each hefted a messenger bag over their shoulders. They had packed some necessities earlier while Ainsley and Indigo and Merdi had been previously occupied. Ainsley's backpack would be left at the tree house since her phone was dead, and without service besides, and her flashlight, in the presence of stars, would be pointless. There was nothing else of much value—though the candy bars would be taken along—that would prove useful on the trip. Rowan instructed her, firmly, to leave the starbud hidden in her backpack at the Tree. If it fell into the right—or wrong—hands, things could turn out badly for everyone.

There was a general buttoning of jackets, gathering of things, and tightening of shoe laces. Rowan unbuckled the gun belt around his hips and turned to Khade.

"Here," he said, holding it out. "You might need this."

Khade stared for a moment. "Won't you?" he asked uncertainly.

Rowan gave a half-hearted smile. Khade apparently had little idea as to what a star could be capable of. "Nah," he said. "I'm set. And Dekk has his swords, and Indie has— well, she can take care of herself. So that just leaves you."

"What about Ainsley?" Khade asked. "She needs to be protected too."

Rowan pushed the gun belt into Khade's arms. "She's more capable than either of you realize. And you're a lot more appetizing, mortal boy," he said, looking the other in the eye. He shrugged. "Not that I'd mind if you got eaten along the way. Besides, you seem so eager to be her personal meat shield."

Khade sighed and accepted the gun belt, buckling it around his hips.

Rowan watched his slight awkwardness, one eyebrow arching. "I never thought to ask, but you do know how to use a gun, right?"

Khade looked up at him, seeming a bit frustrated. "Yes, I do. My dad used to take me hunting sometimes when he was still…" He trailed off and adjusted at the belt a little more. Then he glanced back up like a thought had just struck him. "Are you left-handed?"

"Yes," Rowan replied. "Most stars are." Then, feeling slightly defensive, he added, "Why? Does it bother you?"

Khade raised his hands in front of him. "No. Just wondered. It feels weird." He paused for a second then said, "Why isn't Ainsley left-handed?"

Rowan shrugged. "How should I know?"

"Just asking," Khade said apologetically.

Rowan turned and opened the door that led down the tree to the ground. He hoped Khade would get the message and stop talking for a little while. He could tolerate Khade — for the sake of being civil — but that didn't mean they were friends just yet.

Dekk climbed down the trunk first, as a precaution, and called up that it was safe to come after him. Khade went next, followed by Ainsley, then Indigo. Rowan turned to climb down last, but Merdi stopped him.

She took his hand in one of hers and patted it lovingly. "Be careful, dear," she said, and when he started to reply, she shook her head, cutting him off. "Yes, I know you know. But all the same, try to take care of yourself. And look after the others, even Khade."

Rowan let out a short laugh. "I will," he said. "You know I will."

Merdi reached up and placed her hands on either side of his face. She stayed like that for a moment, just looking at him. Then she let go and said, "All right then, love. Go on."

Rowan climbed down through the door to where the others were waiting.

"So where's our ride?" Dekk asked.

"Always the voice of patience, Dekk," Rowan said.

Rowan stepped forward and closed his eyes, concentrating. Then he stood and waited.

"What are we waiting for?" Khade asked after a pause.

Rowan didn't answer. In the next moment, from out of the trees and into the clearing came five bodies with gleamingly white fur. Iridescent horns spiraled skyward. The creatures stopped before Rowan, pawing gracefully at the ground.

"Unicorns!" Ainsley gasped.

Khade stared. "You've got to be kidding me."

"I don't kid," Rowan said and hid a grin when Khade managed an "Oh".

"They don't look like they do in storybooks," Ainsley noted. The creatures more closely resembled a large deer than a horned horse. They had thin, elongated tails that were tufted at the ends, and the hair around their ankles grew long.

"Well, storybooks rarely get anything right these days," Indigo said.

"Are we gonna ride them or stare at them?" Dekk asked. Then, to prove his point, his hopped upon the closest one, patting its mane and then gripping the hair like a rein.

"Stars do really cool things," Ainsley said quietly, petting the nose of one of the unicorns. Indigo helped her up onto its back, before mounting another herself.

Khade refused any help — Rowan imagined the boy must be slowly losing his dignity — and took some time before he achieved any success. But eventually each unicorn had acquired a rider, and they set out through the trees in the direction of Phoenixdown Village.

The first several minutes passed in relative silence, though Rowan could hear Ainsley mumbling excitedly behind him. Of course she must be in awe of all she had seen and heard in the last two days. Everything that Rowan had grown up knowing was new and unusual to her, even if she had read her fairy tales. Rowan figured Khade was doing well just to prevent his own mental breakdown.

After some time, Khade spoke up. Just as well. Rowan had guessed Khade wouldn't be able to refrain from talking for too long. "So, about how long do you think it will take before we reach this village?" he asked.

Indigo answered, "Probably longer than you want me to tell you. At the rate we're going…" She paused to think. Rowan could practically see the gears working in her head. "I'm guessing no sooner than sundown. And a fair chance it'll be later than that."

Khade made a face which showed exactly what he thought about that information. "I'm all for picking up the pace a little, in that case."

Indie smiled and coaxed her mount into going a bit faster. The others followed suit.

"While we've obviously got nothing else to do," Ainsley said, "I have a question."

"No, you can't keep the unicorn just because it followed you home," Dekk said.

"That's not what I was going to ask, but thanks anyway. I was just wondering. What's with the guns everyone seems to have? What happened to bows and arrows and, you know, medieval fairy tale stuff?"

Dekk snorted. "Someone needs to get out more. What do you even do in your spare time?"

"It's a valid question," Indigo said. "You've seen how our kind is portrayed on her side."

"You've been to the human world?" Khade asked.

"We've been known to get into some trouble now and then," Dekk said, shrugging. "You can get away with a lot when people can't see you. But that's rather beside the point."

"*Anyway*," Rowan said, shaking his head, "Not everyone here uses guns. Most fey do still use bows and swords and the like, especially those who live away from Court. Fey are steeped in tradition, and weapons like swords and daggers are traditional. But fey are nothing if not curious. After watching humans for so long, it was only a matter of time before the fey started trying to copy them in some aspects. The

Gentry — Court-folk, I mean — are usually far more likely to wield human-styled weaponry."

"Our guns are better than yours," Dekk added, sticking his tongue out.

"Different," Indie corrected, guiding her unicorn around a bush filled with black thorns. "We don't use gunpowder like humans do. Ours run through interior mechanics and a bit of dust. They never jam, never backfire. As seamless as the most finely wrought clock."

"The perfect gun," Khade said. "That's either really cool or really scary."

"It's both," Rowan said. "That's what happens when fey get their hands on something."

"Did anyone just hear that?" Dekk asked.

"Very funny," Khade said.

Dekk shook his head, motioning for the others to be silent.

"What is it?" Ainsley whispered.

No one answered her, instead glancing around and listening intently for a trace of a sound that was out of the ordinary. Rowan didn't hear anything, but he felt it. He felt hollow. Not an emotional type of hollow, but a literal type, a sickeningly empty feeling that came accompanied by a slight lightheadedness. It felt a bit like all the light had been sucked out of him. And then he saw what had made him feel that way.

Dark, shadowy shapes swam along the ground from among the trees behind them. A few pairs of white eyes locked with his.

"Shades!" he cried, yanking his unicorn's mane hard enough that the creature pulled back. He didn't have time to feel apologetic. "Get out of here!"

The shadows, having been revealed, abandoned all attempts at stealth. They separated from the mass into about a dozen vaguely humanlike shapes. Their white eyes were hollow. In unison, they sprang forward in a black wave, roiling toward the unicorns and their riders. Rowan and the others turned to flee.

They weren't fast enough.

A piercing wail ripped through the air. Rowan twisted his unicorn around hard in order to see what had happened. Ainsley's unicorn was being dragged to the ground, the Shades' sharp, foggy nails digging into its sides, leaving bloody trails in the white fur. Ainsley was kicking at the Shades, but her feet only passed through their forms. Rowan urged his own unicorn toward her just as she and her mount were drawn to the ground and disappeared beneath an inky cloud of bodies.

Rowan jumped to the ground, attempting to run before his feet had even touched down. He pitched headlong toward Ainsley, summoning whatever stardust would come forward. Something hissed past his face and through the body of a Shade. He whirled, expecting another threat. Khade held Rowan's pistol in extended hands, staring toward the Shade with an expression of astonished panic. The barrel smoked with pale glitter.

"You can't shoot them!" Rowan yelled back, turning and reaching the mass of shadow. Without thinking, he reached into the cloud with both hands. The Shades, sensing yet another source of their lost dust, seized him.

For a moment, all he could see was black. The world seemed to twist sideways and upside down, and he couldn't breathe. Then reflex took over, and he let out a burst of glittering light. The Shades tumbled backward, away from both him and Ainsley. Rowan's knees started to buckle. He felt a hand grip his upper arm and tug him upwards. He turned to see Indigo leaning down from her unicorn, her face anxious but unwavering.

"Hurry," she said, pulling. "Climb up."

Rowan twisted around to see Dekk hefting an unconscious Ainsley onto the front of Khade's unicorn. Both of Dekk's swords were out, stuck in the ground by his feet. Once Ainsley was secured, Dekk jerked the swords back out of the ground, and Khade's unicorn surged forward past Rowan and Indigo.

"Come on!" Indie shouted, tugging harder at Rowan's arm. Rowan turned and clambered up behind her. They both looked back to see the Shades starting to reassemble, but Dekk had remounted as well now. Dekk whipped his unicorn with the flat of one blade, and it took off in a gallop after Khade. Indigo dashed after them both.

Rowan glanced back once to see whether the Shades had followed them, but they hadn't. Rather the black fog was gathered around his and Ainsley's unicorns. Both creatures were now white, gory masses lying among their attackers. The bit of dust within their horns would be enough to stave off the Shades for the moment, but the image of their bodies would not soon be forgotten.

Rowan looked away. He wrapped his arms around Indie's waist and rested his head on her shoulder, feeling sick.

FOURTEEN

"I believe in everything until it's disproved. So I believe in fairies, the myths, dragons. It all exists, even if it's in your mind. Who's to say that dreams and nightmares aren't as real as the here and now?"

—John Lennon

Night had almost fallen by the time Phoenixdown Village was in sight. Everyone was exhausted. Rowan had almost fallen off the back of Indigo's unicorn twice. Khade had a sort of haunted look that lingered around his eyes. Dekk had been watching every angle around them, eyes darting here and there for any sign that the Shades were back. Indigo had been wearing an expression of carefully concealed fear for the last couple of hours, ever since they had slowed to a cantering walk. Ainsley had regained consciousness, but she felt awful.

"It's because of the Shades," Rowan told her. "That's what they do. Their own dust has been stolen, so they search out other sources — stars, sprites, pixies, unicorns. Usually whatever they can get. Doesn't work though, they can't hold onto it. The dust just sort of—" he shrugged "—passes through them or something."

Ainsley nodded, sitting sidesaddle in front of Khade, with her arms wrapped around him. She felt him sigh in relief when they reached the gates to the village.

Dekk dismounted and waltzed up to the gates. He looked the wooden panels over, started to raise a hand to knock, then changed his mind and kicked them a couple times instead. No one answered at first, so he kicked again, harder and louder.

A small window slid open. An angular face peered out. "Yes?" asked the face, eyes shifting quickly over everyone. They settled for a moment on Dekk's sheathed blades and Khade's holstered gun.

"Let us in," Dekk said.

The face lifted one eyebrow. "Not likely. What's your business here?"

Dekk glanced back at Rowan. *Should I tell him?* Rowan just gave a weary shrug. Dekk turned back to the window. "We're looking for Neverens'il," he said. "We were told he lives in this village."

The eyes widened for half a second before returning to normal. "I don't know who that is. You have the wrong place."

Dekk opened his mouth to say something that would almost undoubtedly be unpleasant. Indigo smoothly intervened. "We're not from the castle," she said. It was almost a lie, Ainsley thought, but she knew how Indie had meant it. "We need his help with something. Please."

The face behind the window watched Indigo for a moment. Then he sighed as if he was going against his better judgment, closed the window, and opened one of the gates. Ainsley got her first glimpse of who the face belonged to. She figured he wasn't a sidhe, judging by the way his pointed ears were shorter than Indie's or Dekk's were, but then, she didn't really know. He was tall and knobby limbed, dressed in rough brown clothing. His hair was silvery and stood up around his head in disarray. Ainsley wasn't sure whether he was old or if he'd always looked that wrinkly.

The faery stood aside and gestured for them to pass. "His house is on down the lane a ways, the one with the lettering round the door."

Indigo flashed him a smile from under heavy lashes. The faery returned a somewhat dazed grin and waggled his fingers in a wave.

When they were out earshot of the faery, Rowan made a face at the back of Indie's head and asked, "Why do you do that?"

"Just part of my charm," she answered. She let the words hang for a moment before adding, "And it's not like we want him spreading around news of our arrival." No one could really argue with that point.

To Ainsley, the village of Phoenixdown looked like an illustration from a book she had read when she was younger. The houses and

125

buildings were lined up neatly, like a sort of large fantasy neighborhood. The shops were hung with bells and wind chimes, and little patches of mushrooms grew in between buildings. A few open-air stalls were set up, displaying an assortment of items for sale. An older-looking woman, bent low, made eye contact with Ainsley as they passed the woman's stall. The woman smiled mysteriously at her. Ainsley felt as though the old woman had just seen through all her secrets.

Neverens'il's house turned out to be a shop on the front half and a house on the back half. The door was painted black, and strange letter-like symbols arched around it in white. Something about the letters seemed vaguely familiar to Ainsley, but she couldn't place where she had seen them and then the thought was gone.

Everyone dismounted, and Indie stepped forward to open the door into the shop. The interior was dim but comfortable feeling, lined with shelves of books and scrolls and parchment. A pair of crossed swords adorned the wall behind the counter. Also behind the counter was a young man who appeared to be in his late teens or early twenties. However, his slender pointed ears, Ainsley knew, meant he could really be much older than he looked. He was tall and thin, built much the same as Rowan. His hair was blond but not in the pale, whitish blond that was Ainsley's. His was a golden yellow shade, and it stuck out to one side as if he had swept it over on purpose. A pair of large, filmy wings was folded behind his back. His eyes were a dark green, and then, all at once, they weren't.

He looked up when they entered. "Can I help you?" he asked, a bit warily. Apparently, seeing five people enter his shop at the same time was a little out of the ordinary. Of course, Ainsley figured, they *were* out of the ordinary after all. Not to mention, a bit bedraggled looking at the moment. She wondered if it was normal for people to walk around armed, as well.

"Are you Neverens'il?" Rowan asked.

The faery tilted his head. "Depends on who's asking, I guess," he answered.

"We're asking," Khade said. "And there's more questions where that comes from."

The faery nodded somewhat appraisingly. "I might just like you," he said to Khade. And then to everyone else, "I go by Never, in recent years. What d'you need?"

Ainsley had expected him to look older, more naturally associated with wisdom perhaps, but she didn't say that. Instead she blurted, "We need to know whether or not the Blue Wand is real."

A silent moment reigned. Then Never said, "Who sent you? The castle?"

"Merdi. From one of the Pixie Trees," said Rowan. "We know Zake displaced your family. You have your reasons to be against him. We have ours. Your help would be appreciated, but if you don't want to give it, we can leave." He shrugged. "It's your choice."

Never gave a small amused smirk. "You people are pushy, eh?"

"We're on a deadline," Rowan said.

"Possible emphasis on 'dead'," Dekk added.

"Fair enough," Never said. "Yeah, the Blue Wand is real."

"How do we find it?" Indigo asked.

Never held up a hand. "I feel at a bit of a disadvantage here," he began. "You all know who I am, but I don't know any of you really. Introductions, anyone?" He smiled wryly.

Khade gave out their names, pointing to each one of them as he went along. Ainsley noticed a strange look come over the others' faces. When all had been introduced, Never's eyes lingered on Ainsley.

"Ainsley, huh?" he mused. "Queen Say's granddaughter, perhaps?"

Ainsley nodded, staring at him. "How did you...?"

"I know a lot of things," he said. "Knowledge passed down from generations of Unseelie. I'm not as young as I look. Not to mention, you favor her just a smidge." He smiled sharply and turned to Rowan. "Judging from tell of things, Zake isn't much fond of family relations at all, really."

Rowan blinked. "What?"

"Well, I haven't heard of him treating you all that *pleasantly*," Never said. He spread his hands. "And we all know what he did to Say and her family."

"What does that have to do with me?" Rowan asked, shaking his head in confusion.

Never stared hard at him. "You mean you don't know?"

"Know what? I have no idea what you're on about."

"Cruel fate," Never muttered in a low voice, and then louder, "So I guess you never knew you and Ainsley were cousins then."

To Ainsley, who had learned more about her life in the past two days than she had learned in fifteen years, this revelation didn't seem as surprising, or else she was starting to get used to secrets being unearthed. Rowan, however, looked as if he had just been slapped across the face. He stared back at Never, wide-eyed and still. He opened his mouth to speak and then closed it again, seeming to be waiting for his brain to catch up with Never's words. The only thing he could manage to say was a small "What?"

"Well, I guess you two would be more like second cousins or something," Never explained, "Since Zake is Ainsley's great uncle. Your father was his and Say's younger brother, by a few good centuries, I think. Strange that he never told you, in any case."

Rowan's face was white. Ainsley thought he was probably horrified. What Rowan said next, however, proved her very wrong.

"We're *related?*" he said angrily, shocked expression disappearing. "All these years, and we're *related?* I didn't know I could think any less of him!" He was talking to himself now, it seemed. "The next time I see him, I swear I'm gonna—"

"—Do nothing until we get our hands on that wand."

All eyes turned toward Khade. The haunted look was still lingering around his eyes but seemed to have faded slightly. "We can't rush into anything right now. We've already been attacked once. Who knows what else he's sent our way?" He shook his head. "Our priority is getting to that wand before anybody else does."

"No one asked for your input, Khade," Rowan snapped at him. "We don't even need you here."

Khade took a deep breath as if trying to contain himself. "That's fine. I'm not here for you. I'm here for Ainsley. And she may not need me either, but I'll be damned if I let you keep her away from me. Besides, she's not just your princess anymore. She's family too. Don't you want her to be safe?"

"And what? You're going to keep her safe by giving away her name and everyone else's to a stranger just because he asked for them?"

Ainsley looked back and forth between Khade and Rowan, expecting at least some marginal amount of violence to break out. The two only stared at each other, both in silent contemplation.

Never waved a hand through the air. "Hate to break up the family reunion, but here's not really the best place to continue our little conversation." He walked to the door and turned the lock. "I've got a lot of information to share, and you don't have much time to hear it. Follow me into the main room and I'll tell you how to get to the wand."

Dekk and the girls followed Never into the next room — Dekk was watching Never with thinly disguised interest — but Ainsley peeked back through the crack of the door. She watched as Khade reached out and grabbed Rowan by the elbow before he could leave. Rowan tensed but didn't pull away.

"Look, I know you don't like me," Khade said. "I'm not fond of you either. But if we're going to get anything accomplished, we've got to work together. Zake's not working alone, and neither should we. Both of us have people we want to protect. We don't need to get in each other's way of that." He let go of Rowan's arm, waiting.

Rowan gave a sarcastic laugh. "Now you choose to start making sense."

"Someone needs to," Khade replied. "Besides, family is a noun, not an adjective. It doesn't define you. Just because you guys are related, it doesn't—" He hesitated and then said, "It doesn't mean you're like him."

"What is that supposed to mean?" Rowan asked quietly.

Khade sighed. "Let's just say I've had my share of family issues too. You really don't want to turn out like them. But that's what makes you different, right?"

Rowan turned around and stared him in the face for a moment. "You don't suck as much as I thought you did after all," Rowan said finally. He still managed to sound insulting.

"Why thanks," Khade returned. "Just remember, you might be Ainsley's cousin, but that doesn't mean I have to like you."

"Right," Rowan agreed. "And I'll still beat the hell out of you if the need arises."

Ainsley managed to scramble back away from the door just as they opened it from the other side. Never and the twins were sitting around a plush carpet and looking over a map. Dekk glanced up when the door opened.

"What took you guys so long?" he asked.

"Nothing," Rowan answered. "We were just discussing something."

A devilish smirk curled across Dekk's face, and he opened his mouth.

"Shut up, Dekk," Rowan said dismissively. "Do we have a plan?"

"We've got directions," Indigo said. "A plan? Not so much." She held out the map and Rowan took it, scanning over the notes she had written across it.

After a moment, he looked back up. "Are you serious?"

"What's the matter?" Ainsley asked.

"It's underwater," Rowan said. "The wand is underwater. Nobody's getting it, unless someone is part fish."

"Could we get a mermaid to bring it to us?" Ainsley suggested. "Mermaids are real, right?"

"Yeah, they're real," Never said. "But they're ruled by a moon, Earth's moon in particular. Luna, Queen of the Tides, so jealous of the stars that she tried to steal their light for herself." He shook his head. "No, they're not going to just hand it over to you. And they'll drown you if you try to get it yourself."

"Then what do we do?" Khade asked, looking around at the others.

"Hey, diddle, diddle, the cat and the fiddle," Never started singing. "The cow jumped over the moon. The little dog laughed to see such sport, and the dish ran away with the spoon."

"That's not what I had in mind," Khade deadpanned.

"It's not what anyone has in mind," Never said. "Because it's wrong. The words were changed to nonsense over time. Here's what it should be." He snatched the map from Rowan's hands and started scribbling on the back. When he was finished, his message read:

Hey, Diddle, Diddle,
The cait with the fiddle.
The kelpie jumped up for the moon.
The little wolf laughed in the sea. Such sport!
And the fish swam away from the tune.

"I don't understand," Indigo said, reading it over. "What does that mean? It still sounds like nonsense."

"It's in code," Dekk said. "It makes perfect sense."

"Do explain," Khade said.

"Okay. Diddle is apparently a name because it's capitalized. It's probably the name of the cait sidhe who plays the violin."

"Cait sidhe? What's that?"

"Cat faery," Dekk answered. "And a kelpie is like a horse that lives underwater—they drown people for fun—so it might be Luna's pet or something. So it would jump up for her because it obeys her. The fish are probably merfolk and nixies and whatnot. The tune they're running away from has to be coming from the violin. The only part that doesn't fit is the wolf. I don't know what that part means."

"Whoa," Khade said. Ainsley stared in awe. Dekk looked around at them.

"What?" he asked.

"Impressive," Never said. "So you're not as dumb as you seem."

"Hey!" Dekk shouted in anger.

"He's actually a part time genius," Rowan said hotly. "So what about the wolf then?"

"It's a sea wolf," Never explained. "It guards the wand. You want past it, you've got to answer its riddle."

"Why is it always riddles?" Khade asked, throwing his hands up.

"Faery folk like riddles," Never said. "They amuse us." His eyes seemed to glint for a moment, and then it was gone. "Anyway, you need to go to the village of River Rock. There's a family of cait sidhe there, the Diddle family, been around for ages. Cats have nine lives, you know. The Diddles have been famous for their musicians. Chances are you'll find a violinist there. Take them with you to the sea. Have them play the old song about the moon and the star, and the sea folk will stay away from you. If you see kelpies pulling a water carriage, get out of there. Luna will almost certainly be in that carriage."

"That sounds easy enough," Rowan said. "Except that none of us can breathe underwater or hold our breath forever. You could fly an airship through the holes in this plan."

"Never will you ever hear Never say never," the faery announced cheerfully. He rummaged around in a chest of drawers for a moment before pulling out a set of seashells strung on cords. "Wear one of these and you can breathe underwater to your little heart's content. Problem is I only have three, so two of you will have to stay on shore."

"We'll tackle that issue when we come to it," Rowan said, taking the shells and stashing them in a jacket pocket. "Now then. I know all this comes with a price. What do you want in return?"

"My crown," Never said. "I want Unseelie rule returned to me and that bitch of a pretender, Morag, off my throne."

Rowan looked back at Ainsley, who shrugged. "Fair enough then," he answered. "You'll receive your title after everything's been dealt with."

Never seemed to consider whether he trusted the wording of Rowan's statement then nodded in agreement. He looked around at the windows. "You can all spend the night here if you want. It's safer than braving the dark, after all, even for a star."

"Especially for a star," Rowan added quietly. Ainsley nodded in agreeance.

Never had only one bedroom, so everyone wound up sleeping in the main room on the floor. Never moved piles of rugs and blankets and pillows into the room to help soften the hardwood. It didn't matter anyway how hard the floor was. They were all asleep as soon as they closed their eyes.

FIFTEEN

"Government is not reason; it is not eloquent; it is force. Like fire, it is a dangerous servant and a fearful master."

—George Washington

Somewhere between sleep and wakefulness, Rowan's mind registered that the air seemed strangely hotter than it had previously. At the scent of smoke, he opened his eyes. His first coherent thought was of a lit fireplace. When Dekk was suddenly in his face, however, he knew something was wrong.

"Hurry up! Get up!" Dekk urged, pulling at Rowan's shirt. "The whole village is on fire!"

Rowan rubbed at his eyes. "What?"

"Everything's burning! It's only a matter of time before the flames spread to Never's house. We've got to go now!"

The last bit of comprehension sparked to life in Rowan's mind. Pulling his boots on, he scanned the room to see everyone else shoveling things into bags and throwing jackets around their shoulders. Rowan gathered up the few things he had brought with him and shoved his jacket through the strap of his bag.

Never waved everyone over. "Follow me out! This way!"

He led them through a back door and out onto a side street of the village main. The majority of the surrounding buildings were already in flames. Sparks licked at the corners of Never's back windows. The night was still strong, and the only light came from the fires and a tiny sliver of the moon, nearly blotted out by smoke.

They hurried down the street, hands over their mouths, trying not to choke on the overwhelming black ashes that kept roiling across their path. Never led them in sharp dizzying turns and through alleys that were so narrow, everyone had to pass through in single file lines. Fleeing villagers jostled past them, separating them a few times and knocking Ainsley down once. Never stopped dead at the end of one alley, slightly wider than the others so that they could all crowd around to see why he had stopped.

Rowan was stuck at the back but, being the tallest in their party, could see what was holding them up. Lit by flames, standing there watching the village burn to embers, was Fince. Joel was standing right beside him. Rowan felt his face burn in anger. So Joel was responsible too. Had Joel's caring been an act all this time?

"We have to go around," Khade said. "They'll see us if we don't."

"But we need to get to the woods," Indigo said. "We can see the forest from here. We're only one street away. If we go back now, there's a fair chance we'll only wind up being blocked in by the flames."

Dekk rapped his knuckles against the left wall of the alley. The sound that returned was hollow. He faced the others with a pleased expression. "We could go through here."

"He really is a genius," Never remarked, shrugging.

Dekk picked a hidden lock and pushed a section of the wall open. There were no lights in the room, but the fires cast eerie dancing illuminations across the floor. Dekk led everyone through the empty house to a door on the other side. He twisted the handle and the door swung open.

"Looks like we're on the right track then," he said, sliding through the doorway. He checked every direction before waving for the others to follow. Never took the lead again through a last alley that ended on a wide path. Just across the path was an expanse of forest.

"Okay, we don't know who else is here from the castle," Never warned. "So we've got to be quick. When I say, start running and don't look back. Don't stop once we get into the woods. Keep going. I'll let you know when we've gone far enough. All right?"

Uncertain glances mingled with understanding nods, but no one spoke any disagreement.

"Okay then." Never nodded back and glanced around the corners of the alley. "Ready? Now!"

Everyone burst forward in unison. Rowan made certain to keep himself behind everyone else in case any sort of threat should arise. He could only protect them if he could see them. They were within the trees in mere seconds and no one was chasing after them so far. Still they kept running. After a few minutes, the village was only a plume of smoke in the past. They ran for at least another fifteen minutes before Never slowed and held up a hand, waving at them to stop. The lot of them hit the ground in breathless heaps.

Rowan's lungs felt like they were going to fall apart. Every breath stabbed through him like a knife. He lay on his back on the ground, eyes closed and trying not to hyperventilate.

"Not dead, are you?"

Rowan turned his head to see who was talking to him. Khade was lying a few feet off and managing to appear both exhausted and smug at the same time. "Nah, I'm good," Rowan said. "Not gonna lie though, I was hoping we'd have lost you a few miles back."

Khade sat up and grinned. "Not a chance."

"Yeah well, you keep wishing too then."

"So what now?" Indigo asked. "You saw what they did back there. I don't think finding the wand is enough. It's going to take an army to overthrow Zake."

"Yeah, and we don't have an army," Ainsley added.

Rowan sat up, folding his arms on top of his knees. "There has to be a way. We can't have come this far for nothing."

"I might have a solution," Never said, "If you're willing to take some risks."

Dekk laughed. "You say that like we're not taking risks already. What do you think we're doing? Taking goodies to grandmother's house?"

"Okay, technically the grandmother got eaten in that story," Khade pointed out.

"It doesn't matter, guys," Rowan said. "What's your solution, Never?"

"We get ourselves an army," Never said.

A moment of silence passed. "You can't just *get* an army like that," Khade said. "Where would we even start?"

"Look, as a whole, the Unseelie are happy with what they've got, right?" Never said. "We're a backstabbing lot of turncoats. As long as Zake gives them a bit a free rein from time to time, they're happy. The Seelie—" he held up a finger "—are not. They want *their* freedom too, and Zake hasn't been giving them very much. The problem is the Seelie are afraid to rally against Zake without a leader. If they failed, Zake would wipe them out without a second thought."

"So they need a leader," Dekk mused. "Or not necessarily a leader, just someone to give them a cause. If they had a name, they would fight for it. I know they would." He looked to Indie and Rowan, a rekindled light forming in his mismatched eyes. His point clicked in their minds at the same time, but Indie was quicker to say it.

"Ainsley."

Ainsley glanced around at them in confusion. "What?"

"Don't you see?" Rowan asked. "You're the leader. You're the name they would rally behind. The Seelie and Unseelie were equal when your grandmother was queen."

"Technically she's also your aunt," Ainsley pointed out. "You could lead them better than I could anyway."

Rowan shook his head. "If *I'm* just finding out we're related, then I'm not putting much faith in very many others knowing or remembering that. You're her heir anyway. The crown would have fallen to you in her absence. And *everyone* is aware of that fact. *Your* name is the one that will get them moving."

"But we still need to find the wand too, right?" Indie asked. "Before Zake does. We can't do both. We won't have that much time before he sends more Shades after us, or worse."

"I'll go," Never said. "I'll go around to the Seelie villages and recruit for you. Meanwhile, you can all continue on to get the wand. Then you can accomplish both at once."

Everyone else exchanged glances with one another. Rowan knew they were all thinking the same thing: could they trust someone they hadn't even known for a full night?

"I can go too," Dekk announced. "Then I can help Never."

Rowan managed to catch Dekk's eye, trying to convey what he couldn't say out loud. *What are you thinking? Can we really trust him? Sure, he didn't murder us last night or leave us to be roasted alive, but we outnumbered him then.*

"I know it might not be the best idea, splitting up, but what choice do we really have?" Dekk said. "If I go with Never, we can have a little extra strength in numbers. And with one less trying to get to the wand, the rest of you will have that much less of a chance of being seen. Besides, it's not like Rowan and Khade are going to let either of the girls go. So I'm really the only one who *can* go."

Rowan thought over Dekk's words. True, he wasn't letting Ainsley out of his sight. She was the center of everything. Khade wouldn't let Ainsley out of his sight either, so he wouldn't leave without her. Indie going was out of the question. Rowan wasn't about to send her off with some random guy, whether she could take care of herself or not. If Rowan himself was to go with Never, and the others were to encounter Fince along the way, he wasn't sure any of them would be able to stand up to a river troll armed with stardust. Dekk would be fine even if things took a wrong turn. The sidhe was smarter than he let on. He could get out of almost anything. Hopefully, he just wouldn't flirt too much.

"You're right," Rowan said. "You're the best one for it. It should take at least another few days to get to the wand and a few to get back to the castle." He turned to Never. "Is that even enough time?"

Never gave a wicked grin, and for the first time, Rowan got a good look at his teeth. Each one came to a jagged point, locked together like some sort of bright white stitch work. Rowan was suddenly glad that Dekk was the one going; he was the only other one of them who could come anywhere close to pulling a smile like that. "I've got my own little travel tricks," Never said. "I'm the one with the secrets, remember?"

"Speaking of which," Khade said, "Which way and how far to this River Rock place?"

"Straight off that way," Never said, pointing somewhere off behind Ainsley's shoulder. "Not far either. Probably three and a half, four hours' walk. You could be there be just after dawn if you started now." Never gave a catlike stretch, only further securing Rowan's previous comparison of him with Dekk. "Alright then, if there are no more questions, we'll be off. We have our own business to attend to, after all."

"Be careful, Dekk," Indigo said quietly.

Dekk shrugged. "You know 'careful' isn't in my vocabulary."

Indie's brow furrowed. "That's why I worry."

"See you guys later!" was all Dekk said as he followed Never off and away from everyone else.

"I don't like this," Indie murmured to Rowan.

"I don't like it either," he said. "There are a lot of things I don't like about this. We just have to deal with it for now." He put an arm around her shoulders before turning around to Khade and Ainsley. "Let's get everything together. We're on to River Rock."

"Can't we rest for a little while longer?" Ainsley asked. "I'm still tired, and we ran forever."

Rowan shook his head. "We can't. They'll be after us as soon as they realize we're not in Phoenixdown anymore."

Ainsley sighed. "Okay."

They had only been traveling a total of twenty minutes when Ainsley stumbled and fell for the tenth time. Rowan turned and walked back toward her. "This is ridiculous," he said. "We're not going to get anywhere at this rate."

"Well, I'm sorry," Ainsley said. "I'm tired, it's dark, and I can't see the ground."

"You're a star," Rowan deadpanned. "Being in the dark is an occupational hazard."

Khade came up behind him and shoved him out of the way. "Don't talk to her like that. You have no right to—"

"*Boys*," Indie called. "Knock it off. We have a problem. Fix it."

"Fine," Rowan said. Ignoring the murderous look Khade sent to him, he bent down and pulled Ainsley to her feet. Turning his back to her, he ordered, "Get on."

"Hey, wait a minute," Khade started.

Rowan cast him a withering look. "You want to carry her?" he asked. Khade blushed. *Didn't think so.*

"I don't need to be carried," Ainsley insisted.

Rowan turned to her. "Look, Ains, we don't have that much time. I'm trying to help here."

144

Ainsley stared at him. "Only my grandfather calls me Ains."

Rowan blinked. "Oh, sorry then."

She shook her head roughly as if she were trying to get a leaf out of her hair. "No, it's okay. I mean…you're family too, right?"

"Yeah, I guess so," he said quietly. He gave a small laugh. "Haven't had one of those in a while."

Ainsley put her hands on his shoulders and forced him downward. She wrapped her arms around his neck and allowed him to heft her onto his back. "Well, start getting used to it then," she said, "Because I don't plan on disappearing anytime soon."

Rowan pretended not to have seen Indigo smile as he carried Ainsley past her.

SIXTEEN

"Fairy damsels met in forest wide
By knights of Logres, or of Lyones,
Lancelot or Pelleas, or Pellenore."

—John Milton, *Paradise Regained*

Ainsley found herself being lulled to sleep by the soft, bouncing rhythm of Rowan's footsteps. She lowered her head down to rest it on Rowan's shoulder. He wasn't as soft as she had hoped he would be. Truthfully, he was rather uncomfortable. He was incredibly bony, and the bouncing steps he took did nothing to help the fact. But the dark was inviting, though she knew it shouldn't be, and she was exhausted. It was at least better than sleeping in a prison cell, she thought and let her eyelids give in to their weight.

Half-asleep, she realized something had changed. Light seeped in from beneath her closed eyes. Opening them, she discovered three things. First, the sun had risen to cast a fiery morning glow over everything. Second, down the hill, a village rose up, looking warm and quaint and holding the potential for breakfast; just past the village lay a wide river. Third, she noticed that the head in front of hers was not covered in wild, red hair, but rather short, dark brown. She shifted in surprise, and Khade almost dropped her.

"Good morning, sunshine," he said, lowering her off his back onto solid ground. He stretched, and she could hear the sound of his joints popping.

"Have a nice nap?" Rowan asked.

Ainsley looked over at him. He looked terrible. Well, Khade and Indigo didn't seem spectacular either, but Rowan looked practically dead on his feet. And here she had been sleeping, for what was likely several hours, while they took turns toting her through the forest like she was a princess.

Well, she amended. She was a princess, but that wasn't the point.

"I'm sorry," she blurted. "I didn't mean to fall asleep. I just—"

"It's okay," Rowan said, cutting her off. He gave her a weary smile. "Khade enjoyed it, anyway."

Ainsley stared back at him, feeling a hot flush creep up her neck to her cheeks. Beside her, Khade made an indignant noise while Indigo chuckled lightly from Rowan's other side.

"Just as well you're awake now, though," Rowan continued. "We need a plan this time, a little more stealth. At least until we find who we're looking for. I'm not fond of the idea of a repeat of what happened in the previous village."

Ainsley shook her head.

"From the sound of things, there's a festival or something going on," Indie said, peering off down the hill.

Now that she mentioned it, Ainsley could hear it too, the faint sound of music drifting up to where they stood together in the last bit of tree cover. "I hope they have food," she said. She couldn't recall eating anything since they had left Merdi's tree house. And Rowan hadn't eaten anything then, she remembered.

Indie laughed again. "We'll stop at an inn and get something to eat. Then as soon as we find our fiddler, we can go back to the inn and sleep for a few hours."

"Or a few hours *more*," Khade added, grinning.

"Shut up," Ainsley said and pushed him. He stumbled over sideways, laughing.

"There are no gates on the outside of the village this time," Rowan pointed out. "Either that, or the gates have been left open. This village is Unseelie, unlike the last one. The Seelie villages are going to be more suspicious of us, naturally, since we're from the castle." He shook his head in doubt, as if he had said something he didn't quite agree with. "But who knows what kind of news may have traveled so far. If things start to go badly, I can Blink us out."

"Hmm," Indie frowned.

Rowan glanced at her but didn't say anything.

"Why are the villages grouped like that?" Ainsley asked, "Seelie and Unseelie? I always imagined each would have their own territory, not be scattered around like they are, all mingled together."

"They should be like that. Separate, I mean," Rowan answered. "Before Zake, Say ruled over the Seelie Court, and Never's family ruled the Unseelie Court. The territories were separate, but they coexisted peacefully. Or at least, as peacefully as rival fey can exist, meaning there were only wars every century of so. When Say disappeared, Zake allowed the Unseelie free rein across Avyn. It upset the balance between the Courts. Unseelie overran Seelie villages and moved into them themselves. The Seelie villages that managed to hold their own set up walls and gates around their homes for protection."

"So the Unseelie are bad?" Ainsley asked.

"No, we're not bad," Indigo said. "At least not all the way. But neither are we good. The Seelie are more like us than either side really wants to admit. If they're day, we're night. The day may have the sun, but the night has the stars. Neither is good or bad, only different by association. Nothing can be all of one or the other."

149

"Since you and Dekk are Unseelie, though," Ainsley mused, "You both must prefer it this way. I mean, isn't it kind of in your favor that the Unseelie came out on top this time? No offense."

Indigo turned to her with an expression mixed with both defiance and confusion. "The Courts are off balance. In the long run, things will only get worse for both sides. We can't exist like this. And…I have a reason to fight for your side too." She twisted to look off over the village down the hill. "I only want to end this with as little bloodshed as possible, on both sides."

"And in order to do that, we need you," Rowan added. "You and the Blue Wand."

"Aren't we sort of starting a war though?" Khade asked. One of his eyebrows was raised in a doubtful manner. "What if this just makes it worse anyway?"

"We can only hope it won't," Rowan said. "Hopefully Zake underestimates us. He probably won't think of us splitting up and Dekk and Never visiting Seelie villages. He'll think we all stayed together. He may not even know we made it out of Phoenixdown. He obviously knows we're after the wand. Otherwise he wouldn't have sent Fince and Jo—" He cut himself off and paused for the shortest second. "He wouldn't have messed with Phoenixdown."

"That didn't really answer my question," Khade muttered.

"It doesn't matter," Ainsley said. "Things can't go on the way they are, so it doesn't matter." She shrugged, hoping to give off a sense of careless cheerfulness. "Besides, the worst that could happen is we all die, right?"

"For a star," Rowan said, effectively popping her thought bubble, "There's such a thing as a fate worse than death."

"Oh well, that's one way to put it," Indigo said. She turned to Ainsley, whose dark eyes were wide. "We're only in trouble if we get caught. And we'll only get caught if we're not careful." She motioned down towards the village. "So let's be careful while we're going down this hill." She started climbing down with the grace of a cat, reminding Ainsley of a less creepy Dekk.

"Ladies first," Khade said, mock bowing and waving a hand for Ainsley to pass in front of him.

Rowan intervened. "It would be better if one of us went first," he said. "That way, if she slips going down, we could catch her."

Khade turned to him with an exasperated scowl. "Look, I know you're really into this role and all, but the whole shining protector act is starting to get on my nerves."

Rowan fixed him with a flat stare. "Fine. You worry about her then."

"That's what I'm here for," Khade countered, but Rowan was already climbing down the hill after Indie.

Khade made a frustrated noise and turned to Ainsley. "You know, the more I think about it, I realize that I'm completely fine with you being related to Uncle Psychopath. It's the fact that you're related to *him*," and he motioned in irritation down to Rowan, "that I find so hard to deal with. I mean, come on. How do you and he share *anything*?"

Ainsley tried not to smile. "It probably got passed down from the 'psychopath' side of the family. The gene must have passed me up. Like blue eyes or something."

"Yeah, he's got those too."

"So do you," Ainsley said.

Khade opened his mouth to say something then closed it back. He shrugged. "Fair enough."

Ainsley laughed and started down the hill. Rowan and Indie were already a little ways down, slipping on rocks and bare earth where the grass had been washed away by rain. Behind Ainsley, Khade stumbled over something and swore.

"I heard that," she said.

"Well, I—"

But instead of finishing his sentence, which was sure to have been some sort of excuse, he let out a surprised cry and went tumbling past her. She reached out to grab him, managing to snag the elbow of his shirt sleeve, but he weighed more than she did. Coupled with the downward acceleration, the only thing she succeeded in doing was getting dragged down along with him.

Everything whirled past her eyes in a rapid show of color. The rocks and dirt, and then morning sky, and rocks and dirt again. She tried to keep a hold of Khade's sleeve, but he was falling just ahead of her, and

152

the jostling forced her grip to loosen too much. She closed her eyes against the dirt in her face.

"Ains!"

She heard the voice call out to her and then she felt herself slam into something. Instead of stopping, however, she kept rolling, taking the obstacle with her. She felt a pair of arms wrap around her tightly, desperately trying to hold onto her. Though her back was still left mostly unprotected, she could feel her face being shielded.

Finally she felt the rocks change to grass beneath her, and the tumbling slowed to a stop. The thing on top of her rolled off into the grass beside her. Breathing heavily, she turned her head to see who it was. She met eyes with Rowan, breathing just as hard as she was while fixing her with a somewhat bemused gaze.

Khade staggered over and dropped to his knees beside Ainsley, as Indigo half-ran, half-slid down the hill the rest of the way to join them.

"I'm so sorry," Khade said, eyes wide, looking Ainsley up and down. "I didn't mean to. Are you okay?"

She took in his appearance. His clothes were dirty — well, dirtier than they had been — and there was a cut on his forehead that leaked blood down between his eyebrows. "I could ask you the same question," she answered. "But I'm fine." She checked herself over just to make sure. The knees of her tights were ripped, and she was sure she would have some bruises later, but everything otherwise felt intact. She sat up and, from the corner of her eye, saw Rowan do the same.

"What about you?" she asked him. She glanced over him as well. The back of his jacket was covered in dirt, and one of the lenses of his goggles was cracked. She figured it was a wonder they had even managed to stay on his head. A large bruise was already showing up under the freckles below one eye.

He shrugged. "I suppose stars should get used to falling. Personally, I'd prefer we not do it again." He sounded annoyed, but he was smiling.

Indigo jogged over to where they all sat. "I thought I told you all to be careful," she said.

"I was being careful," Ainsley said, grinning. "But you know these two, they don't listen to anything."

Indie tilted her head back to look up at the sky and sighed. "It's not funny. You could have gotten hurt."

"On the bright side," Rowan offered, "We got down the hill faster than we had planned."

Indigo only stared at him, eyes narrowed. Then she turned and headed briskly toward the open village gates.

"Come on, Indie," Rowan called to her. "Don't be mad. I was just kidding." He jumped up, staggering a little, and ran after her. Ainsley watched him walk backwards in front of her, pleading with her.

"You've got to go down on your knee, Rowan!" Ainsley shouted, her hands cupped around her mouth.

"She's right, though," Khade said. "It's not funny."

"Oh, okay, fine," Ainsley conceded. "You win." She stood up, brushing dirt from her dress and tights.

"I don't want to win," Khade said. "I just want you to be safe."

Ainsley felt heat rise to her cheeks. She proceeded to pretend to smooth down her hair in order to hide her face from him. "Well, I am safe," she said. "And so are you. So I guess we both win."

Khade took a deep breath beside her. "Yeah, I guess we do." A silent moment passed briefly before he said, "We should go before they leave us behind."

"Yeah," Ainsley said and then smiled. "Rowan might need our help getting back out of the hole he's digging himself into right now."

Khade snorted. "Or we could make everyone happier and just bury him in it."

Ainsley shoved him sideways, but she was laughing.

SEVENTEEN

"We may have forgotten how to feel. Nobody is teaching us how to live happily ever after, as we've heard in fairy tales."

—Yakov Smirnoff

No guards were stationed at the gates to River Rock, even though the gates were wide open. If fact, no one spared more than a first glance at the strangers who entered. The crowd of faeries started a few yards within the gates and spread out through the rest of the village, getting thicker and wilder as it went along. It was like walking through a tangle of under-growing vines as they moved through the throng in search of an inn. Indigo led the way, followed by Rowan, then Ainsley, then Khade. Everyone was holding onto the person in front of them, gripping tight to an arm or the back of a jacket, so no one would get swept away in the waves of party-goers.

After pushing through the crowd for what felt like an eternity, so much that Rowan was starting to feel a bit claustrophobic, Indie turned around to him and pointed over heads to her left, shouting to be heard above the music and laughter.

"There's an inn over there," she said. "Come on."

Their little train turned off in the direction of the inn, struggling through the multitude even more now that they dared to venture against the others. As they reached the door, Rowan glanced up to read the sign above one of the windows.

The Dragon's Breath

Inn and Tavern

Glamoured payment not accepted

Indigo pushed open the door, and they all filed in behind her.

The inn was busy but felt spacious compared to the atmosphere outside. Several tables remained unoccupied. Indigo led everyone to a little booth in a corner, set a bit apart from any of the taken tables. In a matter a seconds, a barmaid had scurried up to them. Her hair hung half up in disheveled strands around her brown face. Her cheeks were mottled with darker spots like a toad's skin, and her fingers had little suction cup-like tips. She beamed around at each one of them with too-large black eyes.

"What can I get everyone?" she asked amiably. Her voice was strangely pitched, not deep and not light, but rather gravelly. Croaky, perhaps.

"Do you make pancakes?" Khade asked. His expression was ridiculously hopeful.

The frog-maid noticed. She giggled. At least Rowan took it as a giggle. It sounded like a *ribbit.* "If that's what you'd like," she answered.

Flirt, Rowan thought.

"Yeah, that sounds good to me too," Ainsley said.

Indigo shot Rowan a questioning glance. *Will you eat it if I order it for you?* He gave a small nod back to her, and she turned a smile on the frog girl. "Pancakes all around then," she said. "With honey, please."

"Sure," the girl replied and waltzed off. Rowan noticed her brown feet were bare and her toes were long and splayed apart.

"There are some…interesting people here, aren't there?" Khade asked hesitantly.

"You say *interesting*," Ainsley said. "But your expression says *freakish.*"

"I didn't— I mean, that's not what I meant," Khade objected. His eyebrows knitted together. "I'm just…not used to them, is all."

"I sort of want to ask her if she can climb walls," Ainsley said, grinning and leaning around Rowan to try to get another glimpse of the frog girl.

Rowan pushed her back into the booth seat. "Stop," he said. "We don't need to do anything to draw attention to ourselves." He glanced around the room at the other patrons. "We already look out of place. Especially him." He pointed across the table at Khade.

"Me?" Khade, in turn, pointed at himself. "Why me?"

"You're human," Indie answered, seamlessly carrying on Rowan's train of thought. "We can tell."

"How can you tell?" He looked suddenly very self-conscious. "Am I giving off some sort of vibe or something?"

Rowan snorted, hiding a grin by pretending to keep an eye on their surroundings. Indie giggled. "No, it's nothing like that," she said. "It's your ears."

"My ears?" Khade exclaimed. "Seriously?"

"Yes, your ears," Indie said. "Different types of faeries have differently shaped ears, and no faery has ears like a human, at least not unless they have quite a bit of human blood in them." She paused and gave a small laugh. "Well, that and you gape around at everything as if it's on fire. Ainsley does too, for that matter, but she comes across differently than you do."

"Is it her ears too?" Khade asked with vague sarcasm.

If Indigo planned on answering though, no one else ever knew, because the frog girl reappeared with four plates loaded with pancakes and set them down on the table. She vanished again shortly before coming back with glasses and a pitcher of water.

"Can I get you anything else?" she asked, but they all shook their heads, and she traipsed off to a different table and its occupants.

159

For a moment, no one spoke, choosing instead to work at the stack of pancakes in front of them. The stacks were steaming hot and drizzled in butter and honey, and the plates were almost empty when Indigo said,

"I was thinking..."

Rowan glanced across the table at her. He knew what that tone of voice meant. It meant she had an idea and she knew that he was almost certain to disagree with it. "And?" he prompted, ignoring the fact that his and Ainsley's elbows kept knocking together. He wished he'd thought to have sat on the other side of the table, but then, he had forgotten Ainsley wasn't left-handed too.

"I was thinking that maybe Ainsley and I could find the fiddle player while you and Khade get a bit of sleep," Indigo said, picking at her plate with the edge of her fork, not meeting his eyes.

"No." Rowan didn't even have to think about the answer. It was automatic. "Not a chance."

Indie looked up without raising her head, watching him from beneath thick dark eyelashes. It made him want to keep her that much closer. "Think about it, though," she said. "Face it, I know you're exhausted. And so is Khade. He's not used to this, and you've been pushing yourself even harder than usual." She raised her head, alternating a steady gaze from Rowan to Khade and back. "If you keep going like this, neither of you are going to be worth anything, with or without me and Ainsley around."

Rowan stared back at her. Letting Indigo and Ainsley go out wandering around a village full of reveling Unseelie was the last thing he wanted to do. Well, considering the circumstances, perhaps not the *last* thing he wanted to do, but it was nevertheless quite a ways down the list.

"I'll go with Ainsley," Khade volunteered. He seemed to second guess himself quickly. "Actually, Ainsley can stay here, and I'll go with you instead. I don't really know what a kite-caught-cat thing looks like."

"Cait sidhe," Rowan corrected automatically, but Khade didn't pay him any attention and kept on talking.

"If I go with you and Ainsley stays, then at least you'll both have someone to look after you."

Indie smiled, somewhat condescendingly in Rowan's opinion, but since it was directed at Khade, he didn't mind. "Your selflessness is commendable, really," she said. "But I fear you greatly underestimate my capabilities." The smile turned sharply feral.

Khade shrank back in his seat a little, though whether because of Indie's words or her expression, Rowan wasn't sure. It was very likely a combination of both. Khade was probably one of those people who had only ever heard of nice, sweet little fairy tales, the kind in which the hero always wins, and the faeries are pretty little balls of light and the stars stay up in the sky where they belong.

But this wasn't a fairy tale, and even if it was, it wasn't that kind. Here, things didn't always work out. There were no heroes, just people on different sides of the Courts. Faeries might be little balls of light, like sylphs, which were nice enough. But they might also be will-o'-the-wisps,

161

which would lead the unwary hopelessly astray and usually into danger. Faeries were fickle, ever shifting patches of light and shadow that couldn't be simply pinned down and deciphered. They were creatures with sharp teeth and sharper wit, and one had to learn quickly not to put curious fingers between the bars of their cages. Indigo may have been more humane than some of her kind, but she was still a faery, and Unseelie at that. She was a part of them.

So are you, Rowan reminded himself. *Say may have ruled the Seelie, but you never knew that side. You're just as Unseelie as the rest, desensitized to the cruelties you've seen.*

Well, that was fine then. If that was his lot, then there would be no harm in playing along with Khade's fear. "She's right, you know," he said, giving Khade a sidelong glance. "She could eat your face right now if she wanted to." He crossed his arms and leaned back in the booth seat. "Fortunately for you, she only feasts on small children."

Khade furrowed his eyebrows and stared back at Rowan, like he wasn't sure whether or not to take him seriously. "Is the faery world really as bad as you make it out to be?" he asked.

"Not if you know what you're doing," Rowan answered. "And you don't."

Indigo's face had since returned to its lulling innocence. "So does that mean you agree with my proposal?" she asked Rowan.

"Yes," he said. "I know exactly what you're capable of."

She gave him a narrow-eyed grin that he felt sure was mirroring his own.

The frog girl came back to their table and started clearing away their finished dishes. "Can I get you anything else?" she asked, shifting her armload of sticky plates.

"We need a room, please," Indie said. "One with two beds, if possible."

The frog girl gave a wide toothless smile. "Of course. Let me get rid of these," she nodded to the dishes in her arms, "and I'll take you upstairs."

"Thank you," Indie said, and the frog girl bustled off.

"Are we all going to share one room?" Ainsley asked, looking vaguely apprehensive.

Indie caught it. "What's wrong? It isn't as though you haven't shared a bed with Khade before." Her two-tone eyes crinkled in delight. "We know what happened at Merdi's tree house."

"Nothing happened!" Khade cried.

"Shh, not so loud," Rowan said, waving a hand at Khade and trying vainly to keep from laughing at Ainsley's reddened face.

The frog girl came back over to their table. "Is everything all right?" she asked. Her expression was caught somewhere between a smile and confusion.

"Boys," Indie answered smoothly. "You can't take them anywhere."

The frog girl giggled and bounced on her splayed toes. "Come with me, and I'll take you to your room."

They followed her up the stairs onto the balcony and past a few doors. Everything was black woods and ivy carvings and deep red accents. The frog girl opened up one of the doors down the hallway and stepped back to let everyone enter.

"Here you are then," she said. "Will you be needing anything else?"

"No, this is fine," Rowan said. He stuck a hand into his bag and rummaged around before pulling out several golden coins and giving them to the frog girl. More than enough to pay for everything and decidedly not glamoured. Her eyes gleamed. "If we need anything, we'll come down."

The frog girl eyed him with her head tilted to one side. "You are from the castle, aren't you? I thought you seemed familiar."

A weight settled in the bottom of Rowan's stomach, but he kept his face composed. "I've never met you before. You must have me confused with someone else."

"I visited the castle once," she said, "Years ago. You were little then, but I remember you. I remember how sad you looked. I wanted to pet you. You looked so soft. Not like him at all." Her voice and eyes were far away. "He called me ugly. The king. I was neither lovely nor horrid enough for his taste. He called me a toad. I wanted to rip out his eyes." She turned suddenly back to Rowan and the others standing in the doorway. "I won't tell anyone who you are. You can be my secret."

"Promise then," Indigo said. "Swear it."

"Fair enough," the frog girl said. "I bear no reason to bring you harm. I swear to keep you my secret, until death should claim me or my sworn unbind me." She curtsied and then looked up at Rowan with glittering black eyes. "Have a good day."

As soon as they were in the room and the door was closed behind them, Ainsley turned to Indigo, who had started rubbing the dirt off her face in the mirror at the dresser. Rowan and Khade were tossing bags into a corner.

"Why did you make her promise?" Ainsley asked. "What good will that do? People break promises all the time."

"Not here. She's bound by her word," Indie said. "The laws here will force her to keep it. A promise means a lot in this world."

"Laws?"

"The laws of magic we have. They're not written down or made up by someone. They just…exist. Come in here and get cleaned up a bit." She waved a hand for Ainsley to follow her into the powder room.

"I thought she was kind of a creep, that girl," Khade said. "I mean, she was nice enough at first, but what she just said back there…" He shuddered.

"She's not a creep," Rowan said, taking off his jacket. He saw the dirt covering the back and started dusting it off. "She's a faery. It's not the same. You just don't know any different yet." When his jacket was clean, he pulled off his boots and then set to work unbuttoning his shirt.

"You act like I'm stupid or something," Khade remarked, shrugging off his jacket as well before taking off his sneakers.

Rowan folded his shirt on top of his other things. "Maybe I'm not acting," he countered. He turned to face Khade, but instead of a response to the jibe, he got a strange look. "What?"

"How many layers are you wearing?"

Rowan arched an eyebrow. "Do you honestly care what I'm wearing?"

Khade blinked. "No. I just thought you'd be hot."

"I am. That's why I have a girlfriend, and you don't."

Khade didn't miss the jab this time. He casually extended a choice finger in Rowan's direction.

Indigo and Ainsley came back out of the powder room, looking cleaner and more refreshed. Stray hairs had been tamed back into place, and the dirt on their clothes had all but disappeared. Rowan figured Indie had done something special to achieve that, though it seemed Ainsley's torn tights were unable to be mended, as he could still see her pale scraped knees under the stripes. Maybe Indigo didn't want to waste glamour just for...well, glamor.

"We're off to find a fiddler," Indie announced. She bounced over to Rowan and, stretching up on tiptoe, gave him a quick kiss on the lips. He almost wished she hadn't kissed him at all. It only made it harder for him to let her go.

"Be careful," he said quietly. He brushed a hand across her cheek and through her hair, feeling the knife tip of her ear under his fingers.

Indie smiled up at him, fingering the dagger tucked into her belt. "You know I will be. We both will be."

She turned and walked out, and Rowan let his hand drop. Ainsley gave a nervously excited wave to him and Khade before ducking out after Indigo and closing the door.

Rowan sighed and let himself fall into the bed nearest the powder room. He heard the other bed creak lightly as Khade sat on the edge of it. He could feel Khade staring at him.

"You really love her, don't you," Khade said, but it wasn't really a question.

"I could ask you the same thing," Rowan said. "I'm fairly certain the answer would come out the same."

Khade didn't say anything for a moment, and then, "Am I that obvious?"

"To her?" Rowan said. "I don't know. I can tell though, and I'm positive Indie can too. But then, she picks up on a lot of things."

Khade gave a short laugh. "I noticed." The bed creaked a little more as he stretched out on it. "Do you ever wonder what you'd do if you lost her?"

Rowan was surprised by the question, but more surprised by the fact that he had an answer. "I think, for us, it's more the other way around."

"Why would she lose you?" Khade asked, and then, when Rowan didn't reply, "I'm sorry. I'm prying, I know."

"Yeah," Rowan said with a laugh. "Just a little."

"Do you hate me?"

Rowan laughed again. "I haven't decided yet."

"Oh." He could hear the smile in Khade's voice. "Well, let me know when you figure it out then."

Rowan rolled over, grinning, and that was the last thing he remembered.

EIGHTEEN

"Human speech is like a cracked kettle on which we tap crude rhythms for bears to dance to, while we long to make music that will melt the stars."

—Gustave Flaubert, *Madame Bovary*

As soon as Ainsley and Indigo walked out of the inn, they were ambushed by the sudden return of the pulsing crowds and the drift of airy, floating music. Indie turned to Ainsley.

"Where do you look for a musician at a party?" she asked, her eyes bright.

Ainsley shrugged and shook her head, feeling confused.

Indie's shoulders slumped in disappointment. "Playing the music, of course," she explained. Her expression perked back up mischievously. "You're not the brightest star in the sky, are you?"

"Hey!" Ainsley cried, but she couldn't help smiling at the bad joke. Or perhaps, it was a good joke. She didn't know anymore. "So we follow the music then, O Smart One," she said ceremoniously.

Indigo grinned in triumph and jerked her head in the direction of the music, farther down the street. "This way, court fool."

The two girls made their way through the crowded streets, following the sound of the music. As they came nearer to the source, Ainsley started picking out the sounds of different instruments. Some kind of flute, a tambourine, and there—a violin. The sound of it led them to the town square. A stage was set up in the center of the cobbled walkways. Three musicians were on the stage: a faun man with a wooden flute; an antlered girl with white freckles and a tambourine; and a small, dark faced violinist with furry ears and a tail and cropped black hair that covered one eye. Around the stage, faery couples danced. Among them, one couple stood out, dressed entirely in white, with tiny flowers and vines wrapped around their heads.

"It's a wedding," Ainsley said, looking to Indigo for conformation.

Indigo nodded dreamily. "Isn't it lovely?" she asked.

Ainsley smiled. Underneath it all, Indigo was still just a lovestruck girl. "It would be rude to interrupt," Ainsley said.

Indigo nodded again. "We'll wait," she said, and the two of them sat down on a nearby shop ledge to watch.

When the song stopped, the crowd stepped back from the wedding couple and applauded. The wedding couple bowed and then sauntered off to mingle and converse with the guests. Ainsley and Indigo saw their chance and hurried to the stage where the cait sidhe sat tuning her violin.

"Excuse me," Indigo said.

"We'll be taking requests in a few minutes," the antlered girl answered.

"I was just wondering if I could have a moment with Miss Diddle, please," Indigo asked. She opted to raise her eyebrows inquiringly instead of smiling. Ainsley was secretly glad. She found Indigo's sharp smile somewhat unsettling.

The antlered girl and the faun exchanged glances before turning to the cait sidhe. The cait sidhe looked back at them and then to Ainsley and Indigo. Her visible eye was a vibrant amber with a black slivered pupil.

"I'm a bit in the middle of something," she said. "Any chance it could wait?" Her *i*'s had an *ah* sound to them, as if she were yawning as she spoke.

Indigo put on an apologetic face. "It'll be but a minute, Miss Diddle."

The cait sidhe sighed, putting down her violin. "Alright then," she said, putting the same *ah* sound into her *e*'s. "But please, call me Yveena."

"Yveena," Indigo repeated, dropping into a light curtsy. "My name is Madda. And this is my friend, Lain."

Yveena returned the curtsy. "Madda. Lain. Nice to meet you both."

Indigo turned and led Yveena a little way off from the stage, into a little alley where they could be fairly sure no one would pay them any attention. Ainsley followed quietly, testing out her fake name in her mind.

When the three of them were out of earshot of most of the main crowd, Indigo faced Yveena. "I've heard you're one of the most talented violinists in all of Avyn, a true musical prodigy," Indie gushed, her charm set at full force. "I feel honored to be speaking with you."

Yveena blushed. Ainsley could tell by the way the cait sidhe's ears turned pink on the inside. "It runs in my family. It's nothing, really," Yveena muttered, but Ainsley could tell she was pleased with both the compliment and herself.

"As you're the best, I knew we could have asked for no one better. We've traveled a long distance to find you." Indigo paused for a moment before adding, "We really need your help."

Yveena seemed to know the direction this conversation had been heading in, but she didn't show any hesitation. "With what?" she asked.

"We're searching for something," Indie answered. "The legendary Blue Wand. Have you heard of it?"

Yveena looked thoughtful for a moment. "I have, but I thought it was a myth."

Ainsley didn't mention that, where she lived, every single person she'd met in the last few days would be considered a myth. Funny, the thought of a mythical world with mythical stories of its own.

"We want to find out if it's real," Indigo replied. She didn't tell Yveena about Never or the fact that they needed the wand for a coup d'état. It just didn't seem like the type of thing to bring up in polite conversation.

Yveena looked uncertain and suspicious. "You mean you don't know for sure?"

Indigo never faltered. "But imagine," she said, eyes large. "You would be known as the fiddler responsible for unearthing a legend. You would become a legend yourself!"

One of Yveena's ears twitched. Her slitted eyes narrowed in thought. "What if it's not real?" she asked. "What then? It's all a waste of time."

The hint of a smirk arced its way across Indigo's mouth. "I might be able to ensure a place for you as musician of the Court. Your choice of Courts, possibly, if things go as planned."

Indigo's smirk gained energy and jumped across to Yveena's face. "When do we leave?" she asked.

"Meet us at sundown at The Dragon's Breath. There will be two others with us."

Yveena nodded. "Sundown then." She glanced back out into the crowd. "I'd best be getting back to the wedding. They'll be looking for me."

Indie nodded, and she and Ainsley watched Yveena disappear into the throng. When Ainsley started to walk out as well, meaning to head back to the inn, Indigo grabbed her by the arm. "Wait. Just in case."

Ainsley didn't understand, but she didn't question her. Instead, she asked, "Why was she so quick to agree to go with us? I mean, she doesn't know what kind of trouble we could be getting her into."

Indigo shrugged. "Cats and curiosity, you know. It's a good thing she's got nine lives." She paused for a moment. "Although she's probably gone through a few already if she's this eager."

Ainsley furrowed her eyebrows. "Nine lives? You mean cats really have nine lives?"

"Well, cats don't," Indigo replied. "But cait sidhe do. They'll die and come back until their lives are all spent. If they live to old age each time, they can be around quite a while. A lot of them get into trouble at least once or twice though."

"How long does one life last if they live to old age?" Ainsley asked.

"Anywhere from eighty to a hundred years, usually. And not every life is the same length. Luckily for us, she is so curious. Otherwise, we'd be without a fiddler." Indie leaned around the corner of the alley and glanced from side to side. "Okay, we can go now."

The walk back was silent, at least on the part of the two girls. The crowd was still full force, the music had started back up, and Ainsley kept one hand tight on Indie's white bustle so as not to lose her.

When they ducked into the inn, they found the scene had changed drastically. With the breakfast rush over, there were only a few tables occupied. They passed the frog girl on the way to the staircase. She was behind the counter, wiping out goblets with a white cloth. She looked up at them as they crossed the room and dipped her head in their direction. Her eyes were glinting from somewhere in their dark depths. Ainsley got the feeling she seemed to enjoy knowing their secret. Or at least, one of many.

When they reached their room, Indigo opened the door as quietly as possible, then closed it and locked it behind them. The boys were both asleep, each in a bed of their own. Khade was sprawled out on his stomach, arms and legs everywhere, hanging over the edge of the bed, sticking out from under the covers. On the other bed, Rowan lay on his right side, facing the wall. He had his knees pulled up and one hand over his face. He had kicked the blankets off, and he was shivering.

"Ainsley," Indigo called quietly.

Ainsley turned. Indigo had stripped out of her purple jumpsuit and was now standing in nothing but her underclothes. Ainsley must have looked shocked, because Indigo said, "They're asleep. It's not as if they're looking."

175

She tossed Ainsley something white. When Ainsley unfolded it, she saw that it was some kind of long shirt.

"I managed to grab some things before we left," Indie explained, putting on something similar to what Ainsley held. "I didn't think you'd want to sleep in that." She gestured to Ainsley's dress.

"Oh. I guess not," Ainsley said. She hadn't thought about it until now.

She changed out of her dress and into the shirt quickly, in case one of the boys woke up. She didn't know why she couldn't have gone into the powder room to change, but Indigo was staring at her, silently telling her to hurry up. She left her tights on, trying to hold on to her dignity in any way possible.

She sat down gingerly on the bed she would be sharing with Khade and watched as Indigo shinnied under the covers in the other bed, pulling the blankets over Rowan and herself and tucking her face into the back of his shoulder.

Ainsley lay back on her pillow, trying to emulate Indigo's complete lack of hesitation, but she felt awkward. She was keenly aware of Khade's even breathing beside her, and she turned on her side to try to block out the thought of him. She had never been to a sleepover before, never spent the night away from home without her grandfather, and now, she seemed to be catching up on the nights she'd missed in rapid succession.

She felt a sudden pang at the thought of her grandfather. She had never thought she would miss home, but now she found that she did. She hoped she would get to see it again.

Sunlight poured in from one of the windows in the room. Ainsley gave a deep sigh, pulled the covers over her head to shut out the light, and closed her eyes.

NINETEEN

"All the ancient classic fairy tales have always been scary and dark."

—Helena Bonham Carter

The sky was alight with stars, and Rowan was standing among them. There was nothing beneath him for miles, and yet he was suspended in air, floating amid the thousands of spots of light.

One of the stars faltered for a moment and then started to descend, slowly at first and then more rapidly. It fell past Rowan, and it was close enough that he could make out its features. It looked just like Ainsley. It held out an imploring hand as it passed him.

As if on cue, other stars began to drop, one after the other, falling past him. Rowan tried to move but found his wrists and ankles bound. The stars took on the faces of others he knew: Khade, Indigo, Dekk, Merdi, Joel. Some he didn't quite recognize: a tall blond man and a lady with red curls. All were staring at him as they fell, eyes blank and empty, hands outstretched.

A crack of thunder, and Rowan was falling too. He opened his mouth to shout, to scream, but no sound came out. The chains that bound him tightened. He fell until he felt himself hit water, and he tasted salt. Waves crashed over his head and pushed him under. He sank farther.

A mermaid peered at him curiously then smiled with a mouthful of sharp teeth, grabbing him by the shoulders and pulling him down headfirst, deeper and deeper into the sea. He couldn't stand it anymore and took a breath. Salt water gushed into his lungs.

Another peal of thunder, loud and nearby, and Rowan sat bolt upright in bed. His breaths came in rapid disorientation. The room was dark in between flashes of blinding lightning. Indigo made a sleepy noise beside him and sat up, rubbing her eyes with the tips of her fingers.

"What's wrong?" she asked, a haze of sleep marring the sound of her concern. "What's going on?"

Rowan shook his head and covered his face with his hands. Indigo must have taken his silence as a bad sign, because she asked, far less sleepily, "Are you okay?"

Rowan sighed. "Yeah, just dreaming."

"Again," she said. It wasn't a question.

Rowan turned to look at her. In the dark, with her dark hair and tan skin, she seemed like a speaking shadow beside him. He focused his eyes on her mouth so that he wouldn't have to see the concern in her eyes. But her lips were twisted into a downward arc, so Rowan just stared at his hands in his lap instead.

"Do you think she has them too?" Indigo asked. Rowan felt her shift to look over at Ainsley, still sleeping soundly beside Khade.

Rowan shrugged. "I doubt we have the same dreams, Indie." But really, he had no idea whether she had the same dreams or not. He only knew that his own dreams were terrifyingly realistic, and they haunted him at least once a night, making him wake up in a cold sweat and hyperventilate in terror. This time, he'd had two, though the first one hadn't caused him to wake up Indigo.

Rowan shook his head, sighing. "At least, I hope she doesn't," he muttered.

Indigo rubbed a hand over his shoulder. "So do I." She gave a small, rueful smile. "Sandman must not like you much, eh," she said.

"Wouldn't know," Rowan said. "Never met him. But nightmares aren't really his style, I don't think."

"The Sandman is real?" asked a voice from the other side of the room.

Rowan and Indigo turned to see Khade propped up on an elbow in bed, staring back at them with a curiously confused expression. Lightning illuminated his blue eyes.

"That's the guy that supposedly brings dreams to everyone, right?" Khade asked.

"Yeah," Rowan said. "That's him. He's real, just like all the other things you didn't believe in."

Khade's expression changed to something almost hurt. "Hardly my fault," he muttered. "So what is he? A faery or something?"

"He's a star."

"Hmm," Khade mused. "Of course he is."

Rowan arched an eyebrow at him. "Well technically, he's not fully star. He's the son of Leo and Luna, the sun and the moon respectively. His dust isn't like that of your average star. It has the power to influence sleep, choose dreams. Usually, they're good dreams, but he can get a little bored sometimes, I guess. He is the son of Luna."

"Yeah," Khade said. "Isn't that the crazy lady who drowned that one star guy because of a magic wand?"

Rowan shrugged. "The dark side of the moon. In a literal sense."

"Witty," Khade deadpanned. "Let's hope that cat girl you guys went looking for knows what she's doing."

Indigo gasped and hurdled out of bed, causing Rowan to nearly jump out of his skin. She started throwing things back into their bags, picking her clothes up off the floor.

"You guys get up!" she said, disappearing into the powder room with her armload of clothing. "I told the cait sidhe to meet us downstairs at dusk. It's practically night now!"

"Great," Rowan said, detangling his long legs from the sheets. Nightmare ridden though he might have been, when he stood up, he couldn't deny that he felt infinitely better than he had before. Sleep had done him well.

He fished around in the dark for his discarded clothes. Khade was shaking Ainsley awake.

She rubbed at her eyes. "I had the worst dreams," she said.

"Me too," Khade replied. "Seems to be going around lately."

Rowan finished buttoning his shirt in silence.

Indigo came back into the room, dressed now into her violet jumpsuit again. She picked up Khade's and Ainsley's clothes and threw them onto the bed. "Look alive, you two. Places to be and all that."

Ainsley stumbled sleepily into the powder room to change. Khade looked displeased at being so bossed around but put on his shirt and jacket and shoes without arguing.

By the time Ainsley came back out of the powder room, her hair still tangled in a half-up mess, Rowan and Indigo had finished packing everything back up and were ready to leave.

"Remember," Indigo warned all of them, "Yveena Diddle doesn't know any of our real names. Or at least, I haven't told her. Ainsley, you're Lain. Khade, you're going to be Jess. Rowan, you're going to be Fellan, and I'm Madda. As long as we remember that, I won't have to beat you senseless for messing up my plans."

"Yeah, no problem," Khade mumbled quickly.

Rowan agreed with him.

When they got downstairs, the cait sidhe was sitting at the counter, waiting for them. Rowan took in her appearance: her dark fur, the agitated flicking of her tail, the twitching of her left ear toward the occupied tables. Her eyes darted around the counter, but she never turned to look behind her. She was dressed in a pair of midnight blue pants with black boots that were laced up to her thighs. Her shirt was deep gunmetal silver, heavily ruffled around her wrists and laced down the front. Her dark shoulders and a fair amount of her chest were exposed. Her violin had been packed into a hard leather case and strapped around her back.

Her ears flattened backward when Indigo stepped up next to her at the counter. "You're late," the cait sidhe said. There was a faint note of hissing in her voice.

"My deepest apologies," Indigo said. "My companions and I overslept. We had traveled all night."

Yveena turned around, taking in the appearances of Khade and Rowan. Her visible eye lingered a moment longer on Rowan before flicking back to Indigo. "So who are the additionals?" she asked.

"This is Jess and Fellan," Indigo said, gesturing to each of the boys. "Guys, meet Yveena Diddle, the finest violinist in Avyn."

Yveena seemed pleased, but she was trying to hide it. "Buy me dinner," she purred, "And I'll forgive you for being two hours late."

***

The frog girl wasn't their waitress this time. Instead, their waitress was thin and grey-skinned, with hollowed eyes and stringy black

183

hair that hung in tangles around her gaunt face. She wore a long white dress that dragged the floor, and when she walked away after taking their order, Rowan saw that the hem was stained with what looked like old blood.

As long as she doesn't start screaming, Rowan thought, *We'll be just fine.*

If anyone else was unsettled, they didn't mention it.

Yveena and the others discussed plans, such as the best routes to take and how to get to the shore quickly and without being seen. They stopped only for a moment when the grey lady came back, with bowls of mushroom and carrot stew for everyone, and then delved right back into conversation. They ate quickly, speaking between mouthfuls, but Rowan had little idea what they were really saying.

Ever since he and the others had sat down at their table, he'd had this strange sense that someone was watching them. Or more precisely, listening to them. Even though they were speaking softly, they still weren't exactly whispering.

He had spotted the person quickly enough, sitting two tables over, all alone. There were several empty tankards strewn over the table; some had been knocked over and had dribbled their contents onto the scarred, wooden table. The person was dressed in differing tones of grey, and five or six black-hilted daggers hung around his belt. His head was resting on his arms on the table. Pale, pointed ears knifed up through gold-white hair that fell to the middle of his back. To any other passerby, he would have looked like just another passed-out patron. And for a while, Rowan tried to convince himself that he was exactly that.

Still, something about the guy was irritatingly familiar. If only he could see his face, then maybe—

Rowan's eyes traveled downward to the faery's boots. Embossed into the side of the black leather was a symbol: two crossed pistols and a crowned star. And suddenly, it clicked in Rowan's mind just why this person seemed so familiar.

That was Zake's crest.

Haviss. He'd sent Haviss to keep tabs on them. Or kill them. Neither prospect was good.

As calmly as he could, as quickly as he dared, Rowan turned around to face the others at the table. "We need to leave now," he whispered, digging through his bag. He pulled out a few coins and slid them onto the tabletop. "I mean, right now. Hurry. Be quiet."

Rowan got up silently, watching Haviss carefully to make sure he wouldn't hear them leaving. The others followed closely behind. No one questioned his command. He was far too serious.

Once they got outside the inn and onto the streets, he broke into a full out sprint toward the woods. The little village was now barren of all other signs of life, save for the glowing windows of houses and shops. Normally, nightfall would not be reason enough to end a wedding celebration, but the storm had managed to drive the crowds back indoors. Now the only sound to be heard over the rain and thunder was the clamor of voices and footfalls behind Rowan's own, letting him know that the others were following right after him.

Not a moment too soon either.

The inn door slammed back open, and Rowan felt a knife hum past his cheek. He propelled himself forward even harder, finally reaching the edge of the village where the cobblestone stopped and the trees began. A few yards in, a low, thin branch slapped him wetly in the face, throwing him off balance, and he failed to see the tangle of roots protruding from the earth. He hit the ground hard, threw his hands out in front of himself, and felt rocks and twigs bite into his skin. He stayed on his knees for a moment, chest heaving, holding his bloodied palms together to try to stop the stinging.

The crash of underbrush behind him told him that the others had caught up to him.

"Geez, Rowan," Indigo panted. "Some of us don't have legs as long as yours."

"None of us do," Khade interjected. "Would it kill you to slow down a little?"

"It's a definite possibility," Rowan countered. "Do you have any idea who that was back at the inn?"

Khade's face fell. "Who at the inn? Was someone watching us or something?"

"Or something," Rowan said. "Did no one notice the guy sitting a couple tables over from us? The one sitting all alone?"

"Wasn't he asleep?" Ainsley asked.

"No, he wasn't," Rowan said. "That was Haviss. He's Zake's champion, which means he's also his assassin."

Indigo gave a little gasp. "I didn't even recognize—" She didn't finish the thought.

"What do you mean by *champion*?" Ainsley asked.

"He's his personal fighter," Rowan answered.

"I thought that's what Fince was," Ainsley said.

Rowan shook his head, a look of disgust plastered over his face. "Fince is Zake's muscle, his bodyguard and lackey. He's the promise that a threat will be carried out. Haviss is far more refined. He's not just brute force. It's his job to fight in place of Zake himself."

"That frog girl probably sold us out," Khade muttered.

"I told you, she can't break her promise," Indigo said. "Maybe someone else alerted them, but not her."

"You're all from the castle," Yveena said. "Every one of you. That's why you could offer me a court position." Her eyes shrank to slits. "So which side are you on anyway?"

"Which side are *you* on?" Khade countered. "I think that would be a better question."

"I'm not on a side," Yveena said. "What Zake does is his own concern."

"Hardly his own only," Rowan retorted. "You have no idea what goes on in that castle."

"Maybe not. But I can trust you all no more than I could trust him. I don't even know your real names."

"That's something we can't afford to share right now," Indigo said. "But you have to understand why. Our lives depend on how this quest ends. I was serious when I said I could give you a court position, but I can't fulfill that offer unless we're able to get the Blue Wand before anyone else gets it."

"You're not looking for the wand just for the hell of it, are you?" Yveena asked. She sounded as though she already knew the answer.

Rowan stared her defiantly in the eye. "No, we're not. Are you still in, or aren't you?"

The cait sidhe stared back at him. Her left ear flicked. With either agitation or interest, Rowan wasn't sure. There was a strange gleam in her eye.

"I'm curious to see how this pans out," she said after a moment. "I'll go with you." She held up a finger. "But be warned. If this goes south, I bail."

"Fair enough," Rowan conceded. "Let's go then."

And thank the stars for curiosity, he thought.

Yveena led the way through the trees. Rowan picked himself up off the ground and dusted at the knees of his jeans. His clothes were spattered with mud, and he was soaked to the skin from the rain. His knees didn't get any less muddied, but he did succeed in getting dirt into the cuts on his hands. He hissed when they started stinging freshly again.

Indigo reached a hand out to him. "Let me see," she said.

She looked pretty pathetic herself. Her wet hair seemed almost black and hung in dripping locks around her face. Droplets of water were suspended in her long eyelashes. Her white bustle was soaked and limp and polka-dotted with bits of mud. The sight of her like that struck something inside Rowan.

He jerked his hands away from her and crammed them into his jacket pockets. He set off after the others in quick, long strides, not looking at Indigo even when she hurried up beside him.

"What did I do?" She sounded as though she didn't know whether to be angry or hurt.

Rowan stared at the ground. He could see her sandaled feet flash in and out of his peripheral vision. She had to take two steps for every one of his.

He shook his head, hunching his shoulders against the rain.

"What's wrong?" Indigo asked. Her voice was now so quiet that Rowan could hardly hear her over the wind and thunder. She sounded so unsure, and that was something Rowan never wanted to associate her with.

Rowan stopped, and Indigo stopped beside him. Rowan took a deep breath and sighed toward the sky, breath leaving in a small puff of frost. None of the stars were visible through the clouds.

"This is never going to work, is it?" he asked.

"What do you mean?"

"This whole quest thing," he clarified. "There's no way we're going to get away with what we're doing. Everywhere we've stopped, we find someone tailing us." Rowan threw his hands out. "Fince was in Phoenixdown. Now Haviss is here. And this whole thing is my fault because I was too stupid to see what Zake had laid out for us in the first place! Anything else want to go wrong?"

Lightning flashed brightly, and thunder sounded off so closely and so loudly that Rowan jumped a foot into the air.

"I didn't mean that!" he cried.

Indigo stifled a giggle. "I wouldn't tempt fate if I were you. It seems a little less than fond of you lately."

Rowan cut a glance skyward as if the clouds had undermined him on purpose. "Yeah, no kidding. I'm on everyone's favorites list, it seems."

"We should catch up," Indigo said with a little grin. Her lower lip was trembling, and for a startling second, Rowan thought she was going to cry. He didn't think he could handle that at the moment. Then she shivered, and he realized she was trying to keep her teeth from chattering. The cropped jacket she had on was cloth and stuck to her skin.

Rowan stripped off his leather jacket and held it out to her. "Put this on," he said. "It'll keep at least part of you dry."

She shook her head. "I'm fine."

He grabbed her jacket at the shoulders and tugged it off backwards. "It wasn't an option," he told her. He held his own jacket back out. "For the sake of my fragile state of mind."

She sighed, beaten, and took his proffered jacket and pulled it on. She knew he would do almost anything she asked of him. She also knew there were some things she could never win against him. "Appreciated," she said softly.

He smiled back at her. Then he looped her sodden jacket over the strap of his messenger bag, stuffed his hands into his jeans pockets, and started after the rest of their entourage. He felt her wrap a hand around the inside of his arm. Despite the fact that all three of his shirts were soaked through to his skin already, he felt infinitely warmer.

TWENTY

"I shot across the sky's expanse,
A meteor, blazing bright.
Now fallen, I sprawl in the grass—
Who'll help me to my feet?"

—Johann Wolfgang Goethe, *Faust*

Nearly four hours later, the storm had let up to a thick mist. Ainsley didn't find this ideal, but she couldn't argue that it was far better than the deluge they had been traveling in previously. She was also glad of the fact that her companions had decided that, as they hadn't yet been ambushed and murdered, it wasn't likely that they had been followed. Or

192

at least, not closely followed anyhow. Nevertheless, they had agreed that they could stop for a few minutes and rest. The next village was only about twenty minutes away and had an airship port where they could catch a ride on a fishing vessel that could take them to the sea.

Rowan had started a small fire, but it kept sputtering and going out. He would relight it, cursing the damp twigs and branches he was using until they flared to life, only to go back out again. Indigo took pity on him after seven or eight tries and threw some sort of blue powder onto the bundle of wood. The flames instantly sparked up, gaining energy until they were burning nicely. Rowan gave Indigo a sarcastic glare that Ainsley knew was underlain by gratitude.

Khade busied himself with checking over the pistol he'd gotten from Rowan, emptying the magazine and reloading it, multiple times. Yveena was licking the backs of her clawed hands and fussing at the lock of hair that fell over her face. She smoothed furiously at the fur on her ears, mumbling something angrily about water. The fur on her tail was sticking out in random directions, reminding Ainsley of the cartoons she'd watched back at home. Those animated, talking cats paled in comparison to what was sitting across the fire from her.

"So, Jess," Yveena said lazily, "You're not from around here, are you?"

Khade seemed to take a minute to realize she was talking to him. "Oh, um," he stuttered. "Not really. I'm from a… a village on the other side of the castle. You probably haven't heard too much of it. It's pretty small."

"Try me," Yveena said, and her cat teeth flashed in the firelight. When Khade didn't answer, she scoffed. "Liar," she said, but she sounded more amused than accusatory. "I know you're a human from the City. Don't try to pretend you're something else." She tilted her head at him. "Besides, fey can't lie, and you're much too clumsy anyway."

Khade looked slightly ruffled, like he'd been insulted for being something she thought was beneath her. "I'm not the one licking myself," he said.

Rowan started coughing suspiciously. Ainsley bit the inside of her cheek to keep from laughing.

Yveena flattened her ears. "I'm finished talking to you," she said and curled her tail around herself.

Khade shot Ainsley a look that she translated as saying, *Why'd we bring her along again?*

But something had piqued Ainsley's interest. "What's the City?" she asked.

Yveena didn't reply. Apparently, her annoyance with Khade was contagious to the others as well.

"The human side of the world," Indie answered. "Or at least, what we call it now. It's had many names before. Midgard is another common one, but mostly we just say the City."

"What is this side of the world called?"

"We usually refer to it as the Wood or simply Faerie. But there's also Faeryland, Tír Na nÓg, Álfheim, among others." Indigo shrugged. "There has never been only one name for something as infinitely

194

beguiling as the world. The Norse had a name for it, the Celts had another. Modern humans pick and choose among those that exist. Sometimes they make up new ones, new names for old things. They try to pin things down with names, like butterflies under a glass. The fey choose their own names for it. And the world just keeps on going, completely heedless to it all."

Ainsley nodded thoughtfully and stared up at the sky. The clouds had cleared just a bit, and a few scant stars could be seen from where she sat. A couple of them looked somehow brighter than the others. Maybe brighter wasn't the word. Perhaps *closer* was a better description.

Her eyes widened when she saw them both falter and dim then go whizzing across the night sky. As they fell in an arc, one after the other, their light intensified.

"Guys, look," she whispered.

"What?" Khade asked and then gasped.

"We need to go," Rowan said. Ainsley turned, confused by his words, to see him kicking dirt onto the fire to put it out. His face was grim. "There's nothing we can do."

"Is it me, or does it look like they're falling toward us?" Yveena asked.

Ainsley turned back around. Surely enough, the two lights seemed to be curving right in their direction.

"Scatter!" Indigo cried.

Everyone ducked and dove out of the way. The two stars swept over the tops of their heads a few yards in the air, hitting the ground through the trees somewhere a little ways off from where the fire had been.

Ainsley sat up, rubbing at the elbow she'd landed on. "That did not just happen."

"Is everyone okay?" Khade asked.

No one was hurt. Rowan was helping Indigo off the ground. The fur down Yveena's spine was standing on end.

"You're right," Yveena said. "We need to go."

"I changed my mind," Rowan said. He followed the trail the stars had burned through the trees.

"Oh, come on," Khade moaned. "We're gonna get ourselves killed."

"He's right," Indigo said. "We can't leave them when they're this close. Not if they're still alive." She disappeared into the trees too.

Ainsley followed her tentatively. She could hear Khade behind her. She trusted the cait sidhe was coming too, if for no other reason than sheer curiosity.

The site where the stars had fallen was hot, far hotter than it should have been, given the weather and time of year. Ainsley could smell something burning, not grass or leaves or anything else she'd ever smelled, but something strangely familiar all the same.

One of the stars was female. She was wearing a glossy silver dress with tiny gold bells around the waistline. Her coal black hair was splayed out around her head like a dark halo. The other star was male, dressed in blue and gold, with the same black hair that probably would have been shoulder length had he been standing. Both of them were lovelier than any other person, faery or otherwise, that Ainsley had ever seen.

Rowan was kneeling over the girl. "Check the other one."

Khade hurried to the other star. Indigo was right behind him.

Ainsley wandered cautiously over to Rowan and the girl. He was pressing a hand against her neck. He sighed and sat back on his heels, shaking his head. She didn't have to ask to know what he meant.

He stood up to move to Khade and Indigo, but Ainsley stayed where she was, staring down at the star girl. Her face was porcelain pale. Her eyelashes looked like black brush strokes. Ainsley inclined her head reverently to the girl and moved away.

The other scene she encountered was far more hopeful. The star's breath was coming in gasps of pain, but he was very much alive. Indigo was trying to calm him down.

"Don't worry," she was saying. "Everything will be fine."

"Don't lie to him, Indie," Rowan whispered. He turned to see where Yveena was, to make sure she hadn't heard him use Indigo's name. The cait sidhe was watching a bird preen itself in a tree. She stared at it like she wanted to eat it. Ainsley wouldn't have been surprised if she did.

"As if I could," Indigo said.

"The other star," Ainsley said, shaking her head. "She didn't make it."

Indigo sighed and looked away.

"What do we do with him then?" Khade asked, gesturing toward the star in front of them.

A snapping twig sounded from somewhere off in the woods. Birds scattered into the air. Raucous voices were audible, but barely.

"Starshooters," Rowan breathed.

They had only a few minutes at the most. Rowan looked around at the others with a torn expression.

"It's your choice what we do with him," Indigo said, but she looked uncertain too.

"It's hardly my decision alone," Rowan said.

"We can't just leave him here. Not now," Khade said, and Rowan gazed at him, a shocked expression on his face. "What? I have a heart."

"Apparently so," Rowan admitted, grinning a little. "Alright then." He shrugged off his messenger bag and passed it to Ainsley, who slung it over her own shoulder.

The star's eyes were fluttering weakly. He was barely conscious. Rowan slid one arm under the star's shoulders and the other arm under his knees and lifted him up with a grunt.

"Come on, hurry," Rowan said. "Yveena, lead the way."

Yveena seemed to have no problem with getting out of there as swiftly as possible, whether or not anyone else did. When Ainsley turned to follow her, she found that the cait sidhe had climbed up a tree and was sitting on a high branch on all fours, tail lashing back and forth. Her amber eye glittered.

"No time," she hissed. "Hide yourselves somewhere."

"Where?" Khade quietly demanded.

Yveena didn't answer, only disappeared higher up into her tree. Khade jammed his middle finger in her direction.

"Over here," Indie whispered. She motioned around a large tree trunk, at least ten feet in diameter. "Get behind here."

There was no time to search for somewhere better. Certainly not with the extra weight they had acquired. Everyone crowded behind the trunk, pressing up against the bark, against each other, whatever it took to make themselves nonexistent.

The owners of the voices came into the area with the fallen star. Ainsley couldn't see them, didn't dare to try to snatch a peek. She had seen starshooters before, and she could live without seeing any more of them for the rest of her life.

"Well, shit," one of the voices said loudly. "She's dead. How are going to explain that one to his lordship?"

"We tell him she died, naturally," another voice said. Ainsley stifled a gasp at the sound of it, lilting and feminine. It had never crossed her mind that some of the starshooters could be female. "It's hardly our fault that she didn't survive the fall."

"We need to get rid of the body," a third voice said, deep and gravelly. "Here." Ainsley could hear the sound of something being thrown, a wind-cutting hum, and then hitting what she suspected was leather. "Burn it."

"Burn it here?" the loud voice asked. "Now?"

"Yes, here," the gravelly voice answered. "We don't need anyone else finding it. And contain the flames. Burning down his lordship's lands would not settle well with him."

Ainsley heard the sound of something striking and then the crackle of flames. The smell of burning flesh and cloth filled the air soon after, followed by the feeling of something being tugged from multiple directions. Some kind of magic pulse. With the combination of senses, Ainsley felt sure she was going to throw up. Beside her, Rowan's face was ashen pale. She couldn't see Khade's or Indigo's faces from where she crouched among them.

"Now to find the other one," the female voice said. She sounded bored beyond belief.

"My thoughts exactly," the gravelly voice said. Whether he sounded annoyed or amused Ainsley couldn't tell. "Let's go this way first. Make sure the fire is burned down to ashes before you leave it. And go the other direction. We might be quicker split up."

The owners of the female voice and the gravelly one ambled off through the trees, cracking twigs as if they meant to make noise.

The loud voice was talking to himself. "Oh, sure I don't mind being left behind. Left with the body no less. I thank you for that. Jackass."

He fell silent then, though Ainsley wished he would have kept talking. She was terrified even to breathe too deeply, in case he should hear her. She dared not move for anything, though her right foot was falling asleep and tree bark was digging into her elbow. She only wished for the body to burn faster, as morbid as she felt for thinking it and as much as she tried to ignore the sound and the smell.

Yet it burned on. For what seemed like ages, they sat there, until the crackling sound of flames had gone soft, until Ainsley had grown accustomed to the smell, and the bristling pulse of magic had disappeared. Only then, finally, did Ainsley hear the sound of dirt being kicked and flames sputtering out. Footsteps faded away into nothingness.

Still, no one moved for a long while. Yveena came down from her tree at last, and the invisible hold over everyone was broken. A collective sigh rippled through them.

Ainsley stood up, joints cramping, both legs tingling with needle-point sharpness. Khade groaned next to her, arching his back in an uncomfortable-looking stretch.

"This dream just keeps getting worse, doesn't it?" he said. He twisted his head toward Ainsley, giving her a humorless smile.

"Well, we haven't died or anything," she replied.

"Yet," Yveena interjected. Her smile was far worse than Khade's in every way.

"So much for optimism," Khade muttered.

Ainsley sighed. "Shut up."

Rowan had hefted the star into his arms again. "I hate to interrupt this lovely banter, but we need to move. Now."

"Before they decide to search this way," Indigo added.

They came back around the giant tree trunk, heading in the direction of the place they had stopped to rest. The misty rain had stopped completely now, but Ainsley would almost have preferred it to these most recent events.

No one said anything about the charred area of grass that lay behind them.

TWENTY-ONE

"The fault [...] is not in our stars
But in ourselves, that we are underlings."

—William Shakespeare, *Julius Caesar*

The walk to the next village, which should have taken around twenty minutes at the pace they had been traveling, ended up taking a little over an hour. The added company weighed them down considerably. They had to stop several times to put the star down for a moment. He hadn't stirred since they had set out with him.

By the time they reached the village, Rowan thought his arms were going to fall off. The village inn was quite a ways into the heart of the little town. The windows were glowing with the light of burned-down candles. The streets were quiet, but that didn't keep everyone from being on edge.

Before entering the inn, Rowan and Khade situated the star between them, one of his arms slung across each of their shoulders.

The inside of the inn had a sleepy feel to it. The only person in the dim room was a spindly, brown-skinned faery who was dozing in a chair behind the counter. Rowan explained to him that their *friend* had drank a bit too much faery wine, hence the reason for his passed-out state, and the walk back to his home would be too long to drag him back there. So they needed a room, and make it two so they could keep an eye on him overnight.

The brown faery didn't contradict their story, didn't nod in understanding or comment on their bedraggled appearances. He just yawned, handed them keys, and accepted their payment. Then he dropped his chin to his chest, leaned back in his chair, and waved them away.

They dragged the star out of the room and down the hallway until they found their rooms, side by side on the left. Rowan and Khade settled the star into a bed in the first room while the girls dropped off their things in the second room.

Rowan waited until Indigo came into the first room with him before he left. Not that he didn't trust Khade. Well, if he were being completely honest, he didn't trust him a hundred percent, but he knew Khade was trustworthy, at least when it came down to Ainsley's safety.

Rowan just didn't think Khade was the best candidate for taking care of an injured fallen star.

Rowan ran a hand through his hair, fingers catching in tangles, as he watched Indigo tend to the star. "I'm going to the air docks to see who I can finagle into giving us a ride," he said. "I'll try to be back by first light."

Indigo barely glanced back at him, bent over her work, and gave a little nod. At least she would be kept busy and wouldn't sit and worry about him while he was gone.

Rowan paused on his way out the door. "Don't leave Ainsley alone with the fiddler for too long. She's far more fey then Ainsley's used to. And don't let her promise anything, either."

Khade was out the door before Rowan could even open it himself.

***

The village streets were darkened and bleak. Little balls of light floated down the lanes in the distance. Hushed voices called out, beckoning softly in lulling tones, but Rowan knew better than to follow will-o'-the-wisps.

The night was chilled from the recent rain. Rowan shoved his hands into his pockets and hunched his shoulders, shivering a little and wishing he had thought to get his jacket back from Indigo. He hoped she, at least, was warm.

The air docks loomed above the other buildings and houses, rising in the distance, the glint of moonlight catching just barely off brass

205

gears and furled sails, just enough for Rowan to see them. He estimated it was another few miles' walk to it.

Rowan cut through every available alley in order to quicken the travel. By the time he reached the docks, he had warmed up considerably, and there was a tear in the knee of his jeans.

The wooden docks spread out and up like a dead spider that had been electrocuted, all flat slats along the center and ramps sticking into the air in seemingly random array. Several of the ramps led to tethered airships. Despite the odd hour, the docks were host to several crews of sailors, all bustling along with various chores and paying Rowan little heed as he pushed through to the ships. He got as far as the top end of one of the ramps before anyone showed him any attention.

The sailor who had been left to guard the ship stepped in front of Rowan and stuck out a hand, barring the way onto the deck. The faery was burly but not very tall, wearing tattered pants and no shirt or shoes. He seemed unbothered by the chilled air. Tattoos of black leafy vines curled down his body, pulsing lightly under his skin.

"You're not a member of this crew, and we don't need any more," he said matter-of-factly. "If you're looking for work, try elsewhere." He looked Rowan over. "Though I doubt you'll find much luck around here. Sky captains like their crew members a little more…sturdy."

Rowan's face heated at the remark. If only this sailor could see him pilot an airship, he'd be begging for flying lessons. Rowan forced out a deep breath.

"I'm looking for passage, actually," he replied. "To the shore. And trust me, if I had my own ship, I wouldn't be asking you."

Instead of becoming angered, the sailor only laughed. "You couldn't handle your own ship, boy."

A strange fire lit in Rowan's eyes. He was never one to let himself go unproven. "A deal then," he proposed. He paused for a moment. He would have to word this carefully. "Let me and my companions have safe, comfortable passage to the shore, and I will pay double the normal price of passage."

"The other half?" the sailor asked in interest.

"You let me fly," Rowan said. "If I earn your captain's approval, we travel for no fee."

The sailor tilted his head thoughtfully. He was silent for a long while.

"Let me check with the captain," he said finally.

Rowan nodded, and the sailor disappeared onto the deck and into the cabin. Rowan sat down on the ramp to wait. He leaned his head back against the hull of the ship. Lately, it seemed each day was becoming longer than the one before. He closed his eyes and pressed his fingertips against them, attempting to rub away the fatigue. Then he breathed out in what he supposed was a laugh. How strange that normal stars were awake at this time, while he had become so accustomed to being awake during the day. He wondered absently what it must be like to be a star in Skyline. He had only the slightest inkling that he had ever been there before, when he was very young. But then, it seemed his whole lie of a life had been unraveling at the seams these past few days. Who knew what else he might find out in those to come?

The sailor came back with a tall faery that Rowan could only imagine was the captain. He was dressed in a long nightshirt and black pants and had a sort of sky-weathered face. His eyes were pale brown, and his long white hair was tinted violet and hung around his face in sleep-tangles. When he spotted Rowan, his expression broke into pure shock. Rowan pushed himself up, even though his body willed him not to move.

"I've got it from here," the captain said to the sailor, though his eyes never left Rowan's face.

The sailor nodded. "Yes, sir," he said, and he turned and left.

The captain gave a sorrowful smile. "You look just like your father."

Rowan gripped the railing hard. "What?" he said. It came out barely more than a whisper.

"Well, your father was blond," the captain reiterated, "but still."

"No, I mean— I don't—" Rowan stammered. He backed down the ramp unsteadily. He'd been recognized. And they had been so close.

The captain grabbed Rowan's arm, wrapping a hand above his elbow and pulling him back. "Hey, wait a minute!"

Rowan pushed desperately at the fingers that held him, but it was useless. The fight had been worn out of him over the last few days, and he was exhausted. His knees started to buckle under him. The faery captain quickly grabbed Rowan's other arm and lowered him to the floor.

"Whoa, easy," the faery said. He leaned back a little. "You don't know who I am, do you?"

Rowan shook his head. "Are you going to turn me in?" He sounded defeated even to his own ears.

"What? Of course not," the faery said. "Your father was one of my closest friends. I learned a lot of sailing tips from him." He smiled. "But of course you wouldn't remember me. A little after Errin met your mother, they both went back to Skyline. I met you only days before they were…" He paused and glanced away for a second. "Well, before things changed." He gave a little salute. "The name's Lorin."

"I'm—"

"Rowan, I know," Lorin finished. "You've grown a bit since I last saw you. That hair hasn't changed though. Just like your mother's."

"I don't really remember them all that much," Rowan admitted.

"It's okay. They remember you. Wherever they are."

Dead, most likely, Rowan thought, but he didn't voice it. He'd come here with a mission. "I don't mean to sound forthcoming, but my companions and I really need a ride to the shore. We can pay—"

Lorin waved his hands. "Errin and Jiri's boy needn't pay for anything of mine. I have only one request."

"What's that?" Rowan asked.

Lorin grinned at him. "You show me those piloting skills you were bragging on about."

Rowan's eyes widened. "Seriously? That's it?"

"That's it," Lorin said. "How many do you have coming?"

Rowan counted them off in his head. "Including me, five, maybe six. They're somewhere else right now though. Can I bring them back in a few hours?"

"We don't set sail till about nine o'clock. The rest of the crew's still asleep. Can they be ready by then?"

"Yes," Rowan said. He estimated the time was around two-thirty in the morning. Back to the inn, sleep, eat breakfast, and back to the docks. Not an enormous amount of time for everything, but then he hadn't much choice in the matter. "We can do that." But he couldn't stifle the reluctant feeling he still had.

Lorin seemed to sense it. "You can trust me, you know."

"No," Rowan admitted. "I don't know. But I don't have much of a choice right now."

"There's a choice in everything," Lorin said. "If it's a promise you need, I would gladly make it."

Rowan shook his head. "No." The offer alone was as good as proof. A trickster would never give an offer of a promise for fear of being taken up on it and being forced to either deny it or swear it. "I'm a little more certain now, I think."

"My crew will say nothing either," Lorin added. "They fear me above Zake. I'm the one who pays them."

Rowan laughed softly. "You must be terrifying."

"An absolute horror," Lorin said, standing and smiling. "Now get out of here. I'm going back to bed, and you're going back to your friends. We'll have time to fill in the gaps of your parentage later."

Rowan rose from the floor. "I really appreciate it," he said, trying to convey just how much he really meant it without saying 'thank you'. He knew Lorin wouldn't want to hear those words.

"It helps to have friends in high places," Lorin remarked. "And my ship can take you pretty high."

Rowan sighed at the bad pun, but there was a hopeful smile on his face.

***

The brown-skinned faery was still asleep behind the counter when Rowan crept back past him through the inn. He was snoring now and about to fall out of his chair. Rowan briefly wished that Dekk were there to push the faery over, and then he wished he hadn't thought of Dekk at all. Hopefully, the sidhe was having an easier time of things than the rest of them were. He hoped their own luck might be turning around as well.

Down the hall, Rowan knocked lightly on the door of their first room before he entered. The interior was dim, with a couple of candles lit, and the window was open. The moon seemed darker from inside compared to how bright it had seemed at the docks. The star was still on the bed, pale and motionless. Everyone except Yveena was sitting around the room. Rowan knew something was wrong as soon as he walked into the room.

Indigo ran to him with tears in her eyes and buried her face in his arm. Rowan looked around at the others. Ainsley's eyes were red, and Khade seemed strangely sobered.

Rowan wasn't sure he wanted to know but he asked anyway. "What happened?" And then he knew the moment the words came out. He looked over at the star on the bed. There was no rise and fall of breath, no stirring eyes beneath closed lids, no sign of life whatsoever.

"There was nothing I could do," Indigo whispered into Rowan's shirt. Her tears were hot through the cloth.

"It isn't your fault, Indigo," he said, hugging her close. A strange fire stoked itself inside his chest. Determination rekindled anew within him. "It's Zake's fault," he said. "This is all Zake's fault. It always has been." He pushed Indie away and held her at arm's length. Her eyebrows were knitted tightly together as she stared back at him. "Go to the other room and get some rest." He glanced at Ainsley and Khade. "You two, as well. I've gotten us passage for tomorrow. There's an airship crew willing to take us to the shore, but they depart at nine. It will take several hours once we're under way, and who knows what we'll encounter when we get there. We need to be ready."

Indigo nodded and slipped away. Ainsley followed quietly out behind her. Khade, however, came up to stand next to Rowan, folding his arms and focusing stubbornly on neither the star on the bed nor the star beside him.

"You know," he began, "I just can't seem to figure out your girlfriend. Sometimes she seems just as dark and cruel as the other creatures we've run into here, and then other times, she's an emotional wreck of benevolence. I don't understand her."

Rowan raised his eyebrows at the awkward attempt of taking the spotlight off the dead body in the room. He suspected Khade wasn't sure what else to say — he couldn't blame him — so Rowan gave in and answered.

"She's fey. You could spend your entire short life trying to understand." He shook his head and shrugged. "But you're not fey, so you can't understand. It's just what they are."

"So explain it to me. You're fey too, right?"

"No, I'm not." Rowan made a face. "I mean, I am, but— It's complicated."

"You're telling *me* this?"

"Just…listen, okay? Stars are *fey* but not *faery*. We're part of the faery realm, but at the same time, we're not. We come from somewhere else too. That's because stars carry different principles, ones unlike those of either faeries or humans. We're related, like how wolves and whales are both mammals and completely opposite. Then there are humans. We all have similarities — no matter how much a faery would say otherwise — but we don't think the same. Does that make any sense?"

Khade nodded, but he still looked confused. "Yeah, a little. But why are faeries so adamant that we're not alike at all?"

Rowan shrugged. "Again, you're asking a star, not a faery. Stars and humans think and act a little more alike. We kind of have more similar ideals, even though stars are still distinctly fey. True faeries are just a breed of their own. Completely untamed. They're closer to nature."

Khade was silent for a while. Rowan knew he had been gathering up the nerve to ask — what to do about the dead star.

"We're going to need a shovel," Rowan said. "Two, if possible."

Khade nodded, sighing. "Okay." And Rowan was glad he didn't have to explain.

Between the two of them, they pilfered through the basement and the little shed behind the inn, but they only came up with one shovel. While one would dig, the other would search for small stones. The work was long, even splitting it as they did, but eventually, they had created a deep hole in the ground. Once they had lowered the star into the hole, they covered him with dirt and Rowan began placing the stones around the perimeter of the grave. Khade never asked what he was doing or why, and Rowan was grateful for that. Khade would see soon enough.

When the last stone was in place, Rowan put a hand to one on the corner of the grave. He closed his eyes and concentrated. The stone beneath his hand glowed a pale, watery blue. On either side the glow spread from stone to stone, until the entire row of them was glowing with soft light. Rowan stood and backed away a few feet. Khade stood in awe beside him.

"I wouldn't mind being buried like that," Khade remarked quietly.

"Careful what you wish for," Rowan said.

Khade turned to him with an indignant expression on his face, but Rowan held up his hands.

"I'm just saying, nothing's keeping you from being next. No one's invincible." He walked away, back to the inn, calling over his shoulder. "Come on. We've got a couple hours to sleep. Then you can try your luck in the air. Maybe you could jump off of something."

Khade fisted his hands and stalked off after him.

TWENTY-TWO

"He ran, he flew, he shouted: 'Star of gold! Brother!
Wait for me! I'm running! Don't go out yet!
Don't leave me alone!"

—Victor Hugo, *Et Nox Facta Est*

Ainsley woke feeling oddly depressed. At first, she couldn't figure out why she felt that way. Then the events of the previous night came back to her, and she buried her head back into the pillows. The person next to her shifted suddenly, hitting her in the face with a failing, furry tail, and then there was nothing else to be done. She was completely and irreversibly awake.

She slipped out of the bed she had shared with Yveena. She was still wearing her dress and stockings. She hadn't cared to change last night. She stretched, glancing around the room.

Indigo was asleep in the armchair in the corner, curled up. Pale morning sunlight drifted across the floor. The room was warm and cozy. Surely Ainsley had dreamed up everything that had happened just hours ago.

Picking up her sneakers, she padded on stocking-feet into the hall and into the other room.

This room looked much the same as the one she had just left, except the bed was unoccupied. Khade was asleep on a pile of blankets on the floor. One arm was across his face, as if he had slept fitfully. Rowan was sitting against the wall, holding something shining in his hand and staring blankly at it.

Ainsley cleared her throat gently.

Rowan's head jerked up, but he relaxed when he realized who she was. He tilted his head away from her in a come-on-over sort of gesture. Ainsley tiptoed past Khade and sat down, bringing her knees up to her chin and pulling the skirt of her dress in close.

"How did you sleep?" she asked, forcing a smile. Rowan only shook his head. Ainsley's brow furrowed. "What is that supposed to mean?"

"I didn't sleep," he said. "Too much to think about."

"Where is the star?"

"In a better place, maybe," Rowan said. "We buried him in the back. Khade and I did."

A silent moment passed between them. Khade tossed in his sleep, rolling away to face the wall.

"What are you doing now?" Ainsley whispered.

Rowan held up a dagger carved with glittering designs. The handle was the darkest, deepest black Ainsley had ever seen.

"That's beautiful," she said.

"It's made of celestial silver, from Skyline. Star metal, but it looks like it could be faery craftsmanship. A rare blend. The star was carrying it."

Ainsley gaped at him. "You took it off a dead guy? You can't do that."

"I'm fairly sure he no longer has a need for it." He studied her expression. "Is it wrong to do that as humans are concerned?"

Ainsley nodded, wide-eyed. "A little bit. It's disrespectful." *And creepy*, she thought.

"Disrespectful would be not using this to exact vengeance," Rowan replied. "But I digress."

"Yeah, I guess so." Ainsley glanced back at Khade. "So what now?"

"Wake up your stray dog," he said, standing. "I'll handle Indigo and the feline. We have a ship to catch."

***

The trip took a little longer with all of them than it had with only Rowan. Ainsley mentally complained of all the side streets that he was leading them down. Then there were the fences they were forced to climb over. He insisted it was faster this way, but Ainsley only wanted to crawl back into bed for a few more days. Indigo and Khade looked as though they felt much the same way. Yveena, however, appeared to be well-rested, pouncing around and over obstacles in the catlike way she had. Rowan seemed strangely rested as well, even though Ainsley knew he hadn't slept at all. She couldn't make the effort to ponder why that was.

They arrived at the docks ten minutes late.

And then, despite her fatigue, Ainsley felt awe wash over her at yet another of the sights this foreign world held.

It was like she had entered the faery version of *Treasure Island*. Sailors were everywhere, some with wings, some with green- or blue-tinged skin. Some had clothes that she could swear were made of scales. One particular sailor she caught sight of had a fish tail and webbed ears. She blinked around at them all, vaguely remembering that she was supposed to be following the others. She had to hurry to catch back up with them.

Rowan was leading the way up to a large airship bustling with crew members. Down the side of the hull, the name *Cloud's Bounty* was etched into the wood and bronze. Beneath that were several more etchings, each one in strange but different alphabets. Ainsley stumbled along the ramp that led up to the ship. She made sure to walk down the middle, determined not to look over the edge.

"Rowan!" a voice called as Ainsley walked out onto the deck. She caught a glimpse of Rowan's face as he whirled toward the sound.

"So it's Rowan, is it?" Yveena purred in contented triumph. Rowan winced as she said it. "I wonder how long till I can figure the rest of your names out."

Rowan sighed and strode toward the faery who had called him out. The faery was dressed in a long, tailed red coat with brass buttons down the front. His black pants were tucked into tall boots with tiny gears detailing the sides. His white and violet hair was smoothed into a ponytail tied with golden ribbon.

"Everyone, this is Captain Lorin," Rowan announced. "He's agreed to let us stowaway on his ship for a little while." He leaned forward to whisper in the faery's ear, and Lorin inclined his head slightly toward him. "The cait sidhe doesn't know all of our real names, and I'd rather it stayed that way. If all of this works out like I hope it does, we'll tell both of you. We owe you that much, I know, but still…"

The faery captain held his hands up and shook his head. "It's fine. I understand." He looked apologetic. "I suppose I may have already given yours away."

Rowan shrugged. "It's okay."

Lorin nodded then said in a louder voice, "Well, let's get all of you settled then, shall we? You are a bit late, after all." He arched an eyebrow at Rowan, but he was smiling.

Lorin led them around the deck, pointing out areas to them and sounding as proud as if he were speaking about a successful child of his — "That's the helm up there. She turns as smooth as a wisp of fog." —

and then he led them into the galley — "Anything you want to eat, provided we have the means to make it, you can just ask Miss Qate."

Miss Qate was on the plump side, with skin that was greenish and mottled in places and pale in other places. Her eyes were shiny-black like beetles, and her ears were pointed but broad. Her teeth were dagger-sharp when she smiled. Something in Ainsley told her that Miss Qate must have had some goblin blood in her.

"Pickin' up strays, captain?" she rasped, stirring something in a giant pot and adding what Ainsley considered to be questionable ingredients.

"Nothing so much like that," Lorin answered. "Closer to fulfilling a favor."

"You shouldn't make bargains that involve humans," Qate said. "Though he might make a good stew." She reached out to Khade with a hungry look in her eyes.

Lorin didn't bat an eye. "He's a friend of a guest and, as such, falls under the captain's protection." He settled a hand on Rowan's shoulder, daring Qate to defy him.

Qate said nothing more on the matter, but her beetle eyes lingered on Khade for a second longer. Ainsley felt him squirm next to her. The faery turned to Rowan instead.

"Well, look what we have here then," she said. "And aren't you the replica of your father?" She glanced aside at the captain. "Small favors, sir."

"No trouble, Qate," Lorin warned. When he turned to leave the galley, Khade was sure not to be the last one out.

The next stop was the cabins. Lorin took them to his personal cabin, where he had set up a small area for them to rest and keep their things. "I hope this will be sufficient," he said.

"Of course," Rowan answered, and at the same time, Indigo said, "It's lovely."

Ainsley took in her surroundings once again. Lorin's cabin was all in reds and bronze and wood. The large partitioned window was hung with scarlet curtains on either side. An enormous wooden desk was in front of the window. Laid across it were charts and books and feather pens. His bed occupied one wall. The blankets were stitched with embroidered gears. Expensive looking rugs made the wood floors plush and comfortable.

"This is amazing," Ainsley breathed.

Lorin seemed pleased. "I'm glad you find it to your liking. Have you never been on an airship before?"

Ainsley wondered if she gave an impression of being an outsider. Still, she hadn't been the one that the ship's cook had tried to serve for dinner. "I have, actually. Twice. But the first time was not fun at all, and the second time was only a little better."

"I see. Have you eaten?"

They all shook their heads. Khade spoke up quickly. "I don't trust your chef."

Lorin chuckled. "I will personally ensure that you don't eat any cousins."

Khade didn't laugh. "The faeries are making jokes now. Wonderful."

Ainsley bit her lip to hide a grin. Lorin's eyes were sparkling with amusement. "I'll have one of the crew send you something you'll find…edible." He smiled rakishly. "Now, if you will excuse me, I have a ship to get underway. You're welcome to follow if you'd like. Rowan." He gestured with a hand. Rowan followed him out onto the deck.

Khade sighed. "Is it just me, or is every faery we meet out to give me hell just for their own twisted amusement?"

"It's not only for amusement," Yveena answered. "We merely enjoy playing with our food."

"That was a rhetorical question," Khade mumbled.

"The truth is, Khade," Indigo said, "You're awkward and naïve, and we just like messing around with your head."

"Oh, thanks," he said.

"They're just leading you on, you know," Ainsley said, trying to straighten her hair while using a windowpane as a mirror. She had to admit — there were days she had looked better. "And I think Merdi told us not to say *thank you* to anyone. But I don't really remember anymore." Being at Merdi's tree seemed like so long ago now. She felt as though she were losing grip on the passing days.

"I don't know," Khade said, shrugging behind her in the reflection. "Sounds vaguely familiar."

"You'd do well to remember it," Yveena said.

Ainsley gave up on her hair and turned around. Yveena was pilfering curiously through the things in the room. Ainsley wondered if she would be bold enough to steal something. She couldn't completely doubt it.

"Words are empty by themselves, meaningless," Yveena went on. "Unless it's a lie, a promise, or a name, there's just no power to it. *Thank you*—" and she said it with distaste— "is hollow. If you're really grateful, swear a favor. That shows true appreciation."

"Do you feel the same?" Ainsley asked Indigo.

"Yes," the sidhe said. "I've yet to meet a faery who thinks otherwise. It's our way."

"Rowan sort of explained it to me last night," Khade said. "About how we're different. I still don't understand all of it though."

"And we fey can't understand how you humans can attach so much meaning to those two little words, yet you throw names around as if they're nothing," Yveena said.

"It's our way," Khade repeated, giving her a look.

Yveena returned his look with a withering one of her own. "Hence the reason you remain inferior."

Khade opened his mouth to say something else, but Yveena cut him off, saying, "Your argument is invalid, human."

Khade shut his teeth together with an audible click. Yveena opened her violin case and started tuning the strings on her instrument. Khade made a disgruntled noise in his throat.

Ainsley needed to get them separated before they tore each other apart. "I'm going to go enjoy the view on deck. Anyone want to join me?"

Khade nodded, shooting a glare at Yveena. The cait sidhe didn't answer, only began to run the bow along the strings of her violin and play. Ainsley assumed that was a *no* on joining her on deck.

"Indigo?" Ainsley asked.

Indigo shook her head. "No, I don't think so. I'm going to stay in here for a while. Clear my head a bit." She ran her fingers through her hair and began picking spots of dried mud and dirt off her clothing.

Ainsley could understand that, though she couldn't stand to waste this free time that had miraculously fallen into her lap. She felt safe for the first time in days. Besides, she knew that relaxing to "clear her head" would only cause her to think about everything even more.

She gave a little wave. "Okay, then. I'll keep an eye on Rowan for you."

"I'm sure Khade will help," Indie said with a raised eyebrow.

Khade made a face and pushed open the cabin door. Ainsley followed him out.

On deck, there was a flurry of activity now that they had left the docks and their journey had begun. Lorin passed Ainsley on his way to the upper deck. She stared at him in slight confusion.

He noticed her expression. "Are you looking for something?" he asked, and though he said it quickly, Ainsley didn't think he meant it rudely.

225

"Oh, no," she said. "I just always assumed that the captain would be the one to steer the ship."

Lorin smiled at her. "No, not usually. We have the helmsman for that. I've been known to take occasional control though. At the moment, I don't have a crew member at the wheel at all." He turned to walk away up the stairs and Ainsley followed, trusting he meant for her to. Khade tagged along behind them both.

"Did he just say no one's driving this thing?" Khade whispered to Ainsley.

She shrugged. "Let's hope not." The safe feeling she'd had just moments ago was shriveling up and dying inside her.

At the top of the stairs was the wheel. And behind it was—

"Rowan?" Ainsley asked. "What are you doing?"

"I'm inclined to ask you what it looks like I'm doing," he replied, grinning. "I'm settling a bet."

One of the sailors stood behind him, leaning sullenly against one of the masts. The sailor's vine tattoos writhed under his skin.

"A bet?" Khade asked.

Rowan shook his head. "Long story."

"Who's winning?" Ainsley asked.

Rowan grinned wider, and Ainsley felt as if she were seeing the real Rowan for the first time — brash, carefree, and a touch cocky, not weighted with responsibility and worn down by years of abuse. She liked this version of him.

"Yours truly," he said.

"Don't rub it in," the vine-covered sailor grumbled. "You've proved your point well enough."

"What?" Rowan said, turning to the vine faery. "D'you want the wheel?"

The faery shook his head. "I'm going to pretend I don't hear you."

Lorin chuckled. "Oh, come now, Vestun," he said to the sailor. "Don't be a sore loser. Perhaps next time, you'll make your bets based a little less on physical appearance."

"Or perhaps I'll check with you to see whether or not their relatives happened to be pilots as well and whether the boy practically inherited his skill." Vestun crossed his arms and looked away.

Lorin shrugged and turned to the others. "My first mate," he said as if in explanation. "He'll get over it. Though I can't promise he'll learn from it."

"No problem," Rowan said. "I'm sure I can find something else to prove him wrong in."

"I'm sure you can," Lorin said, lifting one eyebrow. "Now keep your focus on what you're doing." He walked over to a small desk a few feet away and sat down in the chair, peering over what appeared to be maps or charts. A large sextant sat on top of the desk.

"So you two took bets on whether or not you could fly a ship?" Khade asked.

"I'm sure dumber bets have been made," Rowan said, slipping a backwards glance at Vestun.

"I'm sure I could say the same of you," Vestun countered. "Why else would you be so far from the castle?"

Rowan's brow furrowed. "Just how much do you know about me?" he asked. His guard was slipping back into place.

Vestun lifted one shoulder in a half-hearted shrug and said in a quiet voice, "Just what the captain told me last night, about who your parents were and how he knew them. But we've made runs to and from the castle before. I've seen you there in the past. I had thought you looked familiar, but I didn't pay it too much mind. When the captain brought you on last night and mentioned your father, I finally put it together." He gave a humorless smile. "And who you are might have remained a secret — our noble king Zake has made sure of that by keeping you in the castle — but tales of his little stray dog are known all over the place. You're famous, and no one even knows you're practically an heir to the throne of both Courts."

"Did Lorin tell you that too?" Rowan asked.

"Everyone knows Saydie, Errin, and Zake were siblings. They just don't all know you're still alive. Say and her human husband, Errin and Jiri, the little Ainsley and her parents—" Ainsley felt a strange twinge at being mentioned, though surely he couldn't recognize her— "all of them disappeared. Most still don't know whether or not they're even alive, but it's not likely. It was easy to assume you vanished with the rest of them." He shrugged again. "The ones who knew — they were silenced one way or another, I'm sure."

"Silenced?" Ainsley asked. "You mean they were killed?"

228

"There's more than one way to silence someone. Those who were trusted or those who valued their lives were probably willing to swear an oath not to say anything. Those who were seen as a threat, however..." Vestun made a face. "You can't force everyone to swear, but you can kill the ones that you know about. Then again, I'm sure he doesn't know about everyone. Even his majesty can't be entirely omniscient."

"Not from lack of trying," Rowan muttered.

"I'm sure," the faery said. "I've idled long enough. You can find me if you need." He waltzed off down the stairs and onto the lower deck, and then Ainsley lost interest in watching to see where he was going.

Rowan was banging his head against one of the spokes on the helm. He sighed and shifted the wheel ever so slightly to one side. "He clearly wasn't one of those sworn to silence."

Ainsley snorted a laugh. "Apparently not." She watched Rowan guide the ship effortlessly. "How did you learn to fly like this if you weren't ever allowed out of the castle?"

Rowan grinned, but his eyes looked troubled. "Joel taught me," he said. "He wasn't supposed to, of course. Zake never wanted me out of the castle. I guess Joel was trying to give me something to do besides hide from Fince and draw. He knew I had a rebellious streak." He chuckled. "Maybe he was trying to keep me from getting into too much trouble. You know, give me a little sense of freedom so I didn't go entirely crazy. So when I turned ten, he started taking me out on the castle airships when Zake was away or busy and wouldn't notice. We never landed anywhere but the castle docks. Joel didn't dare risk someone else seeing us. Dekk and Indie would come along sometimes but never anyone else." Rowan smiled sadly. "Those are probably the best memories I have, all of us out there, getting into trouble. It's the only taste of freedom I ever got."

"Zake doesn't cross me as the type of person to be fooled," Khade said. "Did he never notice?"

Rowan shrugged. "If he did, he didn't ever mention it. But then, maybe he knew and decided to see what it would lead to, if I could be useful to him." His expression darkened. "He's never had an issue with using people for personal gain."

"How long did it take you before you got really good at flying?" Ainsley asked, watching the steady side-to-side motion of the helm, the way mid-morning sunlight glinted on the bronzed wood surfaces of the ship.

"I don't know for sure," Rowan said. "A few months, maybe a year. Took a little longer before Joel trusted me completely, though. It came fairly naturally to me."

Ainsley nodded, thinking. She wanted to ask him, but she wasn't sure what he would say.

He must have noticed her expression. "What? Are you hedging at something?" He raised an eyebrow knowingly and took a step back from the wheel, extending a hand. "Did you want to take a shot at it?"

Ainsley's eyes widened. "Could I?"

Rowan's laugh came out as an amused breath. "I wouldn't have offered otherwise."

Ainsley smiled anxiously. "Okay." She reached out a hand to brush it against the polished wood and then gripped one of the spokes.

"No, not there!" Rowan shouted.

Ainsley jumped back, retracting her hand with a jerk. Rowan burst out laughing.

"I'm only kidding," he said. "Your face was priceless."

"You scared the crap out of me," she said, scowling.

"Joel did the same to me. I didn't think it was funny either. I finally understand his amusement now." He bit at his lip, trying to reign in a smile. "Come on. No more jokes."

Ainsley took a deep breath and grasped the wheel again. "Okay, show me what to do."

Khade sat down against the railing along the deck. "We're all gonna die," he muttered.

TWENTY-THREE

"Say who are you that mumbles in the dark?
And who are you that draws your veil across the stars?"
—Langston Hughes, *Let America Be America Again*

Dekk and Never had been using faery gates — doors which linked the fey and human worlds — to quickly gather supporters over the last couple of days. Dekk thought they were doing fairly well in their mission. Never seemed to know all the right things to say, and the Seelie fey were itching for a fight anyway. Dekk couldn't blame them. His Unseelie nature was anticipating a bit of violence too, and it wasn't even his Court that had been oppressed.

He ducked out the doorway of the building he had been in and stepped into the street. Sunlight glinted off his hair as he looked around for Never. They had agreed to split up to cover more ground in what time they had — which wasn't very much — but Never didn't seem to have come out from the building he had been in across the street. Or maybe he had already finished and moved on to his next mark.

Dekk gave a mental shrug. He wasn't going to wait on the ex-prince. Never could find him when he was ready. And if he had to search a little — well, that was his problem.

Dekk turned and wandered down the street to his left. Other faeries milled about, tending to their morning business. Dekk grinned a sharp-toothed smile as Seelie faeries sidestepped out of his path. He rested a hand on the hilt of each of his swords, reveling in the wide berth they gave him.

His job wasn't to scare them, he reminded himself, but he couldn't help enjoying it. They would have enjoyed it as well, had they been in the opposite position.

Dekk ambled on, keeping an eye out for his next site. He passed an alley on his right, darkened and narrow between a couple of shops, and two shadows moved through it away from the street, speaking in hushed tones. Dekk thought little of it. Dark things happened, even in daylight, so often that he'd grown accustomed to seeing it.

And then he heard a name that made him freeze in mid-step. *Rowan.*

Ducking back around, he peeked around the corner to see if he could get a look at the speakers, but they were too far away to tell if he'd ever seen them before. He knew they could be talking about someone else with the same name, but he had to be sure. He couldn't take coincidence as an easy way out. Silently, he trailed after them. They reached the end of the alley, coming back into the light in a deserted area surrounded by fields. Dekk shimmied up the copper drainpipe of one shop and perched on the roof, peering over the edge. What he saw were two people he'd never thought he would see together: Fince and Never.

Dekk's eyes narrowed. What could those two possibly be doing? He didn't expect it was anything good.

Fince was smiling, a cold, ugly smile that promised trouble. Never looked serious and a little as though he were trying to be intimidating, but his folded wings kept twitching anxiously. Former Unseelie prince or not, he wasn't one now, and Dekk could tell the troll was making him nervous. Dekk smirked to himself.

"Are you positive?" Fince was saying.

"I wouldn't have told you if I hadn't been," Never said, scowling.

Fince chuckled, as if Never's annoyance was entertaining. "All right, then," he said, waving a hand. "Don't get your wings in a twist."

Never's scowl deepened.

"So," Fince went on, "They're headed to the shore then. What area?"

"The banks off the Black Cliffs. They should be there by late afternoon if everything has gone according to plan since we split up."

Never crossed his arms. "I've got a Seelie army on its way as well. Tomorrow, probably. Spilling a little blood of theirs may put them back in their place." He gave a terrible smile.

Dekk pressed himself lower to the roof, frowning and listening hard. Much as he felt dislike toward Seelie fey in general, he hadn't meant to lead them to slaughter.

Fince nodded, showing his teeth. "Good, we'll get Rowan, the princess, *and* the Seelie all in one blow."

"One of the sidhe twins, the brother, is tagging along here somewhere. Rowan's merry band didn't seem to fully trust me. I plan to do away with the sidhe when the opportunity presents itself."

"Ah, good to know. I'll be on the lookout for him." Fince reached for something behind him. "Now then, the deal we had." He pulled out a silver crown and tossed it to Never, who caught it with a pleasantly confused expression.

"Not exactly the way I was expecting it to—" He cut off with a sharp gasp and stared at the dagger buried into his stomach. He had never seen it coming, and Dekk had seen the flash of metal only a second before it happened. Fince wrenched the blade back out, and Never staggered backward into the wall of the shop, sliding down to the ground and gasping. A flutter of dust came down around him as his wings scraped against brick.

"We had a deal," he choked out.

Fince crouched down beside him, and Dekk dared to lean out closer to hear. "We did. You asked for the Unseelie crown in return for information. Congratulations—" Fince pulled the crown from Never's fingers and placed it on the sprite's head— "Your Highness. A deal's a deal. Besides," he said, standing, "Who's to say you wouldn't betray our side, given the chance?"

"You cheating bastard," Never gasped past a mouthful of blood.

"You flatter me," Fince returned. He dropped the dagger near Never's feet and walked off back through the alley.

Dekk waited for Fince to disappear down the street and listened for footsteps while trying to block out the sound of Never's labored breaths. When he was certain Fince would not return, he scampered down the drainpipe and stepped out into the sunlight behind the shops.

Never was slouched against the wall, hands pressed over his wound, looking pale and pitiful in his crown. His eyes were scrunched shut in pain.

"Well, well," Dekk cooed, causing Never to jerk his head up in alarm. "Look what the traitorous cat dragged in. And to think I found you attractive."

Never gave a fierce growl and pitched the silver crown at Dekk, who sidestepped it easily. "Look who's talking," he rasped. "An Unseelie sidhe helping his Seelie friends overthrow his king."

Dekk's eyes hardened. "Both sides suffer from this. The Courts need real leaders, not pretenders. You should've known he'd never give you what you wanted." He shrugged. "Rowan would've made sure you were made Unseelie King. Then you could've done whatever the hell you wanted."

"How could I have trusted you to keep your end?"

"Yeah, because Zake really came through for you, didn't he?" Dekk countered, arching an eyebrow.

Never didn't answer immediately. He just stared back, white-faced and bloodied. Then, "What are you waiting for? Feel the need to watch me die?"

Dekk shook his head. "I don't know what I'm waiting for. I'd planned to make your last moments mocking and miserable, but—" he shrugged— "I think you're having a rough time of things as it is anyway. I guess I'd just like to know if what you wanted was worth sending my best friend and my sister to their deaths. Was it worth their lives? Was it worth *yours*?"

Never met his eyes defiantly. "Is anything?"

Dekk turned to walk away. He didn't have time for this, not if he was going to try to warn the others. "Some things are," he answered. He didn't look back.

TWENTY-FOUR

"A mermaid found a swimming lad,
Picked him up for her own,
Pressed her body to his body,
Laughed; and plunging down
Forgot in cruel happiness
That even lovers drown."

—W.B. Yeats, *The Mermaid*

Rowan had to admit, the princess hadn't done a bad job at piloting the airship. She wasn't a natural — not by far — but she certainly showed promise.

Still, he hadn't been about to let her try to dock the thing. Truth be told, she seemed grateful to be exempt — though she hadn't told him thanks, so maybe she was finally starting to learn — and he had given her several breaks to eat and to rest. Lorin, in turn, had relieved Rowan as well. Vestun seemed disinterested in piloting at all with Rowan's skill having been talked up so much.

So when they neared the cliffs along the shore, the sun low in the sky of late afternoon, Rowan suggested he take back the wheel from Ainsley so that they could survive the ride in order to be eaten by vicious mermaids later. She readily agreed to surrender control of the ship, though she appeared to be a bit leery at the mention of deadly fish-people. Rowan couldn't imagine why.

He steered the ship close to the cliffs so that the other sailors could tie it off to the rocks. Lorin sent a few winged fey to retrieve the lines and make sure they were secure before a rope ladder was tossed out and tied to the cliffs.

Lorin stepped up beside Rowan and motioned for Vestun to come over. The faery grudgingly accepted the wheel from Rowan. Lorin put an arm around Rowan's shoulders and led him away from the helm and over to the railing where the rope ladder waited. Rowan cut a grin over his shoulder at Vestun. The first mate narrowed his eyes, but a reluctant smile lingered around his mouth.

Khade was arguing with Ainsley about who would climb down first. "I'm trying it out before you go," he said. "What if it breaks?"

"Just let him go," Yveena growled, "So we can get off this flying bucket."

Rowan watched Khade climb down the ladder in his graceless, human way. The star's dagger was tucked into Rowan's boot. It wouldn't take much to sever the rope... But then Ainsley was following him, and the desire was gone.

"Are you sure you're ready to be sent off on your own with them again?" Lorin asked, amusement in his tone.

Rowan rolled his eyes. "I've survived him this long. It's the cait sidhe I worry about." He made a face. "Though really, I'm just happy to be getting away from your cook."

Lorin chuckled. "I'd say her bark was worse, but I can't back up that statement with solid evidence."

"I wouldn't mind leaving the human with you, if you're finding yourself short on supplies," Rowan said, grinning. "But really, I appreciate your letting us aboard. I'm not sure what you'd like in return, but—"

Lorin waved a hand. "Don't worry about it. Your father's friendship was more than I ever deserved and more than I could ever repay. Consider us even."

Rowan nodded. "It's been a pleasure flying with you."

"I wish you luck in whatever you've gotten yourself into," Lorin replied.

Rowan smiled and climbed down the ladder. He was the last to leave the ship, and the others were waiting among the rocks. The winged sailors untied the ropes tethering the ship to the land, and then Lorin and the others were floating off away from them all. Rowan gave a last wave to the sailors.

"What now?" Khade asked from behind him.

Rowan turned, but Yveena answered instead.

"We make our way down to the shoreline. Are all of your people so dense and oblivious?"

Khade was biting back a snide comment, judging by the look on his face. Yveena arched a challenging eyebrow and waltzed away down the hill.

Khade let out a breath, joining the others as they followed after the fiddler. "Can we shave her in her sleep or something?"

Indigo laughed loudly. "No, you can't do that. Not unless you want her to carve up your face."

"Yeah, I doubt she's been declawed, Khade," Ainsley said.

"Well, I'd like to murder her," Khade said. "But I know we still need her. And I don't admit that happily."

"You don't do anything happily," Rowan said, edging down a large rock.

"I could push you off this cliff we're on. I could be happy with that."

"Such homicidal intentions you have."

"The better to kill you with."

"Touché," Rowan said. "You're finally getting the hang of this lovely sarcastic banter we have going on."

"Oh, enough with the battle of wits," Indigo groaned. "The testosterone in the air is making me sick."

"That's funny," Rowan said, grinning. "I didn't know Khade's mother was with us."

Khade swung a hand out at him, and Rowan laughed and danced ahead, sliding down the hill and skipping over jutting rocks. Khade darted after him with a yell.

White waves came into view, and the next thing Rowan saw was an up close and personal eyeful of sand as Khade tackled him. Indigo was shouting something he couldn't quite catch, but he figured she wanted both of them to stop rolling around on the beach and flinging sand at each other. Rowan didn't let up until he was certain he had shoved enough faery snails down the front of Khade's shirt. Only then did he back off, watching Khade dance across the beach as he fought to get the slimy, winged creatures out of his clothing. The startled yelps let Rowan know the snails had put their needlepoint teeth in his bare skin.

"Really?" Indigo deadpanned beside him.

Rowan gave her an innocent shrug, and she answered with a sharp cuff to the back of his head. Small price to pay for such satisfaction, he wagered.

"Are we going to do this, or are you two going to continue to waste my time?" Yveena called from atop a large rock in the sand. She had taken her violin out of the case and was tapping her chin with the bow.

Khade flicked away the last snail with an expression locked somewhere between repulsion and irritation. "Yes, of course," he muttered. "Let's not take any more of your valuable time, your furriness."

Judging by her pinned back ears, Yveena had heard him.

"She's right," Indigo said. "We need to get this done with so we can be on our way back."

Rowan fished into his jacket pockets and pulled out the shell necklaces Never had given them. "We have three of these, so we need to know who's going in the get the wand. Yveena has to stay on shore, of course, so she can play."

"I seriously doubt we could get her in the water anyway," Khade said. "She is a cat."

"You're getting on my nerves, human," she returned, hissing.

"I'm not staying here with her," Khade said. "I value my hide."

And yet, you talk so much, Rowan thought. "Fine, you can go then, but not alone. You'd get eaten."

"I think only two should go," Ainsley said. "Then if something happens, we have some sort of backup plan."

"Good idea," Rowan said. "But you can't go with Khade. Then you'd both get eaten."

"You and I will go," Khade said, turning to him.

"I'd *let* you get eaten."

Khade rolled his eyes. "It's the only logical solution." Rowan arched an eyebrow at the thought of Khade becoming logical. "Ainsley and I don't need to stay on shore since we're both unfamiliar with the land, and—" He lowered his voice. "—I don't trust the cat. Therefore, you and Indigo can't go get the wand together. I'm not leaving you and Ainsley on shore while I go with Indigo, because frankly, your girlfriend scares me. And I'm not letting Ainsley go with you into evil-mermaid-infested waters where I can't keep an eye on her." He crossed his arms, the look on his face daring Rowan to find fault in his theory.

Rowan only shrugged. "Okay then." He handed Khade one of the shell necklaces. The other he handed to Indigo, while he slipped the third around his own neck. "Give us a few hours before you come in. Hopefully, we'll find it soon so we can get the hell out of the water. I'm still not entirely fond of this idea."

"Try not to get eaten," Indigo said, a mocking smirk arching her mouth.

"Very cute. I'll try my best." Rowan began stripping out of his jacket and shirts before moving on to his boots and dropping everything in a pile.

"What are you doing?" Khade asked, looking confused.

"Were you planning on going swimming in all your clothes?"

Realization dawned on Khade's face. "Oh. Fair enough." He stripped down to his jeans as well and slipped the necklace over his head.

The ocean breeze was cold, and Rowan could only imagine the water was colder. Might as well get it over with though. He turned to Yveena and nodded.

The fiddler began to play, a haunting song that sounded like the funeral version of the lullaby of the star and the moon. Or the séance version, possibly. Rowan didn't want to find out how she had known what to play. He just glanced at Khade and gave a dark grin. Then he waded into the waves and dove.

The water was cold, and his skin prickled with goosebumps. The salt burned in his eyes. He held his breath, his brain unwilling to believe that he could breathe underwater. He swam out deeper, trusting Khade to follow or else be left behind. After a few minutes, his lungs wouldn't let him hold his breath anymore, and he let out the air and inhaled before he could think. He shut his eyes tightly, expecting to choke. Then he took another breath and another, and relief washed over him. So the Unseelie prince hadn't been lying about the shells, at least.

The farther he went, the colder the water became. Somewhere along the way, the feeling in his skin went numb, but he ignored it and kept his focus on their surroundings.

A garbled sound came to him from his left, and he turned to see Khade, staring back at him and looking expectant. Rowan shook his head and shrugged.

Khade's mouth moved, and the garbled sound came back. "What are we looking for? A palace or anything like that?"

Rowan raised his eyebrows. So they were able to talk underwater too. That was interesting. "I don't know," he said, sounding strange and distorted to his own ears. "We'll know it when we see it, I think."

Khade nodded, and they continued on.

Rowan hadn't been out of the castle other than in an airship, but at least he was vaguely familiar with what the world looked like. At the very least, what the fey world looked like. Under the waves, everything seemed alien to him. He and Khade swam through gardens made of seaweed that grew tall as trees and strange plants that whispered to them. Marble statues watched them pass. Shimmery currents wavered by like heat waves. Creatures with gills and fishlike eyes peered out from among coral the size of small houses. Everything had a sleepy feel to it.

Rowan glanced at Khade. The boy was in just as much awe as Rowan was, though Rowan hoped his own face didn't look as bemused and openmouthed as Khade's did. Khade turned and saw Rowan staring at him. His expression changed, and his face became guarded again. Rowan smiled to himself.

The two of them swam on for what felt like forever. The environment became less novel as they passed through more gardens, more fields of statues, more seemingly deserted ocean terrain.

Where are the mer-fey? Rowan wondered to himself. Was this normal or the work of Yveena's music? Or was it something different entirely?

Something glimmered golden in the distance, distorted by currents. Rowan tapped Khade's shoulder and pointed.

"Let's take a look at whatever that is."

Khade nodded in response.

As they neared the golden thing, it became clear what it was: a large building, surrounded by columns and adorned with crescent-shaped marble details. Two merfolk guards were stationed in the doorway, leaning against sharp tridents. The guards' eyes were closed, and their gills fluttered with deep, even breathing. Their iridescently scaled tails swished steadily back and forth.

"They're asleep," Khade said. "Yveena?"

Rowan nodded. "Probably. This must be the Mer-Queen's palace. Luna seems to really be into this ruler of the tides thing." He tilted his head at the building. "Come on. The wand's going to be in there if it's anywhere."

Rowan swam forward, Khade close behind him. The palace columns loomed high over their heads. The guards didn't move. The boys moved past them, taking care not to jostle their spears.

Together, they pulled open one of the giant, gilded double doors, wincing at the fresh current that whooshed out from inside. The current brushed past the guards, sending a ripple through their tailfins and making them sway, but they didn't wake. Rowan let out a breath of bubbles and swam inside.

The first thing he realized was that there was no ceiling. The entire roof was missing, and, as deep as they were, he could still see the setting sun on the surface on the water. He figured, at night, the moon would be visible as well. The interior of the palace was decorated in columns and statues and potted ocean shrubbery. Several doors lined various hallways to either side. Everything was gold and marble and accented by a strange kind of navy blue fabric that undulated like water.

Rowan and Khade swam warily through the large main hallway until they came to what appeared to be the throne room. Upon a dais, an ornate high-backed chair sat shining silver in the room full of gold. The peculiar navy fabric stretched out on the floor in front of it. To the right of the throne was a shorter one, a slightly reduced twin of the other. To the left of the throne was a silver pedestal, topped by a navy cushion. Atop the cushion sat a thin, shimmery object that pulsed with its own aura.

"The wand," Rowan breathed, words coming out in mangled bubbles. He swam forward to it, just as something large and hairy emerged from behind the throne.

An enormous wolf, grey-furred and blue-eyed, padded around the dais to stand next to the pedestal, staring from Rowan to Khade and back again with a sentient gaze. It glanced up at the navy pillow and its occupant before turning back to the boys.

"What now?" Khade whispered in a gargle. "I thought Yveena's music was supposed to work on everything down here."

Rowan opened his mouth to answer, just as the wolf beat him to it.

"I can hear the sound of the cait sidhe's violin," the wolf said. His voice was deep and husky but clear, despite the fact that he was speaking through water. "But it does not lull me to sleep or chase me away as it does the other folk of the sea. I am immune to the wiles of a cat."

Rowan stared back, surprised but cautious. What was he supposed to say to it? *Hi, we're here to steal that magic wand you happen to be guarding. If you could kindly step aside, we'd appreciate it ever so much.* He found the thought morbidly funny and bit his lip to keep from laughing. Somehow, he didn't think the wolf would find that appropriate.

"How do you know it's a cait sidhe playing that music?" he asked, though he wondered how it could even hear the music at all.

"Cats and water are natural enemies," the wolf said. "It is only logical to assume that one could beguile the other. The sea-folk have their tricks as well, ones used to ensnare foolish felines too curious for their own well-being. I, however, am not so fickle as felines and fish. Therefore, I am affected by neither."

"And here I thought cats just didn't like to get wet," Khade muttered. "Silly me."

Rowan shook his head, attempting to block out Khade's voice. "Not that I wish to offend you in any way, but what are you? If you don't mind my asking, of course."

"I am the guardian of the Blue Wand of the queen's star lover," it replied. "I am the trusted servant of Queen Luna, the Moon of Earth and Gracious Lady of the Tides. I am the Sea Wolf."

Great, Rowan thought. *How do we to get past it?* "We need to borrow the wand for something," he said slowly, testing the waters in a rather literal way before he decided to dive in. "Could you let us use it if we swear to bring it back?" Or, as much as he hated to consider it— "Or we could give you something in return."

"I am not one you should blithely be swearing favors to," the wolf said. "I can assure you that you would not enjoy the repercussions." It smiled, and its teeth gleamed in sharp white relief against its dark face. It was a smile that promised terrible things. "I would ask for one of the shells around your necks. Only one, of course."

Rowan took a steadying breath. They were much too far from the surface. If they gave up a shell, one of them would drown.

The wolf made a barking sound, its mouth wide and its head thrown back. It was laughing. "Of course, I am unable to allow you to borrow the wand in any case, favor or no. I am sorry to disappoint you."

"You don't seem sorry," Khade mumbled, barely audible, and Rowan hoped the wolf hadn't heard.

"We can't leave without that wand," Rowan said. "The fate of the Seelie Court depends on this. We have to keep it safe from Lord Zake, the self-made king who rules both Courts falsely."

"I know who Lord Zake is," the wolf said. "I am not blind to the on-goings of the upper world."

"Then you're plenty well aware of how the upper world is going straight to shit unless something is done about it."

The wolf tilted his head to one side. "I never said that you could not take the wand, only that you could not borrow it."

Confusion gripped Rowan's mind. "What?" he asked, as Khade echoed him with "Huh?"

The wolf barked a laugh again. "I can allow you try to win the wand, but you must pass the test first."

"What is it?" Rowan asked, anxiety building within him.

"A riddle for each of you," the wolf said, "And then a decision for one."

"What happens if we fail?" Khade asked.

A smile full of fangs. "I have permission to eat or drown you. At my discretion, of course."

Rowan and Khade shared a glance, each silently asking if the other would back out. After a moment, Khade nodded and spoke up.

"I'll answer first. What's the riddle?"

"I make you weak at the worst of all times. I keep you safe, I keep you fine. I make your hands sweat and your heart grow cold. I visit the weak but seldom the bold," the wolf said. "What am I?"

Khade's face paled, and his eyebrow lifted. *He doesn't know it,* Rowan thought. He couldn't help him. He knew it would likely be a forfeit if he were to intervene in any way. *I know the answer. Why did he have to volunteer to go first?*

Rowan felt seconds tick by in agonizing sluggishness. Then Khade's expression brightened.

"You're fear," he said, sounding as though he were unsure.

The wolf nodded his head. "Congratulations," he said. "But you have won nothing yet." He turned to Rowan. "You are next. Ripped from my mother's womb, beaten and burned, I become a poisonous killer. What am I?"

Seriously? Rowan thought. *As if that makes any sense.* He concentrated hard. Whatever it was had to be taken out of something.

The ground, maybe? Then beaten and burned to become a killer. What was created to kill? Weapons killed, at least by the hand of their wielder. A sword was beaten, heated in fire and hammered flat. But a sword wasn't poisonous.

At least, not all swords were.

"Iron," he said, surprising himself by the sound of his distorted voice. "Taken from the ground, heated, hammered, used to kill, and poisonous to fey."

"Very well done," the wolf said. "You have both answered correctly. You now have a choice to make. You are free to take the Blue Wand for your own."

"If?" Rowan asked, knowing there was more.

"If you believe you are a blue star."

Rowan felt as though time had frozen, drawn down to that one statement. How would he know that? He had never been told by anyone what kind of star he was, never been told how to find out. He certainly hadn't dared ask someone, not when those with the knowledge were the very people he tried his hardest to stay away from.

"If you are not a blue star," the wolf went on, "You will not survive contact with the glamour that has been set upon the wand's pedestal, and I will eat your companion. My lady, the queen, feels that only a star as bright as her lost love may lay claim to that which he has left behind. If you pass her final test, she relinquishes all entitlement she has to the wand."

Rowan took a deep breath. He'd come too far to turn back now. If the glamour killed him, so be it. He wasn't getting out alive in the end anyway, not without the wand.

"I accept the terms," he said, "Whatever happens." He glanced back at Khade and shrugged apologetically. Then he stepped forward onto the dais and gazed down at the object upon the pillow.

The wand was long and slender, made of a bluish silver metal that didn't appear to be natural to Faerie, yet it didn't look the same as the dagger he had found with the fallen star. At the top was an ornate five-pointed star shape with a pair of wings that fanned out to wrap around the staff. Closing his eyes, Rowan reached out and picked it up.

A sudden rush went through him, nearly knocking him over. *This is it,* he thought. *I'm history, and Khade's going to be dog food.* But the feeling didn't go away. It only intensified until it hurt, a sensation of power flooding into him, as though he had received a Dusting in reverse. As the feeling faded, he opened his eyes. The wolf and Khade were both staring at him, and awe was written plainly on Khade's face.

"So you have proven your worth," the wolf said, bowing low on his front paws. "My lady will be pleased."

"Pleased?" Rowan asked. "I thought she wanted the wand over anything else."

"Do not believe every story you hear," the wolf replied.

"Man, that was cool," Khade said, shaking his head. "This blinding light came up, and I thought you were going to blow up for sure."

Rowan opened his mouth to say something spiteful. Then he noticed to way the wolf's ears pricked toward the palace door. "What is it?"

"The music has ceased," it said. "The folk previously entranced will undoubtedly be waking, and I do not imagine they will be pleased." It turned and padded back behind the throne. "I would go now, if I were you. It would be a shame to die only after achieving your prize."

Rowan and Khade glanced at one another, their horrified faces mirroring the other. Then, without a backward glance at the Sea Wolf, they fled from the palace.

The guards outside the doors were still dazed, and Rowan and Khade took the advantage to dart past them. The boys made it all the way back to the garden of seaweed and marble before the sea-folk caught up to them.

Shiny black eyes and dead-white eyes and gleaming red eyes devoid of pupils were lurking between the tree-trunk-sized strands of vegetation. A school of spear-wielding creatures with orange-yellow skin and spindly arms circled below, gazing upward with bulbous eyes too large for their fishy faces. A pair of shark-tailed fey prowled above, their mouths opened wide from ear to ear, revealing rows of jagged, arrowhead teeth.

Rowan and Khade froze in place. More fey swarmed into the area, leering at them and brandishing teeth and weapons.

Khade was trembling faintly, eyes darting from side to side, though he kept his head still. "What now?" he whispered.

Rowan gave a marginal shake of his head. There had to be a way to scare them off without engaging them. If he and Khade tried to fight, they would unquestionably be torn to shreds by some sort of sentient piranha. He gripped the wand tighter in his hand.

"When I say three, swim straight and don't stop," Rowan whispered back.

"What's your plan?"

"One…"

"Are you going to tell me?"

"Two…"

Khade rolled his eyes. "Guess not."

"Three!"

Khade shot off through the water, distracting the fey, and Rowan brought the wand up over his head.

Time to find out how this thing works, he thought, and let loose every ounce of concentration he had.

The world around him exploded into white-blue light so bright he felt sure he'd been blinded. Through the haze of sapphire, he could see the sea-folk scattering, jolting into each other in their frenzy to get away. By the time the light faded, he and Khade were the only things left in the garden.

Khade stared at him from a few yards away, eyes wide in amazement. "How'd you do that?" he breathed in a stream of bubbles.

Rowan shrugged, blinking away the spots the light left in his vision. "I don't know," he said. He didn't even feel dizzy like he usually did when he used dust in some way. "But I'm not about to complain."

Khade shook his head, grinning. "Me neither."

Nothing else bothered them underwater.

TWENTY-FIVE

"The rude sea grew civil at her song,
And certain stars shot madly from their spheres
To hear the sea-maid's music."
—William Shakespeare, *A Midsummer Night's Dream*

Ainsley watched the surface of the water break as the boys emerged from the waves. She tried not to quiver as she saw their victorious smiles, saw Rowan raise the Blue Wand over his head in triumph, saw their faces pale when they realized what had taken place in their absence.

Neither came forward from the shallows, only stood tense and wary as they took in their situation.

Night had all but fallen now, the moon and stars flickering softly, not yet at full strength. Ainsley and Indigo were standing close to each other. Yveena lay farther away in the sand. Her violin and bow were abandoned beside her. A patch of red stained her shirt across her chest, a pool of blood spreading out beneath her. She lay still, eyes open and glassy. A guard was holding one of Indigo's arms behind her back with one hand, and his other hand, gloved in thick leather, held an iron bar mere inches from her face. Another guard held Ainsley tightly by both wrists. Another dozen guards stood by, and positioned just ahead of them all, flanked closely by Fince and Haviss, was Zake.

He leered at Rowan and Khade as they stood in the shallows, waves hitting the backs of their knees with such force that they swayed in place. "I see you've found it," he called to them. Rowan stiffened. "I was hoping you would, of course. Otherwise, I would've killed all of you quite some time ago. I must hand it to you, though. You are a clever lot." He shook his head, smiling. "Which is why I had to be even more cunning than usual."

"How did you know where we were?" Rowan snapped at him.

"Temper, temper," Zake replied. "I talked to your friend, the prince. Amazing whose loyalty can be bought in exchange for favors."

"Never sold us out?" Khade asked, his expression shocked. "That little bastard."

"Yes, well, he did receive his crown as promised. It just wasn't quite the one he expected." Zake's smile turned absolutely rotten. "You needn't worry about him any longer."

Ainsley felt her insides freeze over. Even if Never had betrayed them, she didn't think he had deserved to die the way Zake was implying.

"Now," Zake continued, "I'm here for a very specific reason, and I don't intend to leave without it." He reached a hand toward Rowan. "The Blue Wand, if you please."

"Go to hell," Rowan said. His voice was icy quiet, and the wand pulsed with a strange light that seemed to catch in his eyes as well.

Zake smiled. "You may want to retract that statement." He spread a hand through the air at Indigo, who struggled feebly from the iron bar. Ainsley could smell the metal, could tell it was making the sidhe girl ill just by being close to it.

Rowan stepped out of the shallows and onto the sandy beach, stopping several yards from Zake. "Leave her out of this," he warned.

"Oh, she got into this of her own accord, I'm sure," Zake said. He turned and nodded at the guard who held the iron.

Without the slightest warning, he set the bar against Indigo's cheek. She screamed and tried to jerk free, but the guard held her too tightly. When he pulled the bar away, she sagged to the ground. An angry, blackened burn mark sizzled on her skin.

Rowan started to run to her, but Zake stopped him. "Not so fast now," he crooned. "Wouldn't want to do that again, now would we?"

Rowan was breathing hard, his face ashen beneath his freckles. Khade stared on behind him, still standing in the shallows, the look on his face one of absolute horror. His eyes trailed back and forth from Ainsley to Indigo and back again.

"Hand it over now," Zake said.

"Don't," Indigo whimpered from the ground. "Please don't let him have it."

The guard held the iron to her skin once more, and Ainsley tried her hardest to block out what was happening.

"This is tiring," Zake sighed, when he realized he was getting nowhere. "Shoot the princess. We'll see what they choose after that."

Ainsley jerked her head around to find herself staring down a gun. Behind it, Haviss locked eyes with her, cold and unflinching.

A sharp "No!" caused her to look away. Khade ran past Rowan, dodging him as he tried to reach out, and headed toward Ainsley. His face was the most serious she had ever seen it before, his mouth set and determined. He reached his pile of clothes and the pistol he had borrowed from Rowan and snatched it up, cocking it and firing in rapid succession. A second gunshot rang out in echo from right beside Ainsley, and she couldn't keep from flinching away. Khade jerked violently and collapsed with a harsh cry. Blood welled up over his chest, soaking into the sand below him.

Someone started screaming, and it took a moment for Ainsley to realize it was her. Tears ran down her face, and she struggled with renewed vigor. The guard forced her to the ground where Haviss lay sprawled, a bloodied hole in his neck.

"I wouldn't," Zake warned as Rowan started toward where Khade had fallen. Rowan stilled and turned hate-filled eyes on him. "Do you still defy me?"

Rowan growled and pitched the wand at Zake's feet. "I hope it destroys you," he spat.

Zake bent and plucked the wand from the sand, turning it over to admire it. "You see, that's why I still need you alive. That's why I've always needed you alive. I can't wield it. Only a blue star can wield it, and I'm not one." He smiled with false sincerity. "I'm going to force you to wield it for me. And if you refuse, I'll kill everyone you've ever held dear, starting with what's left of your merry little band."

Ainsley turned and made eye contact with Rowan. He looked as lost as she felt.

Fince sauntered up to him, and he backed away until he met the waterline. Ainsley could only imagine the troll's sneering grin. Rowan darted to one side, but Fince caught his arm and pushed him to the sand. Ainsley tried to tug free of her guard as she watched Rowan be rolled to his back and Fince put a hand to his chest. Sparks of gold glittered over their skin, and Rowan's struggles ceased altogether after a moment.

Zake turned and began to walk away. "Load them up," he called to his soldiers. "Take measures to ensure the other two don't resist. Leave the human."

Ainsley's eyes went wide at his words. "No, we can't leave him here!" she cried, pulling against the guard that was forcing her to her feet. She stared at Khade in panic. "We can't leave him!" She felt a hand on her chest and screamed with everything in her, kicking and flailing wildly. Dizziness made her sway, and she felt her knees hit the sand once more. Then the ground rose to meet her face, and there was only darkness.

TWENTY-SIX

"Of all the shooting stars I knew, I never fell for anyone but you."
—Ozma

Dekk waited, hidden behind an outcropping of rocks. He was impatient. It wasn't in his nature to be anything else, but he knew he had to stay put. He watched the proceeding events unfold before him, gritting his teeth as he held back. He had arrived just in time to catch the end of what appeared to have been some kind of scuffle.

Zake and his soldiers were loading Indigo, Ainsley, and Rowan into some kind of ornately barred carriage. Both Ainsley and Rowan were unconscious, and Indigo looked as though she were well on her way to joining them. She stumbled and staggered as soldiers pushed and pulled her along, and Dekk bit his lower lip until he tasted blood, scowling. The human boy, Khade, was collapsed in the sand, a pistol just in reach of his fingers. A cait sidhe lay in a pool of blood — Dekk supposed this was the fiddler Never had suggested and cursed the prince to his fate — and another faery was sprawled not far from her. Dekk recognized him almost immediately.

Haviss, you bastard, he thought. *Looks like you finally got what was coming.*

He watched the soldiers depart, leaving the bodies behind, and he sighed. They were all dead then, if they were being left behind. Or at least, beyond help. The sheer amount of blood staining the white sand seemed proof enough. He stood up from behind the rocks, edging through the brush, preparing the follow the carriage. He couldn't waste time here over lost causes either dead or dying. He passed across the beach, past the cait sidhe with the stain over the center of her chest and Haviss with a hole through his throat. Both definitely dead. Last, he passed Khade, shirtless and blood-spattered, and stopped, staring down at him. Dekk couldn't pretend to mourn the others — one he hadn't known, and the other had been a pain in his ass. But he had known Khade, at least for a short while, and he knew Ainsley would be heartbroken when she found out — if she hadn't already.

He sighed and took a step. Then he stopped again, peering closer. Khade's chest rose and fell, slightly, but it was there. He was still alive.

Great, Dekk thought, *A moral dilemma.* Stay and help the human, who would probably die anyway, or go after the carriage that was holding people he knew had the greater chance of survival?

He sighed. Ainsley would never let him live it down if he abandoned her boyfriend.

Dekk knelt and placed a hand on the side of Khade's face, pushing back wet hair and slapping him gently. "Hey, earth to Khade," he said. "Wake up, man."

Khade's eyelids fluttered but remained closed. Dekk sighed again. He looked around and spotted a pile of clothing and crawled over to it. He found what he figured was one of Rowan's shirts and, assuming he wouldn't be needing it, ripped it into long shreds. Then he scooted back to Khade and started to wipe away some of the blood staining his chest. The wound wasn't as bad as Dekk had imagined it would be — he had taken a hit to the shoulder, but the shot looked fairly clean — but still, Khade was going to need more than what Dekk could provide. When the blood had been cleaned away, Dekk wadded up a strip and positioned it over the wound before tying another strip around Khade's shoulder to keep it in place.

Khade's eyelids finally flickered open, and he glanced around with dazed, glassy eyes. Dekk leaned into his line of vision.

"Good morning," he said cheerfully. "Well, night, technically, but you're so out of it, I really doubt you care anyway."

Khade's brow furrowed. "What?" he asked weakly.

Dekk shook his head and waved a hand. "Nothing. Doesn't matter. We need to get you out of here. You've lost quite a bit of blood, and I've reached the extent of my abilities."

"Ainsley and the others," Khade said. "They—"

"I know. I plan to get them back. Until then—"

Khade ran a hand across his face. "I'm so useless. I can't even protect her here."

Dekk sighed. He didn't have time for this. "Look, you can angst later. Besides, I'm sure she's capable of taking care of herself. She's been around Indie long enough, surely."

"I love her."

Dekk's eyebrows shot up. *What am I supposed to say to that?* "I think you're delusional," he remarked.

Khade shook his head, grimacing at the motion. "No, I'm serious. I can't let anything happen to her. You have to go after her."

Dekk scoffed. "Yeah, and then let her skin me alive when she finds out about you," he said. "I don't think so. I'll take care of you first. That way, we both get out alive."

Khade looked hesitantly thoughtful. "But then—"

"Yeah, yeah, I'll go after your girlfriend," Dekk said with a wave.

"She's not my girlfriend."

"Yet," Dekk returned. He pulled Khade to his feet, shifting his weight as the other swayed unsteadily. "Come on. I think I know a short cut. Never showed me how to travel by faery gate. Only thing the jackass seems to have helped us with."

***

By the time they reached Merdi's tree house, the sun was rising in a pink blush across the sky, and Khade was nearly completely unconscious, his breathing ragged and uneven. Dekk had slapped him across the face so much he would probably be bruised later, but then he wasn't exactly a medical expert. Dekk dumped him — and the supplies he'd been able to bring with them — at the roots of the tree and scampered up, pushing his hand against the door. When he found it was locked, he began banging loudly on the wooden panel.

"Merdi, come on," he yelled. "It's Dekk. Open the door. I need you for something."

The door opened with a jerk, and Merdi stuck her face through the hole, glaring down at him. "What d'ya think you're doing, making that kinda commotion," she snapped. "I've already been searched once, you idiot. Don't be the cause of a second visit."

Dekk shrugged as best he could without letting go of the tree trunk. "Way to bite my head off. Good morning to you too."

"Good morning," she scoffed. "And I will bite your head off. Put it into a stew, I will. Cross me again, love."

Dekk sighed. "Look, I just need your help with something, okay?"

"With what?" Merdi asked, an edge still lingering in her voice.

He pointed down at the ground. "With that," he said.

The troll's eyes went wide, and she shooed him back down the tree, following after him and muttering quick words he wasn't able to catch.

She looked Khade over when she reached him, checking his eyes and feeling his forehead and fussing. "What in Faerie have you lot gotten into?" she asked. "I thought you were going to talk to Never, not get into a fight."

"We did talk to him," Dekk said. "He told us where the Blue Wand was and how to get it. He and I went to gather some forces, and the others went to get the wand. I don't know if they found it or not, but I do know that little bastard Never betrayed us to Zake." His mismatched eyes narrowed.

Merdi glanced up at him. "What?"

"He betrayed us, after we offered to help him get back the Unseelie throne, for Zake's offer instead. I saw him and Fince talking, and then Fince stabbed him. I left him for dead. If I ever see him again, I'll be sure to kill him — if he was lucky enough to survive, at least. He did help to gather a Seelie army, but Zake already knows about them too by now."

"What of the others?" Merdi asked breathlessly. "Rowan and Indigo and Ainsley?"

Dekk shook his head. "Captured. Probably taken to the castle, but I can't be sure."

Merdi nodded solemnly, turning back to Khade. "Help me get him inside."

Dekk nodded back, and between the two of them, they lifted Khade slowly up the tree trunk and through the door, before laying him across the bed in one of the rooms.

Merdi scurried around the room, gathering bottles and bandages and whatnot, while Dekk looked on.

She turned to him with a lifted eyebrow. "Just going to watch, are we?"

Dekk shrugged helplessly. "Do you really want me in your way?"

Merdi sighed, turning her eyes upward. "Fair enough point, dear."

When she had her supplies, she began unwrapping the makeshift bandages across Khade's chest, frowning at the wound underneath. Dekk lingered just behind her, watching but careful not to hinder. She dabbed and prodded and muttered to herself, and Dekk finally just sat down against the wall to wait.

***

"Dekk," a voice said, close to his face. "Dekk, love, get up."

Dekk blinked a few times and focused on Merdi's face, directly in front of his own. He had dozed off. He rubbed his eyes fiercely.

"You need to go," Merdi said. "Khade will be fine. He's patched up quite nicely. Now we need to move on to our next problem."

Dekk groaned and stood. "Dekk the Incredible, off to save the world again."

"Don't be ridiculous, dear," Merdi said, not amused. "I'll be tickled if you manage not to break anything."

"Such confidence you have in me. Besides, I'm not going to be breaking anything. I'm going to be breaking *out* something."

She only stared at him. "Get going, love."

Dekk bowed deeply, then turned and fled before she could fling something after him.

TWENTY-SEVEN

"It is often in the darkest skies that we see the brightest stars."

—Richard Evans

Rowan knew his situation was less than desirable before he ever even opened his eyes. As consciousness slowly returned to him, sound and feeling returned as well. He could hear the faint sobbing of someone close by, hear voices farther away. He could feel hard stone floors beneath him as he lay on his back, and his chest felt tight. Cold seeped into his skin, and he finally opened his eyes, before shutting them again with a sigh.

He was in the castle prisons.

He took a deep breath and opened his eyes again, taking in his surroundings. He was in the prisons, true, but he was alive, so that had to count for something. He heard a soft groan next to him and turned his head — which responded in making his vision dance in dizzying circles — to see Ainsley laying there, her eyes still closed but her face scrunched up in discomfort.

Rowan pushed himself up to a sitting position with a grunt and rubbed at the back of his head. He felt as though he had been used as a plaything by a dragon. Well, he amended, by a troll, at least. He looked down at the spot on his chest that still stung. He hadn't exactly had time to put his shirt back on, and the old burn scar that told of past Dustings was freshly red once again.

"I was wondering when you would wake up."

Rowan shifted to stare at Indigo, sitting in the next cell over, her face turned away and her knees pulled up close to her chest as if it made her feel safer. She looked decidedly bedraggled, her clothes and hair in an even worse state than when Rowan had seen her last. And she hadn't been in the best state then either.

"Hey," he said, and his voice sounded weak, even to his own ears. "Are you okay?"

She nodded, not looking at him. "You should check on Ainsley."

He twisted back around to Ainsley. Her face was pale and a little ashen. He put a hand to her cheek. She felt clammy. "Ains," he said, gently shaking her shoulder. "Hey, Ains, wake up."

Her eyes scrunched up and then opened, blinking rapidly before they focused on him. "Rowan?" she asked. She glanced around at their cell and then let out a breath in a disappointed whoosh. "Oh, no," she said, closing her eyes and putting a hand to her face. "Here again?"

"Afraid so," he said. "And I don't know of anyone inside the castle coming to our rescue this time."

She sighed and pushed herself up. "What about Joel? Do you think he knows where we are?"

Rowan turned away from her hopeful face. "I don't even know what side Joel's on anymore. How can we be so sure he's still an ally?"

"You shouldn't judge him like that," Indigo said. "He may be trapped in this mess just the same as we are."

"Maybe," Rowan said. "I don't know anymore. I'm running out of ideas here."

Ainsley gasped all of a sudden, as if she had just remembered something. "Khade!" she cried. "They left him behind! What are we going to do?"

Rowan's eyes widened. He had figured they would've taken him to the infirmary or…something. "Are you sure they left him?"

Tears began coursing down Ainsley's face, cutting trails through the dirt on her skin. "Yes, I'm sure," she said. "You wouldn't remember. I never should have let him come with me." She pulled her knees up and tucked her face into her arms, sobbing.

Rowan turned to Indigo. "Indie," he asked, not entirely sure if he wanted to hear the truth, "Did they really leave him?"

Indigo nodded, but she didn't look at him, only kept her face hidden away as she had been doing since he'd awakened. He shuffled over on his knees to the bars that separated them, reaching through and trying to grab her hand. She only pulled away from him.

"Are you mad at me?" he asked her. "Have I done something wrong? Why won't you look at me?"

Indigo shook her head. Rowan glanced back at Ainsley for aid, but the girl was still crying, her whole body shaking. Rowan sighed and tried again.

"Indie, please," he begged. "Just tell me what's wrong so I can fix it."

She gasped a little, and when she spoke, her voice was small and sounded on the verge of tears. "You can't fix it this time."

"Not if I don't know what's wrong, I can't. Please."

She spun suddenly to face him, eyes glassy and red. Down the right side of her face, under her eye and across her cheek, two deep lines crisscrossed through her skin, blackened and burned. "See?" she said. "I told you, you can't fix it."

Rowan stared in horror. Ainsley gasped in a sharp sob behind him, and Indigo turned away again, trembling.

This is your fault, a vicious voice whispered inside Rowan's mind. *You might as well have held the iron as it burned her. And Khade is probably long dead by now, just like you wanted.*

"Indigo," he murmured, "I'm sorry. I never meant for any of this to happen. I just—"

274

"Don't," she said sharply, and he was afraid she didn't want to hear him anymore. "Don't blame yourself for this, like you blame yourself for everything. Because I don't. Now—" and she turned back to him, teary but determined "—we need to figure out what to do next."

Ainsley grabbed Rowan by the shoulder, her breaths short and scared. He glanced at her, and a shadow fell over them from above. He steeled himself and looked up.

Fince loomed over them, a self-satisfied grin plastered across his face. "Sleep well?" he asked them.

Rowan put an arm in front of Ainsley, though he knew shielding her was pointless. He wasn't too worried about Indigo at the moment. All of Fince's attention was centered on the two captive stars. "What do you want?" Rowan snapped, well aware of the dangers of getting short with the troll. "Come to gloat?"

Fince waved a hand. "Nah, I'm here for a different reason." He yanked a ring of keys off a rack on the wall adjacent — Rowan briefly wondered if he would be able to snatch them away — and began picking through them before casting down a ruthless smile. "Zake has requested your presence in his office."

Rowan's heart sank, but he did his best to keep his face blank as he watched Fince choose a key and stick it through the lock, turning it until it clicked. The lock was pulled away, the cell door opened, and then a guard was entering the room to stand by Fince.

Fince tossed Rowan a white shirt with wide sleeves and waited while Rowan put it on. Then he leaned close to Rowan's face, bringing a wave of pond water scent. "No tricks, now," he warned gleefully. "Or I'll come back for your girlfriend." He leered in Indigo's direction, and she stared back with darkened eyes. "Come on, then."

Fince gripped Rowan tightly around one arm, while the guard did the same to Ainsley, and led them out of the prisons and into the hallway.

The halls were deserted for the most part, excepting the occasional faery who dashed by in a hurry, but Rowan could hear distant shouting coming from somewhere. He couldn't bring himself to ask from where it was coming.

They wound around several corners before Zake's office door lay in front of them, and Fince stepped up to knock, dragging Rowan along with him. Zake's voice sounded on the other side, and they opened the door and stepped into the room.

Zake was leaning against the front of his desk, regarding them with a pleased expression. "So glad you could join me," he said. "I wanted to show you something."

Rowan and Ainsley were pushed forward, so suddenly and forcefully that they both stumbled, and Rowan nearly fell. He recovered as quickly as he could, glaring back at the amused look that had found its way onto Fince's face. Both he and the guard lingered behind, though the guard's face was locked into a blank expression.

"Show us what?" Rowan asked. "The way you're gonna kill us?"

Ainsley made a small panicky noise beside him, as if she hadn't figured out how this all would end. She'd never been prepared for this — *Damn you, Townsley* — and now it didn't really matter anyhow.

"Oh, I don't plan to kill you, dear nephew," Zake said, his tone laced with false sincerity. "I only wish for you to help me in creating my ideal kingdom."

A gleam of dust wavered through the air, followed by the creak and groan of wood. Slowly, the walls behind Zake's desk shuddered and began to separate, pulling away from each other to slide into the adjoining side walls. Through the gap, an entirely new room opened up to reveal walls full of shelving, each shelf holding rows upon rows of tiny glass bottles. Inside each bottle, some sort of glittery substance was glowing, shining with a light of its own. The shimmering powders ranged in color, from deep, dark reds and burnished oranges to sunny yellows and bright whites. In the middle of the room, several soldiers stood guard around an enormous gate that appeared to be made of wrought iron but proved, on closer inspection, to be fashioned from thin, willowy wood.

Rowan glanced at the soldiers and bit down a grin. *A real dream job, that is,* he thought. *Personal guard to Zake's hidden powder room.*

"Are either of you aware of what these are?" Zake asked, running a hand along one of the rows of bottles.

Rowan wasn't sure why they were so important, but he ventured a guess. "Glitter paint?" he answered, silently reveling in Zake's disappointed look.

"Not quite," he deadpanned. "Ainsley, care to take a shot?"

She shook her head, shrugging fearfully.

"How about a riddle then?"

How about not, Rowan thought with a mental sigh. *I'm sick of riddles.*

"At night, they come without being fetched," Zake went on. "By day, they are lost without being stolen. What are they?"

Rowan rolled his eyes. Couldn't they just be executed already, or did Zake really feel the need to torture them first?

"Stars," Ainsley said suddenly, and Rowan belatedly realized she was giving an answer to the riddle.

The grin across Zake's face stretched into something evil. "You, my girl," he said, "Are correct."

The full weight of his reply sank in, and Rowan stared at him in shock. "Stars? What is that supposed to mean?"

"It means that I have been collecting stardust for quite some time, even in the many years I ruled only the Unseelie Court. I have been hiring starshooters to hunt stars down from the sky and bring them back to me. Then I have Fince extract their dust, leaving behind the Shades and storing the dust in the bottles you see around the room. The thing about Shades is they obey whoever is the keeper of their dust. So I've amassed quite the following." Zake stepped close, and it was all Rowan could do not to take a swing at him. "You see, I've been looking for something for a long time. Once I took over the Seelie Court, however, I found it had walked straight into my hands. Since then, I've concentrated on building my army of Shades and waiting for just the right moment.

And with the gate to Skyline sitting behind this office, I've had quite a few stars even recruit themselves."

Rowan felt his heart sink at the thought of a star coming through the gate, only to find himself trapped and turned into a Shade.

"What is it you've been waiting for?" Ainsley asked in a small voice. "Me?"

"Well, you're certainly something I've had hopes of getting rid of, being the heir to the Seelie throne. So yes, in a way. But there is something that has been even more important to me." His eyes gleamed as he turned them back on Rowan. "A rare blue star."

Rowan could feel Ainsley's confused stare on him, but he forced himself not to look at her. "Me," he said. "You need me. Why?"

"Well, you're one of the things I needed," Zake replied. "I also needed this." He lifted the Blue Wand off one of the shelves and held it out for them to see. "I need someone who can wield it. Only a blue star has the capability to use something this powerful. I've been searching for this for a while now. I just had to feed you all the right lines to make you want to go out and get it for yourself, while I sat back and made you think I was trying to stop you. Feel used yet?"

Rowan ground his teeth together and refused to answer that. Instead he asked, "What about the others, Ainsley and Indie and Dekk?" The thought of Khade crossed his mind, but he knew now wasn't the time to be asking after dead bodies. "What do you do with them when you only need me?"

279

"If you don't resist my authority and you agree to wield the wand for me, I won't kill them all," Zake said. He gave a short laugh. "But I'm sure one of you will do something stupid enough to give me reason to bring you harm."

Narrowing his eyes, Rowan took a deep breath. "What exactly do you want me to do?"

Zake grinned. "I want you to help me take over Skyline."

"You—you're crazy," Rowan stuttered, shocked.

"And you haven't a choice, really. This way, please." He turned toward the twisted wood gate, waving a hand for them to follow.

Rowan and Ainsley shared a glance, their faces both wrenched with indecision. Rowan took an uncertain step after Zake, just as a gunshot rang out behind him. He ducked, wrapping his arms around Ainsley instinctively, and whirled in time to see the guard from the prisons drop to the floor.

Fince aimed the gun past Rowan and Ainsley and fired, again and again in rapid succession. Rowan dragged Ainsley down to the floor, shielding her and watching as the soldiers' bodies collapsed one after another. In seconds, only Zake and Fince remained standing.

"What do you think you're doing?" Zake hissed, though his grey eyes were wide. "Have you completely lost your mind?"

"I haven't lost anything," Fince replied, holding the gun loosely now. "In fact, I'm about to win the entire game."

"What are you talking about?"

Fince took a step toward Zake and grinned when the other stepped back. "Think about it. Who's done all your work, quietly and diligently? Who's listened to all your planning, all your secrets? Who has always been the one person you could trust?" He arched an eyebrow. "You only thought it was me. You've always known where Joel stood, known that if you went after the kid, he'd be in the way in the end. But I never gave you reason to doubt me. I've come to the conclusion that you've gone off the deep end. You won't stop until everything falls down around you."

"How do you know?" Zake asked, regaining some of his composure.

"Look at it now," Fince said, spreading his hands. "It's already started. See, I don't want the Unseelie throne. I plan to let Morag have it. And the Seelie lands can go to the highest bidder for all I care. I only want Skyline. I want to be accepted as a true star, not a half-breed mound of river mud that's given no respect. Since no one's willing to give me that, I'll just take it. After all, I've worked for it, haven't I?"

Fince stalked over to Zake, backing him into the wall, and put a hand to his chest, daring him to struggle as he placed the barrel of the gun against Zake's temple. "Guns are nifty little contraptions. Probably the best idea you've stolen from humans. Personally, I hope Morag goes back to fey tradition once she learns she's rid of you." He grinned darkly as dust shimmered around his hand. "It's much more fun this way."

Rowan turned Ainsley's face away and tried to block out the sounds of the struggle. When he could no longer feel the ripple of dust in the air, he twisted back around to look.

Where Zake had been standing, a dark shadow had replaced him, staring ahead with hollow, white eyes.

Fince came ambling up to Rowan, putting the gun away and holding the Blue Wand in one hand. "Still up for that trip?" he asked.

"Go to hell," Rowan whispered.

Fince laughed and then stopped just as quickly. He reached down and gripped Rowan's arm, hauling him to his feet. "I'm not Zake," he snarled. "I don't talk — I do. So you can do as I tell you and not fuss. Or I can turn you into a Shade, and then you can do as I tell you and not fuss. Your choice."

Rowan attempted to jerk his arm away, but the grip was too tight, and he had no doubts that Fince could break his arm if he wanted. "Fine. We'll play it your way," he gritted out. *For now.*

"Good boy." He turned away and jerked his head at Ainsley. The Zake-Shade came forward to put a black transparent hand around the back of her neck. "Let's go then."

Fince pushed Rowan ahead, toward the gate, as the other two tailed closely. He tucked the wand under his arm and laid his free hand on the wood. It smoldered with light for a moment, and Fince pulled it open.

"Welcome home," he crooned in Rowan's ear.

They stepped through the gate, and the world washed out in a swirl of ink.

TWENTY-EIGHT

"Look at the stars!

Look, look up at the skies!

Oh look at all the fire-folk sitting in the air!

The bright boroughs, the circle-citadels there!"

—Gerard Manley Hopkins, *The Starlight Night*

As soon as the darkness spun away and vanished, Ainsley saw her new surroundings through a film of dusky sapphire. Nightlights glittered high above on spiraled posts. The most beautiful people milled about, dressed in pale, silken metallics and illuminated by strange inner lights. A few stopped to consider the new arrivals. No grass grew, only peculiar wisps of smoke that curled up from the ground and tickled Ainsley's ankles. The ground itself seemed to be made of flat, dark clouds, translucent enough for her to be able to see tiny lights far below.

"Fascinating, isn't it?" Fince said, and Ainsley twisted her head to see him staring down at the lights in contemplation. "The brightest souls shine for even the stars to behold. It's downright poetry." He sent her a sidelong glance. "I hate poetry."

Fince pushed the wand into Rowan's hand and let go of his arm. "Don't screw up," he warned.

"Wouldn't dream of it," Rowan said.

Fince chuckled in response and turned to the crowd of onlookers that had gathered around them.

"Ladies," Fince called to them. "Gentlemen. Bow down to your new king." No one moved, but many confused glances were shared. "Oh, good," Fince said. "I was hoping you wouldn't make this too easy for me." He lifted a hand into the air, and an ominous feeling crept into Ainsley's stomach.

With a screech of chalkboard nails, a flock of shadows rose up, hanging above the city of Skyline for half a second, and then crashing down on it like a black tsunami. Stars scattered like fireflies, screaming and pushing. Yells went up to be drowned in darkness. Those who tried to fight were taken down by silent masses. New Shades popped into existence all around. Ainsley could only look on in horror, held in place by the Zake-Shade. She glanced over at Rowan.

He was staring at the wand in his hand. He appeared to be in far better condition than he had been in the prisons, his skin less pale and his face more determined. He looked up and made eye contact with her. He seemed strangely resolute about something, and his gaze was apologetic. He sighed, gave her an uneven smile, and turned to Fince.

"You can do what you want to me," he said, and Fince spun around in confusion. "But I'm not doing anything for you. I will not be your tool." He thrust the wand up above his head, and the pulse of dust rippled out into the air. The Shades pivoted sharply at the wave of power, abandoning the weaker sources, and drifted to Rowan like insects to a flame.

"What are you doing?" Fince shouted, rushing to reach Rowan before the Shades could. "They'll destroy the wand!" He raised his gun and fired. The bullet missed Rowan and ricocheted off the wand, knocking it out of Rowan's hand and sending it spinning along the wispy ground.

Rowan lunged for it, just as Fince caught up to him, grabbing a fistful of his shirt and pulling him backward. Rowan stumbled straight into his grasp. The Shades halted in zombielike confusion, unsure of their next move now that their master had appeared in their line of attack.

Ainsley watched in agonized horror as the next moments passed in front of her.

TWENTY-NINE

"I am not going to die; I'm going home like a shooting star."

—Sojourner Truth

Rowan struggled only enough to convince Fince that he was putting up a fight. But really, he had him right where he wanted him. Fince had him headlocked, one hand around his neck, the other pushed firmly against his chest.

"Have it your way," Fince panted. "You'll be just as useful when you're a Shade. Maybe then you won't be such a thorn in my ass."

I highly doubt that, Rowan thought, concentrating as hard as he could.

He waited until the gold glitter hung around Fince's hand, waited until the black spots flitted in front of his eyes. He could hear Ainsley screaming, tried to ignore it, hoped she knew he was sorry it was going to end like this. She'd be a fair queen once this was over, once she learned more about Faerie, its rules and traditions. She was naïve and young, but she was Saydie's grandchild. If anyone could make things right, maybe she could.

Tell Indigo she's beautiful, Ains, inside and out. No iron can mar that.

Then he let everything go.

He felt the dust burn its way out of him, searing through Shades in a pulsing ring of blue light. Fince yelled in agony behind him, loosening his grip on Rowan and staggering away. Rowan poured more energy into the air, directing it at the Shades that surged toward him in an effort to gain dust. They disintegrated upon touch. Fince writhed on the ground, his skin peeling away to reveal blackened translucence underneath that blew away like sand in the breeze.

Resources spent, Rowan collapsed to his knees with a cry. He blinked hard, trying to clear his vision, but a dim fog covered everything around him. He took a shuddering breath and gritted his teeth in pain.

And then he gave in to the darkness.

THIRTY

"Now the star was only a spark."

—Victor Hugo, *Et Nox Facto Est*

Ainsley ducked instinctively as the explosion radiated outward from Rowan's body. Blinding blue light wrapped around her, dodging her, and attacked the Zake-Shade, crumbling it on impact. Black glitter rained to the ground where it had been standing.

Ainsley took advantage of her newfound freedom to glance around. The explosion — a supernova, she could think of nothing else it could be — darted around and over the other stars as well, targeting the hordes of Shades instead. The army vanished within mere seconds.

Ainsley found herself amazed at the display of sheer power. So that was what a blue star was capable of.

The shockwave pulsed a final time and disappeared, leaving no trace of a shadow behind. Even Fince seemed to have gone.

A pained cry sounded from her left, and Ainsley jerked her head around in time to see Rowan sink to his knees. He swayed forward unsteadily, and the wispy grass seemed to snatch at him.

"Rowan!" Ainsley called in panic. She lunged forward, staggering as she found her feet, and rushed toward him.

A shudder went through him, and he fell onto his side. The ground tugged him under.

Ainsley put on a burst of speed, ducking down to seize the abandoned wand and surging forward again. Rowan's body was half-submerged by the time she reached him. She yanked at his arm, trying to pull him back up, but the ground resisted her.

"Come on," she grunted, doubling her efforts. "Let go!"

In response, the ground opened, sending them both tumbling downward.

Ainsley screamed, watching sky zip past her as they plummeted. The wind stole her voice away, her own ears barely able to hear herself. She spiraled toward the ground, closing her eyes and then opening them again when a wave of dizziness made her head spin. Skyline fell away above, while an arc of white light streamed behind, marking the trail of their descent.

Ainsley reached out to grab Rowan, determined not to lose hold of him again. She tried to coerce the wand into helping, tried to force her own dust to bond with it, and then cursed it when resisted her. So she wasn't a blue star then. A lot of good the knowledge would do her right before she became a pancake on the ground below.

Their speed only increased the farther they dropped, and Ainsley could feel her mind getting fuzzy with vertigo. She had no other choice but to accept her fate.

Please, she thought, as blackness crept into the corners of her vision. *At least let the landing be soft.*

***

Voices drifted in and out, lingering over her, just out of reach. Her body ached as if she had been beaten with something, and she felt uncomfortable, her limbs tangled under her and her head throbbing. One familiar voice rose above the others.

"Ainsley? Hey, princess, wake up." She felt what she assumed was a hand against her face. "You can't die on me now. Your boyfriend'll kill me for sure."

Boyfriend? I don't have a boyfriend.

Ainsley cracked her eyes open a smidge. Bright sunlight poured in, and she scrunched them shut again.

"Oh, good," the voice above her sighed. "I won't be murdered after all."

She made another attempt to open her eyes, blinking rapidly to make them adjust, but something was blocking the light, casting a shadow over her.

Dekk's face hovered overhead, staring at her with a concerned expression he tried to hide with an idiotic grin. "Morning, sunshine," he said. "Way to go skydiving without a parachute. How do ya feel?"

Ainsley took a deep breath. "Like I fell out of the sky," she said, furrowing her eyebrows at him. "What were you saying about a boyfriend? I don't have a boyfriend."

Dekk grinned roguishly. "Not yet, you don't. But it's only a matter of time now. Human boy's already confessed his love for you."

Ainsley blinked. "What? Khade? When did you see...?"

"Found him on the beach," Dekk explained, waving a hand. "He's fine. He's with Merdi at the tree house."

Ainsley's breath came out in whoosh of relief. "He's okay," she echoed, pushing herself up. "He said he loved me?"

Dekk shrugged, helping her to sit. "Could've been delirium, but he seemed pretty cognizant to me."

Ainsley huffed a nervous laugh. She looked into Dekk's eyes, expecting to see happiness for her, but it wasn't there. He looked...sad, she decided, as though he'd lost his best friend.

Oh no.

"Rowan!" Ainsley shrieked, twisting to see where he was. When she saw him, she wished she'd never looked.

He was lying not far from her, his head in Indigo's lap as she brushed his hair from his face almost methodically. His eyes were closed, and his face was much paler than it should have been, making his freckles stand out in stark contrast. His body was very still.

"Is he…?" Ainsley whispered. She couldn't bring herself to finish the words.

Indigo turned to her with wet, miserable eyes. Her breath hitched, and that was all the answer Ainsley needed. Her own eyes filled with tears, and she glanced back at Dekk. He was watching Indigo with the same dejected expression.

"It was Fince," Ainsley said, her voice wavering. "He turned Zake into a Shade. Both of them — they wanted to make Rowan use the Blue Wand for them, because only blue stars could use it. And he wouldn't, he wouldn't do it." Tears rolled down her face. "He took out all the Shades, and Fince is gone. And—"

"It's okay," another voice said, and Joel came into her line of sight. He put his hands on her shoulders. "It's okay. Rowan knew what he was doing."

"He told me about supernovas, but I didn't think—" she said. A sudden thought came to her, and her expression hardened. "It's not okay. Where were *you*? He needed you, and you weren't there! Where were you?"

Joel's expression went blank. "Knocked out and locked in a closet," he said quietly. "But I appreciate your mention of my guilt. I'm sure it'll haunt me for a long time, don't worry."

"Stop," Indigo murmured, and the others turned to her. "Just stop," she repeated. "Arguing won't make things better. I wish it had happened differently too, but you're not doing him any favors."

Joel heaved a sigh and sat back in the grass, while Dekk moved forward to wrap his arms around his twin. But Ainsley had suddenly remembered something, something Merdi had warned her against doing, something she'd done anyway.

She reached down the front of her dress, causing the others to stare at her in bleak curiosity, and drew out a blue flower still in pristine condition.

"Is that a starbud?" Joel asked in amazement. "Where did you get that?"

"I thought you left that thing with Merdi," Dekk said. "You weren't supposed to bring it along. What if someone would have found it? We'd all be dead now." He seemed to realize his poor choice of words and bit his lip, turning away a little.

"Why shouldn't we use it?" Ainsley challenged. "What's the worst that could happen? We get Rowan back?"

The others were very quiet, an uncomfortable silence that made Ainsley want to scream. Why were they so against using the starbud? What were they afraid of?

"Terrible things have happened because of wishes come true," Joel muttered.

"Terrible things happen whether they're wished for or not," Ainsley returned. "That's *why* there are wishes, why there are stars. To light the darkness."

Joel gave her a tired smile. "You are your grandmother's blood, that's for sure. Idealistic to a fault."

"Go ahead," Indigo said, and Ainsley glanced over to her. "We have to try, right?"

Ainsley nodded and held the starbud close to her. She closed her eyes and concentrated on the flower, harder than she had ever concentrated on anything before. She pictured it in her mind, a blue smudge of color standing alone in the dark. She pictured Rowan and tried to connect them, tried to make Rowan light up the same way in her mind. She wished, hoped, prayed for that light, willing it to spark to life.

Please, she thought, *Please, just do something, anything.*

A glow around Rowan flickered faintly and went out. She focused harder, and the light flared up again, wavering unsteadily, blinking in and out. It began to grow at last, shining brighter and brighter until it burned her mind, and she opened her eyes.

Nothing had happened. Joel and Dekk were watching her with pitying expressions. Indigo had buried her face in Rowan's hair. He still hadn't moved.

Ainsley shook her head, unwilling to let herself believe it. "It takes a while to work, right?" she asked. "It'll work."

"The worst thing about wishes," Joel said softly, "They don't always come true."

She felt hollow, like someone had come along and taken her apart and forgotten to put back something important. She couldn't even cry, could only sit and stare at the flower in her hand.

Why? Why couldn't you help me?

She pulled up her knees and dropped her head onto her arms. A sudden, sharp gasp startled her, followed by a harsh staccato of coughing. She jerked her head up to find Rowan's body shuddering as he fought to breathe between coughs. Ainsley lunged toward him, half-running, half-crawling, unmindful of the fact that she was grass-burning her knees. When the fit ended, Rowan took a shivery breath and gazed around with unfocused eyes.

Indigo was crying and laughing at the same time, her tears dampening Rowan's hair as she leaned over him. Joel looked as though he didn't want to believe his eyes in case the scene before him wasn't real. Dekk had a sort of stupid look on his face, lingering somewhere between a grin and confusion. Ainsley felt the missing part inside her slide back into place, joining with everything else and whirring into function like a clock gear.

Rowan blinked and glanced around at them. "Why are you all staring at me like that?" he asked in a hoarse voice. "Do I look that bad?"

Relieved laughter echoed around the group, and Ainsley threw her arms around Rowan's neck. He hissed sharply in pain, and she flinched back.

"Sorry," she said. "Didn't think about it."

"S'okay," he said. His eyes narrowed, locking onto the thing in her hand, before travelling up to her face. "What did you do?"

Ainsley tucked the wilted starbud back into her bodice. "It can wait till later," she said with a nervous smile.

"So, now that Zake and Fince are out of our hair," Dekk said, "Should I call off the army?"

"That was your doing?" Joel asked, at the same time that Indigo said, "Oh, no."

Rowan sighed and closed his eyes. "How far are we from the castle?"

Dekk shrugged. "A few miles, give or take."

"Sounds like a relatively short distance, given how far we fell out of the sky," Ainsley said blandly.

Rowan started to push himself up, and Joel moved forward to help while Indigo steadied him from behind. He swayed a little on his feet, and he was still exceptionally pale, but Ainsley figured it was better than he'd been a few minutes ago.

Something shimmery caught her eye, and she looked down where Rowan had been laying. Among the weeds were the fresh, unfurling petals of a new starbud. Ainsley crouched down to pluck it from the ground.

"Who do you think made that wish?" Dekk asked.

She shrugged carelessly. "Who knows?" she said, but the gleam she saw in Rowan's eyes told her he knew it had been her.

She walked over to where the wand had landed and retrieved it, returning to Rowan and holding it out to him. He regarded it cautiously.

The corner of Ainsley's mouth turned up. "Let's end this for good."

Rowan gave an uncertain grin and took the wand, running his thumb over the dent left from Fince's bullet. "Okay, then."

THIRTY-ONE

"And an open door was to a girl
Like the stars are to the sky."
—Mary Chapin Carpenter, *The Moon and St. Christopher*

As soon as he had taken hold of the Blue Wand, Rowan had felt incredibly and instantly better, just as he had the times before. He had easily outstripped the others, exhausted as they were, on the way back to the castle. He felt freshly rested, however, and it was all he could do not to call back at them to hurry up after every few yards.

He led the others over the field, around scattered trees and through tall weeds that grabbed at their ankles. The sound of battle drifted to them, soft from a distance but growing louder as they grew nearer to it, rising to a harsh uproar. After another little while, they passed out of a final line of trees, and the battlefield lay open before them, a few hundred yards away.

Wails of the wounded and dying pierced the air. Metal screeched against metal, and arrows hissed into the fray from all angles. Some faeries were armed with swords or bows, while others were armed with daggers or spears. A few Gentry carried guns. Others were armed with only teeth and claws. Goblins tore at the ankles of taller Seelie fey, and a large wolf ripped out some unfortunate creature's throat in a spray of crimson. Griffins and half-bird creatures with spindly legs circled in the sky above, clashing into each other and tearing at flesh with talons and beaks. Tiny pixies rose up high to dive down at lightning speed, miniature missiles armed with blades like shiny tooth picks.

Rowan tightened his hand around the wand, feeling a surge of power seep into his blood. He tried to repress the anger he felt at the Unseelie for all the loss they had helped to cause. This wasn't a time for vengeance. They weren't there to fight.

Apparently, Dekk thought otherwise, as he had drawn his swords and stood off to Rowan's right, bouncing and rolling his wrists.

"So," he said. "Got a plan, or are we just going for the ole 'charge into combat with our swords held high and a manic gleam in our eyes'?"

Rowan shot him a sideways glance, one eyebrow rising. "A plan," he said. "Sort of. And it doesn't involve you killing anybody."

Dekk deflated a little. "Well, I'm not sure I like your plan very much."

"What is your 'sort-of' plan?" Ainsley asked.

"Will you take the throne and accept the responsibility of your people?" Rowan asked.

Ainsley stared at him. "I asked you a question first. You can't answer a question with a question."

"I think mine is more important," he said.

She didn't reply for a moment. Then she said, "It scares me, being in charge of so many." She furrowed her eyebrows and stared out over the battlefield. "But I'm not sure Seelie lands can survive another false ruler. I know I have a lot to learn." She turned back and glanced at each of the others. "But I'm willing to give it everything, as long as I can have a little help."

"It'll be there," Indigo said with a smile.

Dekk flashed sharp teeth at her. "Going against our very nature and helping the Seelie is what we do best."

Joel chuckled. "Things can only go up from here," he said.

"Hopefully," Dekk added, and dodged when Indie swung a hand out at him.

Ainsley smiled at them. She glanced at Rowan. "You have to answer my question now," she said. "What's your plan?"

Rowan shrugged. "Stop the fight," he said, and turned and raced toward the battlefield.

Startled cries erupted behind him. He could hear them follow after him but kept his main focus on his objective. If someone didn't stop this, everything would be lost. There was no Seelie ruler, and the only Unseelie ruler, a regent who would seize the opportunity to become a true queen, was currently miles and miles away. At least, Rowan hoped she was. If she were to show up now, they would be in deeper trouble than he was sure they could get out of. And without a queen or king of some kind to call a truce, or surrender or call them off or *something*, the Seelie and Unseelie would completely destroy each other, down to the last faery standing.

Rowan dodged an arrow that flew at his face, not entirely certain whether it had been meant for him or he'd merely gotten caught in the crossfire. Not pausing to glance at the bodies littering the ground at his feet, he propelled himself forward, skipping around corpses when necessary and trying to ignore the smell of blood.

He reached the edge of the battle and slid to a halt, stabbing the wand upward into the air.

Please work, he thought, and released a miniature shockwave over the field.

The faeries swayed where they stood, some stumbling over from the force. Several pixies were sent tumbling away on the wind with high-pitched yelps of bewilderment. All combat ceased, every eye turned toward Rowan. He clenched his shaking hands and paced his way through the frozen mob.

"Zake has been destroyed," he shouted, "As well as many of his closest servants. The true heir to the Seelie throne has returned. Lady Ainsley, granddaughter of Queen Saydie, has arrived to take her place among us. If you are true and loyal Seelie, you will accept her as your queen. If not—" He scanned the crowd "—You are welcome to leave. Any Unseelie who are willing to be peaceful and live by Seelie rules may stay. Otherwise, you are considered to be trespassing. Make your choices now."

Faeries shared glances with one another, still held motionless by the wand.

One faery called out, "How do we know she's who you say she is? You can lie."

"Judge her for yourself then," Rowan said, pointing toward Ainsley, who stood back at the edge of the battlefield.

Ainsley stepped backward, eyes wide, and a ripple of gasps passed through the crowd. Comments of "She looks just like her" and "What power she must have" and "Say's blood, truly" whistled their way into each listening ear. Every Seelie in the crowd went down to their knees, while the Unseelie backed away from her, hissing and raising hackles. Ainsley turned to stare after the Unseelie fey, and the Seelie fighters suddenly surged up as one, racing after their foes.

The Unseelie scattered like birds, some vanishing, some taking flight, none daring to fight back. They knew the power of a true queen. The Seelie army chased them to the edge of the castle grounds and stopped, banging weapons and shrieking, watching as the Unseelie fey retreated.

When they were sure their enemy would not come back, they returned to where Ainsley stood, kneeling once more.

Ainsley muttered something Rowan didn't understand and waved her hands as though she wanted the faeries to stand back up. Rowan sighed, one corner of his mouth turning up in amusement, and went to join her.

"Come on," he said, taking her elbow and leading her toward the castle gates. A few fey gave him a cross look for daring to touch their new queen, but no one said anything. He almost hoped they would. They weren't yet aware of his own royal standing. "We've still got messes to clean up." He glanced over his shoulder at the kneeling crowd. "We still need to search the castle. Spread out and look for anyone that's not supposed to be here." He started forward before stopping again. "And those three are with us." He motioned to Dekk, Indigo, and Joel, who were looking slightly wary and more than a little out of place.

Ainsley allowed herself to be led away. "Where are we going then?" she asked, staring at him. "It can't be this easy, not after everything else we've done."

"It's not," he said. "They accept you now because of the wand. I put a haze of dust over them. They're a little entranced right now."

She jerked her arm away. "What? Why would you do that?" she demanded.

"To keep them from slaughtering each other," Rowan said, gazing back at her. "Hard to be queen when your subjects are all dead."

Ainsley stared at him with cold eyes. "I thought they acted that way because of me."

Rowan rolled his eyes. "They will. But you're not queen yet. Now come on."

He started off down the hall, and her footsteps tailed him, so he figured she wasn't too angry with him.

They wound through halls and around corners, neither of them speaking, until they came to Zake's office. The door was closed, and Rowan had to force his heartbeat to calm before he pushed it open.

The office he had been familiar with growing up remained in perfect condition. Beyond that, the secret room lay in ruins. Every bottle of stardust was shattered. Some were dashed to the floor. Others lay broken on the shelves, razor shards glinting faintly. The dust they had contained was nowhere to be found. The bodies of the soldiers had vanished from the floor.

In their place, standing with a celestial grace Rowan had never seen before, was a tall figure, robed in white, orbited by a faint circle of light.

The figure stepped forward. He had shoulder-length tawny curls that framed his face like a mane. "Prince Rowan. Princess Ainsley," he said, his voice deep and commanding yet soft. "Welcome to the last part of your journey."

Rowan recoiled upon being called by name. "Who are you?" he asked, distrusting.

"Forgive me. I am Leo, High Constell of Skyline." He waved a hand to the gate behind him. "I am one of the rulers of the fire-folk. I and the others are called the Constellations."

Ainsley cut a sideways glance at Rowan. "I thought constellations were connect-the-dot pictures people created when they looked at the sky," she whispered.

Rowan raised his eyebrows at her, shrugging. "My childhood was just as lacking as yours was, as far as heritage is concerned," he whispered back.

Leo smiled at them. "You are unfamiliar with us," he said. "We were aware of this, but it does not matter. You have finally stepped into the roles that have been laid for you."

"Wait, you knew all this was going to happen?" Rowan asked, bristling. "And you didn't do anything about it?"

"It was not our place," Leo replied. "There are many fates one must choose from. Had we interfered, things would not have ended well."

"Enlighten us," Rowan deadpanned.

"I don't think you're supposed to be talking to him like that," Ainsley muttered.

"It is his right to ask," Leo said, before Rowan could answer. "And it is your right to understand.

"If we had intervened, Ainsley would not have discovered her true nature. The treachery of the Unseelie prince would not have been revealed, and he would have raised an army in the future, one that could have been harder to stop. The starbud upon Harper's Hill, the faery gate that Ainsley and the human boy used to enter this world, would not have been plucked, and you would not have obtained the starbud you now have with you. Your courage and wisdom would not have been tested, to prove you worthy of the rule of Avyn. And, perhaps most importantly of all, the Blue Wand would not have found its way back to Skyline."

"The wand?" Ainsley asked. "What do you need the wand for?"

"Luna is not evil. She merely has her dark side, as all moons do. Do either of you know how a moon is created?"

The two of them shared a glance and shook their heads.

A faint smile crossed Leo's face. "All moons were once stars, many of them bright and vibrant. But they are stars who give in to dark desires, who do things that cannot be forgiven. Luna was one such star. She learned of a wand that had been created by a very powerful blue star, possibly the most powerful star that has ever been. She desired this wand greatly, but she was also in love. She could not steal the wand, because it was its maker she was in love with. One night, they had come down from Skyline to take a boat out onto the ocean, her favorite place to visit below. She asked her love if he would allow her to try the wand, to wield it as he did. He refused, saying that its use would destroy her, that she was not powerful enough to withstand what it could do. She dismissed him and asked again, feeling jealousy creep over her at the thought that he could be better than her. Again he refused. Angrily, she stood, yelling at him and causing the boat to rock unsteadily. Merfolk heard the noise and were attracted to it. They began to seize the boat, trying to tip the stars into the water. One managed to grab Luna's dress and pull her to the edge of the boat. Her love ran to aid her, and the merfolk pulled him over instead. Luna became a moon not a long after, now changing the tides as different sides take over, high tide in her dark jealousy and low tide in her moments of grief and regret."

Ainsley let out a long breath. "That's way different from the version I've heard," she said.

"Legends may be true, but that does not mean they have been passed down truthfully. Zake would likely have wound up much the same, had events played out differently." He looked away, lost in thought for a moment.

"You still haven't answered the question though," Rowan reminded him. "Why do you want the wand so badly?"

Leo looked grim. "To destroy it," he said. "We have not been able to get to it in all these years Luna has kept it in the ocean. None of the Constellations are blue stars and so could not retrieve it. Nor have we found anyone worthy of the task." He smiled. "Until now."

He stepped back and swept a hand toward the woven wood gate.

Rowan glanced at Ainsley. She turned to him and nodded.

"Be a shame to turn back now," she said, one corner of her mouth quirking upward.

Rowan wasn't sure what she was finding amusing, but it didn't really matter. He looked back to the star waiting for them and walked through the gate once more.

***

The scene that opened before them was vastly different than it had been on their first visit. Glass houses lay in shattered heaps. Glittering shards stabbed upward from the wispy grass. Lampposts tilted precariously. Some stars had begun sifting through the wreckage, while others sat sobbing or attempting to comfort those who were upset. Most were moving away from the remains of the tiny city.

They were not the same as the fey Rowan had grown up surrounded by. They were not bloodthirsty and violent like Unseelie or mischievous and apathetic like Seelie. They were older and wiser than even faeries. They had no reason to war with anyone. They simply *were*, and now their very existence had been fractured.

Leo was leading them down a silver street littered with debris, and Rowan kept his head down, staring into tiny reflections of himself that winked up at him from a hundred slivers of glass.

"I'm sorry," he said, and he felt Leo glance back at him. "I didn't mean to cause all this."

Leo sighed. "If anything, I should be apologizing to you for lacking the foresight necessary to keep the Shades from coming in the first place. You were willing to give your life to protect others, and you possessed enough control to direct your focus away from other stars. You have no reason to be sorry."

Rowan nodded but didn't reply, and the three of them fell into an uneasy silence. Rowan saw Ainsley glance at him several times from the corner of her eye, but he didn't look back at her.

The wreckage continued farther on as they followed the street, and Rowan found himself in awe of the sheer destruction he had caused. He was so enraptured by the sight that he didn't see the others stop until he ran into Ainsley's back, sending them both pitching forward into Leo. The tawny haired star was hardly moved, glimpsing them over his shoulder with a faintly entertained smile.

Ainsley whipped around to glare at Rowan, not at all pleased at becoming the middle of a star sandwich. Rowan shrugged, mouthing a contrite "Sorry."

He shifted so he could see what they were stopping for, and ahead lay a vast expanse of...nothing. No glass houses or silver walkways, nothing. Even the metallic street they had been following just cut off, a dead end. Beyond it was all open space, wispy grass and more flat foggy ground. Though here, there were also bronze and silver trees that jutted up from the clouds in scattered arrays, millions of glowing glass shards lit brightly in place of leaves.

Leo extended a hand out toward the open space, his form illuminated from the inside out. A veil seemed to shimmer and fall, dropping like a curtain across the field of smoke and lights, and then a castle filtered into view, glass spires rising into obscurity as they reached the sky above. The silver road stretched before them, seamlessly grafted onto its preexisting other half.

Leo twisted around. "Shall we?" he asked, gesturing to the castle.

Rowan forced his mouth to close and followed.

The castle was even larger up close. The enormous mirrored doors were at least twenty feet tall, and Rowan stared into his reflection, vaguely aware of how terrible and worn out he looked, but also highly amused at the look on the face of Ainsley's reflection. He stifled a laugh as the doors opened.

Leo led them inside and down a long hall that was lined with more mirrors and thin pieces of glass blown into winding artwork. The floor was transparent, illuminating the room with the sunlit sky below, and Rowan would have wished he hadn't looked down if he hadn't been in such astonishment.

At the end of the hall, a large circular room opened up, draped in the deepest blues and greys and silvers. A crowd of ethereal creatures stood around the room, not only stars but other things as well. Deer-like unicorns, birds plumed with flame, and willowy figures formed from nothing but smoke. A long, winding dragon lay curled around a dais in the middle of the room, its white scales covered in fur and its crystal eyes showing benevolent sentience. Upon the dais were twelve thrones. The six to the left were occupied by females, while five to the right were occupied by males. One in the middle was empty.

"Welcome," said Leo, "To the Court of Stars, home of the fire-folk and their kin, beings created from the dust of the skies." He motioned to the eleven filled thrones. "These are my fellow Contells and the Constellas."

He introduced them to Rowan and Ainsley, starting from the far end of the females. Taurus, with black hair and short ivory horns; Cancer, her hair vividly red and her eyes beetle-black; Virgo, blonde and wide-eyed; Scorpio, with pale brown hair and a sharp-fanged smile; Pisces, green haired and web-eared; and Capricorn, the High Constella, with soft brown curls and the ears of a goat. Then he started at the far right with the males. Aries, with ram's horns spiraling out from white hair; Gemini, his hair halved in white and black, with one brown eye and one blue; Libra, with bronzed hair and eyes; Sagittarius, with long brown hair and a bow across his back; and Aquarius, with bluish hair and a tunic made of scales.

Leo walked forward to take the empty seat and gazed back at Rowan and Ainsley. "Now it is your turn," he said. "The final thing you need is within these walls. Capricorn will show you the way."

The goat-eared Constella rose from her throne, waving a hand gracefully for them to follow. They shadowed her down a hallway, not unlike the one they had entered the castle through, past doors and around corners that shimmered and glistened from her light. Rowan caught his and Ainsley's reflections across archways and walls, and the floor remained clear as the sky below.

Capricorn stopped before a mirrored door, and Rowan watched in shock as it disappeared in front of her. She didn't have to open it or touch it or do anything at all. It simply faded anyway to reveal a large room draped in blue and yellow, lit by glowing dust-filled lanterns. The room was dim, but he could make out a figure laid upon the large postered bed. It looked almost exactly like Ainsley. Almost.

"Queen Saydie," Rowan breathed. Ainsley took a deep breath beside him.

"Yes," Capricorn said softly, leading them into the room. "She has been trapped in sleep for the past thirteen years, ever since her brother attacked her Court. She attempted to protect it, but her power was not strong enough against him. When she realized all was lost, she came here, to seek help, we assume. But she was in this state when we found her outside the palace. She has been since." Capricorn turned to them. "You may try what you can." Then she slipped out into the hall, and the mirrored door reappeared behind her, sealing Rowan and Ainsley inside.

Ainsley peered over the bed into Say's sleeping face, peaceful and still. "All these years I thought she was dead." She glanced to Rowan at her side. "Then I guess my parents really are gone, if they're not showing us anyone else."

Rowan sighed. That meant his own parents were probably long dead too. He stared down at Say's motionless form, her white-blonde hair splayed out in long waves that cascaded over the pillow and onto the floor. "Yeah," he said. "Probably."

If Ainsley heard the bitterness in his voice, she didn't mention it.

"Do you think we should use the wand?" she asked.

Rowan looked down at the wand in his hand, back up at Say, then finally at Ainsley. He shrugged. "I don't know, but I guess it's worth a try."

He held the wand up, focusing his energy into and through it, directing it toward Say. But nothing happened. He tried again, felt the glow of dust around him once more, concentrated harder. But still she remained unchanged. Rowan turned to Ainsley with a sigh.

"Doesn't work," he said, shaking his head.

"Plan B, then," she said, and reached into the front of her bodice. Rowan knew what she was going for, and grabbed her elbow, stopping her.

"No," he said. "I don't want you to use that flower, not again. I think we got lucky the first time. And yes, I'm fairly certain I've figured out what you did, so don't ask. There has to be something else."

"Well, I'm out of ideas," Ainsley said. "And your ideas suck." She crossed her arms and turned away from him. He snickered at her childishness.

He regarded the figure on the bed again, looking so unlike a queen in her slumber, dressed in simple white, with her hands folded upon her stomach. She seemed so lifeless. He reached out to touch her hand, to convince himself she wasn't dead.

A light flared around her, and Rowan jerked his hand back in alarm. The light receded instantly.

Ainsley shot him a startled sideways glance. "What did you just do?" she asked.

"I don't know," he admitted, a thought forming in his mind. "But I think I may have an idea."

He slipped the wand under Say's folded hands, watching as the wand began to glow. He pulled his hand away from it, feeling a sudden weakness come over him as he released it from his grip. The glow spread outward, enveloping Say and growing brighter until Rowan had to close his eyes to block it out. Then the light vanished, and he opened his eyes again.

"Oh no," Ainsley sighed. "Look."

He followed her gaze to the wand. Or at least, what was left of it. It had shattered into dozens of tiny blue shards, winking faintly in the dim light. He felt his shoulders sag. So that was it then. Their last option was going to be the starbud after all.

A soft noise made Rowan look up to Say's face. Her eyes were fluttering open, revealing pitch black irises. Her sight locked onto the two at her side, and she smiled at them.

"Well then," she rasped in a voice long unused. "I seem to recall the two of you being much smaller last I saw of you."

THIRTY-TWO

"I have loved the stars too fondly to be fearful of the night."

—Sarah Williams, *The Old Astronomer to His Pupil*

The Constellations had congratulated Ainsley and Rowan on waking the queen and destroying the Blue Wand, and for doing both at the same time no less, but Ainsley really had started tuning people out by then. She was exhausted, and from the look on Rowan's face, she could tell he was too. The Constellations had sent an attendant to accompany them back to the gate. Ainsley was fairly certain she and Rowan could have found the way by themselves — follow the silver road, for crying out loud — but she soon realized that the street jutted off in different directions than the one they had first taken, a fact she hadn't noticed previously. Though, admittedly, she had been a bit preoccupied by her surroundings at the time.

She watched their guide lead them down the path, absently taking in how graceful his movements were. He was willowy thin, and his hair seemed to be formed from nothing but smoke, dancing along behind him as he walked. His clothing was in varying shades of smoky grey, and she wondered if her hand would go right through him if she reached out to touch him.

When they reached the gate, their fire-folk escort bowed elegantly and stepped away without a word, making Ainsley curious as to whether he could even talk.

Rowan ran a hand along the door with a sigh and smiled over his shoulder. "Anybody else ready to go home?" he asked.

Ainsley gave a tired laugh. "More than anything."

Say rested a gentle hand on Ainsley's shoulder. "I think that's the best idea I've heard in a long time," she said.

Ainsley looked up into her grandmother's face, free of wrinkles or lines, her un-greyed hair hanging just past her hips in soft, yellow waves, her black eyes shiny with the appearance of youth. She didn't look anything past twenty-five years old, and yet Ainsley knew she must be that age several times over.

Ainsley flashed her a grin and raised an eyebrow. "You haven't been around Rowan long enough yet," she said. "His ideas put everyone else's to shame."

"Well that was just dripping with sarcasm, wasn't it?" Rowan asked. He pulled the gate open. "Ladies first, your royal pain-in-the-butt-ness."

Ainsley snickered and slipped through the gate. She was greeted by the quickly-becoming-familiar swirl of blackness, and when she opened her eyes, she was standing once more in Zake's ruined secret room. She turned to make sure Say and Rowan were behind her before striding forward, feeling a sense of purpose she'd never felt before, but also feeling completely drained.

"I don't know about you, Rowan," she said, stifling a yawn, "But I plan on sleeping for a week after this."

"Do you wish to stay in Avyn or will you be returning to the human side to your grandfather?" Say asked, a strange tone in her voice.

Ainsley stopped and twisted around to face her. "What should I do?"

Say shook her head. "I cannot tell you that. It is your choice and your choice only. What do you want?"

Ainsley thought. She had never felt quite right before she'd been led into this strange new world. There had always been something missing, a hollow spot, a curiosity that couldn't be taken away no matter what she did. She had wanted nothing more than to figure out what had happened to her parents, to her grandmother, and why her grandfather would never speak about them. Now she knew, that he had wanted to keep her safe from the things that lurked in the dark, that he wanted to protect her from the creatures that had killed her mother and father and caused her grandmother to disappear for more than a decade. But now that she knew, what would she do from there?

"You are under no obligation to continue to be the heir to the throne," Say said, watching her. "If this is not what you want—"

"This is what I've wanted for a long time. I just thought it wouldn't happen."

"Careful what you wish for," Rowan called in a singsong voice.

"You're what I wished for," Ainsley returned, and he didn't say anything in reply to that. She faced Say again. "It scares me," she admitted, "Knowing it's real. Knowing I would be in charge of so many people."

Say smiled at her. "You act as though I would hand it all to you today." Ainsley stared in confusion, and she went on. "I see no reason not to train you first. After all, you are young still. I am not asking you to step into the role of queen just yet, only whether you wish to fill it someday."

"As if we'd let you do it alone anyway," Rowan cut in, rolling his eyes.

Ainsley mock-glared at him. "If I say I'll be your princess," she asked Say, "Does that mean I can tell him what to do?"

"I see no reason why not," Say said with a smile.

Ainsley nodded. "Okay," she said and strolled toward the doorway.

"I should've stayed dead," Rowan grumbled behind her. She chose to ignore him.

Ainsley wasn't sure where she was headed, so she hung back to allow Say to walk ahead. Say led them out through the main doors and onto the castle grounds. The battlefield was littered with bodies and debris, but cleanup had already begun. The wounded were being carried away first, followed by the dead. Ainsley held a hand against her nose to block the smell of blood and death.

Saydie sighed. "He always did know how best to make a mess," she said, and Ainsley knew exactly who she was referring to.

A call echoed over the field, and Ainsley twisted to see Dekk running toward her, pointing wildly, while Indigo and Joel trailed more slowly after him.

He reached them, panting, and bowed gracelessly to Say. "Hi," he said. "I'm going to go out on a limb here and assume you're the Seelie Queen, seeing as how you and Ainsley look so much alike."

"And I am going to assume you are not Seelie," Say said, looking him over.

Dekk waved a hand. "Nah, I'm Dekk. I don't follow rules too well." He shrugged. "And my sister's in love with your nephew."

Rowan's face went red when Say cast him a glance. "Really? I have missed a lot."

Indigo and Joel made their way up to where Dekk stood and bowed as well, though with far more grace. Indigo walked up to Rowan and put her arms around his waist, and he hugged her close. Joel went down on one knee in front of Say.

"I hope you can forgive me, my lady," he said. "I'm afraid I've done less than was expected of me."

"You've kept him alive," Say said.

"Barely."

Say shook her head. "What does it matter what margin? It only matters the outcome. Please stand, Joel."

Joel glanced up at her, hesitating, before standing up and taking a step back from her.

"What is that about?" Rowan asked. "Who were you supposed to be watching?"

Joel leveled a look at him. "You."

"Me?"

Joel sighed. "When Zake's armies attacked, Townsley was able to get away with Ainsley, but you were meant to have gone with him too. We knew that you wouldn't have been able to stay very long on the human side – you would have stood out too much – so we were going to have Townsley bring you back somehow, take you somewhere safe. You were only five, after all. Only, you had already disappeared, and we weren't able to find you. Townsley had to leave with Ainsley alone. Queen Say charged me with finding you and keeping you safe. And then she disappeared too. I'm beginning to think it runs in the family." He shot a rueful grin at Say.

"Well, I can think of a few good things that happened while living here," Rowan said, and leaned down to plant a slow kiss on Indigo's lips.

"Am I safe to assume this is the aforementioned Unseelie girlfriend?" Say asked, her eyebrows lifted but the corner of her mouth turned up just slightly.

"Yeah, that'd be her," Ainsley said, wrinkling her nose. "It's gross, but you get kind of used to it."

"No, not really," Dekk said, crossing his arms and receiving a crude gesture from Rowan, who didn't look up from what he was doing. Dekk turned and a grin lit his face all of a sudden. "And look what the cait sidhe dragged in."

Ainsley followed his gaze to two figures on horseback approaching the castle. One rider was short and plump, while the other was taller and thinner. Ainsley squinted to make them out. The taller rider urged his horse into a run, and as he neared, Ainsley was finally able to recognize him. She took off into a sprint, her mind screaming at her that it wasn't real, couldn't be real, but her heart arguing that, with everything that had happened to her so far, why should she have reason to doubt?

The rider pulled the horse up short and leaped down to the ground, stumbling and then running to meet her. They collided then tumbled into the grass, and Ainsley gazed down into Khade's blue eyes. Tears left streaks in the dust on her face.

"I thought you were dead," she breathed, hugging him close.

He gasped in pain, and she loosened her hold, noticing the bandage across his shoulder. He smiled up at her, his expression tight.

322

"Nah, your cousin's creepy-ass friend took me to Merdi. She's terrifying when she's trying to help."

Ainsley laughed and kissed him, withdrawing a moment later when she realized what she'd done.

A look of horror dawned across her face. "I'm sorry, I didn't mean to—"

"Just shut up," he said and pulled her mouth back down to his.

"Who's gross now?" Rowan's voice shouted from somewhere behind them.

Ainsley giggled against Khade's lips.

THIRTY-THREE

"Lightly stepped a yellow star
To its lofty place,
Loosed the Moon her silver hat
From her lustral face."

—Emily Dickinson

Rowan was trying to ignore the persistent knocking on his bedroom door. He slipped his head under his pillow but the knocking continued.

"Prince Rowan," a voice called from outside. "Sir? Are you up?"

If I were, I'd be strangling you right now, he thought in annoyance, but the voice just kept on.

Rowan sighed, untangling his long limbs from the sheets and smoothing the wrinkles from his baggy nightshirt and pants. He padded to the door in bare feet, rubbing his eyes and attempting to flatten his hair into something that didn't make him appear as though he had recently been struck by lightning.

He wrenched the door open to reveal a small, green-skinned faery with bare twigs extending from his back. Rowan thought he looked like a dyed porcupine. "What?" Rowan snapped at him.

"My apologies, sir," the faery said, bowing, "But the tailor requires your presence, sir."

Rowan rubbed his hands across his face. "What time is it?"

"Nearly noon, sir," the faery replied.

Rowan sighed into his hands. "Seriously? I feel like I just fell asleep."

The faery fidgeted, twigs quivering. "Perhaps it would have been wise to have refrained from such large amounts of faery wine last night, sir?" he suggested.

Rowan lifted an eyebrow at him. Last night — and every night over the past week since Say had been returned to Avyn — had been one long faery revel. The days had been spent restoring the castle to fit Say's taste, and hordes of Seelie fey had returned to help. A bit of glamour — and a fair amount of faery wine — had gone a long way into getting things ready for today.

Say had slipped back into rule like no time had passed at all. Normally, a king or queen would have to prove their right to rule by challenging another, or else being so generally terrifying no one wanted to question them. But Rowan supposed the Seelie fey were so happy to have a ruler other than Zake, a ruler who had already proven herself in the past, that they just accepted her authority, no questions asked.

Today, however, Rowan and Ainsley were to be officially introduced to the Court as a Seelie prince and princess, and Ainsley would be announced as the direct heir to the Seelie throne.

All in all, Rowan would rather have slept.

He sighed. He wasn't getting out of it any time soon. "Okay, lead the way."

The green faery bowed and shuffled off down the hall, glancing back over his shoulder every so often to make sure Rowan was still behind him. Rowan ignored him, choosing instead to take in the scenery of the castle. It had changed drastically in such a short time, but with Seelie fey flocking back to the territory as they were, it wasn't all that surprising. The Seelie wanted the last traces of Zake's memory gone, and if that meant they had to pull together with glamour and some stonework, they didn't mind all that much.

The halls were no longer as dark and shadowy, lit with dust lanterns along the walls, and the floors were laid with green carpets woven with leaves. The Seelie coat of arms had been replaced upon the oak doors, a shield inlaid with butterfly wings and stars. There was still work to be done, Rowan knew, but it was certainly a start, and that had to count for something.

The green faery stopped and rapped on one of the wooden doors. The door opened to reveal a tiny little man with a beard longer than he was tall. He barely came up to Rowan's knees, and the man had to crane his neck to look up at him with pale eyes. His beard was tangled with leaves and twigs and what appeared to be a bird's nest. The tailor ushered Rowan inside and closed the door without addressing the other faery.

"You're late." The man looked Rowan up and down. "Stars above, boy," he said. "What, did you just roll out of bed?" Rowan regarded him with a look, and the man shook his head in resignation and shoved a wad of fabric into Rowan's hands. "Well, I'll just have to remedy that, I suppose. Go put that on."

Rowan slipped behind a curtain and shed his nightclothes before tugging on the formal uniform the tailor had been working on. The little man had been crafting formal clothes all week; for the queen, for Ainsley, for Dekk and Indigo and Khade. Indigo and Ainsley had seemed especially excited, while Khade had generally shared Rowan's view of it. Dekk had only been upset that he was being forced to wear shoes.

Rowan stepped back out into the room to be scrutinized under the tailor's careful eye. The man had to climb onto a rather impressive stepstool just to reach Rowan's shoulder, but he seemed pleased with the outcome. Rowan glanced at his reflection in a mirror leaning against the wall. The tailor had done well, to say the least. The sky blue coat was

327

tailed and embroidered with silver around the sleeves and hems, and the buttons were cut into small silver stars. The pants were a darker shade of blue, and the boots were silver, knee-high and made from soft leather. Rowan actually looked like a member of the Gentry now, instead of just a tagalong stray.

"Alright then," the tailor said, shooing Rowan out the door. "I have other things to tend to. So out with you." Rowan stepped into the hall, and the door was slammed behind him.

"The pleasure's all mine," he muttered to the door. Fey were scurrying back and forth through the halls, making final preparations for the event that would be starting in a few minutes, and Rowan had a strong feeling it would last well into the night.

He wound his way through faery servants and guards until he found himself standing outside the throne room. Indigo was already there, flanked by two guards at either side of the door, and Rowan's breath caught at the sight of her. She was gorgeous, dressed in a brilliantly red gown, with a skirt full of ruching and ruffles that trailed the stone floor behind her. The entire bodice was made from nothing but roses and lace that allowed her skin to show through. Black feathers had been woven into her hair.

"You look beautiful," Rowan said quietly.

"I'm sure," Indigo replied, looking displeased. "You look nice too, but you're late. And what happened to your hair?"

Rowan could hear voices on the other side of the door and grimaced. "I was woken up by a green hedgehog. Doesn't that count for something?"

Indigo sighed and rolled her eyes. "Come here." She grabbed his face and pulled him down to her, running her fingers through his hair. A ripple of glamour pulsed around her, and she let him go, satisfied and smirking. "What would you do without me?"

"Look like the aforementioned hedgehog," he replied, holding his arm out for her to take. She slapped at him lightly before wrapping her hand around his arm.

"I can only do so much."

He laughed, and the guards pulled the doors open.

The throne room lay before them, crowded by fey of all kinds on either side of a long aisle that was carpeted by the same green as the halls. The room was bright and open, sunlight streaming in through glassless windows, the whole space smelling of spring and life, even in autumn as it was. All around, fey with antlers and leafy faces and flowers for hair looked on as Rowan and Indigo stood framed in the doorway.

Say stood at the front of the room, in front of a throne formed by branches. Another similar throne sat just to the right of it. The queen had been restored to her former glory, gowned in deep purple and silver with a glittering circlet upon her brow. She smiled at Rowan as she spoke.

"Officially presenting my nephew, Prince Rowan of Skyline, and his consort, Lady Indigo."

Rowan took a deep breath and felt Indie's hand tighten around his arm. "Don't trip me," she warned, and he found himself smiling as they crossed the room to where Say stood waiting. They turned to face the crowd when they reached the front, and Rowan spotted Dekk and Khade almost immediately, standing in the front among the fey. Dekk was dressed in red, like his sister, though his pants were black, and he had found some way to ditch his shoes. Khade was dressed in soft tones of green and silver, with one arm still in a sling, looking entirely out of place among all the fey behind him. Townsley and Khade's mother stood nearby, and while Townsley seemed to blend in with the fey — or at least seemed to be comfortable among them — Khade's mother was incredibly pale, eyes darting around as if in a terrified trance. Rowan couldn't really blame her. She and Townsley had shown up a few days ago, and she'd had trouble taking everything in. She was currently gripping her son's uninjured arm as though she was afraid he'd vanish again.

Rowan turned to Say, and she nodded, facing the crowd again.

"Presenting my granddaughter and the future Queen of Seelie, Princess Ainsley of Avyn."

The doors opened once more to reveal someone Rowan almost didn't recognize. It was Ainsley but not like he had ever seen her before. Her white-blonde hair curled down her back, tied out of her face with bits of twine. A diamond and silver crown sat upon her head. Her gown was fluffy and white, with a corset and sleeves that laced down the sides.

She wore black gloves that sparkled with silver glitter, as if the night sky had been woven into the fabric. She looked like true royalty.

A familiar face was peeking out from beneath the curtain of her hair, his own hair disheveled and his wings beating cheerfully, playing hide-and-seek with the fey that stood around the room.

Wickertwig, Rowan thought, shaking his head with a smile.

Ainsley made her way across the room to stand in front of the throne on Say's other side. And when she turned to face the crowd of faeries watching with intense eyes, the entire gathering burst into elated cacophony.

Once the faery wine started going around, things only got wilder.

***

By the time night fell, the revel of all revels was well underway. Dust lanterns were lit along the walls, and torches cast flickering shadows over the room from atop ornate silver posts. Faery musicians played wild songs, led by the newest Court Violinist, Yveena, of course. Ainsley had been surprised to see her alive, but the cait sidhe merely replied that she had a few more lives saved up in case of emergency. She was mostly only displeased by the fact that her shirt had been ruined with bloodstains.

A section of floor had been cleared away for dancing, and Rowan watched as Townsley and Say swayed around it, having cleared off the other dancers by merely showing up. They looked strange together, he an aged human and she an ageless star, and Rowan wondered if Ainsley knew she and Khade could wind up like that one day, one of them leaving the other behind to mortality.

Rowan wasn't sure, but he figured being a prince meant he could step in and share the floor too. He faced Indigo and bowed.

"May I?" he asked.

She took his hand. "Step on my feet, and I'll murder you in front of everyone," she warned, her expression wry.

He laughed and led her onto the floor, glimpsing Khade take Ainsley's hand and follow them. So he'd finally gotten the nerve to ask. He seemed to have been building it over the past week, ever since the two of them had had an impromptu make out session on the castle grounds. That, and Dekk had proudly told anyone he'd come across that the princess's human friend had deliriously professed his love for her after a case of serious blood loss.

Indigo must have seen the look on Rowan's face. "What's so amusing?" she asked in the middle of a twirl. Rowan shook his head, motioning over his shoulder. Indie peered around him and smiled. "Well, I underestimated him. I thought it would take much more time than that."

Rowan pulled Indigo close, breathing in the scent of roses and woods. "I think it's been a long time coming."

Indie sighed. "I think a lot of things have," she said.

"I can live with that," Rowan said, smiling.

A guard from outside the room paced onto the dance floor, approaching Say with a bow and saying something quietly to her. Indigo halted in their dance, and Rowan stopped to see what was going on. The queen's face looked grim, and she nodded to the guard, who turned and left the room. Say motioned for Ainsley to join her as she approached her throne and sat down, and Ainsley took the throne next to her, wearing a puzzled expression.

Rowan and Indigo shared a look and went to ask Say what had happened, but by the time they reached the thrones, a harsh breeze spiraled through the room, dousing torches and causing lanterns to flicker. A dark figure waltzed down the carpet toward Say and the others, and Rowan instinctively shifted Indigo to his side. He could see Khade standing just behind Ainsley's throne, while Townsley stood off to the side, well aware of where his place was within this world. Several Unseelie soldiers stood in the throne room doorway.

The fey woman now stood before them. Her long, jet black hair stirred in the breeze she had made, and there were no whites to her black eyes. Her lips were the color of dark blood, and her skin was as pale as snow. The corset she wore was made of strips of bleached bone, and her skirt was formed by millions of black feathers. A white crown rested upon her head. She was gorgeous, but not in a nice way. Behind her stood a black-haired faery boy, his green eyes darting around the crowd, never still. Rowan thought he looked rather frightened.

"Well, this is such a nice gathering," the fey woman said, looking like she meant the exact opposite. "I have been throwing quite the ball myself, in order to welcome our new queen. So I felt as though I should congratulate you on your return, Lady Saydie. And look at the sweet little pet princess, a mixed-breed human Seelie star. What a combination, really."

Ainsley's cheeks reddened, but she kept her head high, and Say appeared to be holding her tongue.

Rowan glared at the fey woman. "Lady Morag," he ground out, attempting politeness. He had met her once or twice before when he was younger, and she had been visiting the Seelie territories. She was true Unseelie through and through.

She turned to regard him with shining eyes. "Hmm, I remember you. It's 'queen', now, actually, with your uncle out of the picture. May he rest in pieces."

"What is it you need within Seelie lands?" Say asked, a dangerous tone underlying her words. "Or have you come only to see for yourself your rivals, to test our weaknesses?"

"You wound me," Morag said, holding a hand to her chest. "I prefer to think of it in different terms. I merely came to check up on the competition. You can't blame me, surely?"

"You are not welcome here," Rowan said evenly. "And neither are your subjects." He cut a glare toward the faery boy behind her, and the boy shifted his eyes to the floor.

Morag's eyes narrowed. "Yet you keep company with Unseelie, regardless," she pointed out, glancing knowingly at Indigo.

"She is none of your concern," Say cut in, before Rowan could tell the Unseelie Queen what he thought of her. "I believe it is time to take your entourage and leave."

Morag sniffed. "Very well, then," she said, dropping into a mocking curtsy. "Farewell, your majesties." She cast a last scowl at

Ainsley and turned to glide back across the room. Her faery boy followed reluctantly. The Seelie revel started up once again as soon as the doors closed behind the queen.

"Well, at least she's open with her dislike of us," Dekk said, appearing next to Indigo. "I think we're lower than scum, in her opinion."

"We're Unseelie traitors, as far as she's concerned, I'm sure," Indigo replied.

"Yeah, well, I'm sure we can find a way to remedy that," he said, and a shrewd grin arched across his face.

Indigo sighed. "Can't you just go spike the punch or something, and stay away from people who would enjoy seeing you dead?"

"Nah, too easy."

"Do you think she'll be a threat?" Rowan asked Say.

Say shook her head. "No, I think she was simply curious. I doubt she will become bored anytime soon. She is well aware we will soon become a force to be reckoned with. Besides, she is no longer only a regent of her Court. She will be quite entertained for some time with the task of proving her right as queen and gaining loyalty from her Court." Say smiled up at him. "You need not worry. Enjoy the day. You've certainly earned the right to it."

Rowan smiled back, and then Indigo was tugging him away into a corner. And everything else disappeared when her lips met his.

EPILOGUE

"There you are. I've been looking for you for the past twenty minutes."

Ainsley didn't turn to acknowledge Khade's presence, but she thought she knew why he had come to find her. "Are you leaving now?" she asked.

"Before my mom has a nervous breakdown," he said, coming forward to lean over the balcony beside her. "But I'll be back. Every chance I get. And once I'm done with high school, I don't plan on ever leaving this place again. Not as long as you're here."

Ainsley watched the stars glitter brilliantly above in the black sky, and she wondered if they were watching the tiny souls below them. She tore her eyes away and stared into Khade's. "Are you sure about that?" she asked.

Khade shrugged. "How long have we been neighbors and best friends? I don't even remember anymore. I just know I liked you when I met you."

"That's funny," Ainsley said. "Because I remember hating you when we met."

Khade laughed. "That, I do remember. But you've gotta give me points for determination, at least."

Ainsley chewed her bottom lip. "I'll think about it," she said, a little surprised at her shameless flirting.

"But really," Khade said. "My mom's going to have a nervous breakdown if I don't get her out of here. Your grandmother arranged for us to have an entourage to take us back, so we're going in style. Mom keeps getting approached by satyrs, and she nearly fell over herself when something short and hairy touched her ankle. Personally, I'm not even sure the thing had eyes, it was so furry."

Ainsley chuckled. "Yeah, I'm thinking it'll take a while before I stop being startled by everything around here. I swear I saw a girl with spider legs earlier."

Khade made a face. "I'll be sure to avoid that." He leaned forward and kissed her. It didn't last nearly long enough, and then he was walking away. She turned back to the sky, lost in thought and feeling a bit overwhelmed by everything she'd gotten herself into.

Soft footsteps sounded behind her, and she turned, hoping Khade had come back. She deflated when she spotted Townsley. "Oh, hey," she said.

He came up to where she stood and leaned backwards against the balcony railing. "Well, no need to be so cheerful when you see your old granddad."

She sighed. "Sorry. I just thought you were someone else."

"Hmm, yeah, I passed your boyfriend on the way. He seemed a little to be down about something too. You two get into a fight?"

"He's not my boyfriend," Ainsley said.

Townsley snorted. "Give me a little more credit. I know how that boy's been looking at you for years. It's not my fault you only just noticed it." He twisted around, bracing himself on his elbows. "So spill it. What happened?"

Ainsley felt her eyes burn, but she held back the tears, determined not to let her grandfather see her cry. "He has to leave. He belongs on the human side."

"And why is that?" Townsley asked.

Ainsley blew out a deep breath. "He's human."

"So are you," he pointed out. "At least partly. Where do you belong?"

338

Ainsley stared at him, silent for a moment. Where did she belong? She had never felt quite right growing up in the human world. She hadn't been unhappy, just not completely…right. It had been as though a tiny part of her was missing. She just hadn't been aware of how large that tiny part had been. Here, she felt something, some sort of connection that linked her with everything else, with everyone else. Sure, she had spent a lot of time running for her life — and for the lives of a lot of other people as well, for that matter — but she had felt *right* here. And how could she turn her back on the people she had met so far, the creatures she had bonded with? She had a real, whole family here. She had answers here. How could she go back to the life she had lived before, back to plain old routine and days without the thrill of magic and stardust?

"Here," she said at last, feeling surer of herself than she had felt in a long time. "I belong here. Khade said he would come back. I've waited this long to meet my grandmother. I guess waiting a little while longer for him shouldn't be too terribly unbearable." Townsley gave her a look. "You know I only kept all of this a secret because I wanted to protect you. Right?"

Ainsley nodded. "I know." She cast him a sideways glance. "But in the future, if you don't want me being led away by a pixie to a land filled with god-complex stars and flesh-eating mermaids, you might want to tell me exactly why you're keeping it a secret."

He laughed and wrapped an arm around her shoulders, hugging her close. "You are undeniably Say's granddaughter. Of that, I can be certain. Quite a lot of your mother and father too, come to mention it."

"Really?" she asked. "Will you tell me what they were like one day?"

"I don't see why not. Besides, if I don't do it, Say will, and she's always been full of embellishment when it comes to telling stories. And I'm fairly certain Merdi intends to give me grief to no end over the fact that I've kept things from you for this long."

"Merdi intends to give everyone grief to no end," Ainsley said.

"I'm sure she does," he muttered.

"She threatened Rowan with a spoon once."

Townsley snorted. "I can believe that as well. I never really got to know Rowan that well, since he and his parents lived in Skyline, but I've gotten the recent impression that the boy can be a bit hotheaded at times."

"Yeah, that's why Indigo sticks around," Ainsley said. "To keep him and Dekk in line."

"Well, that one just scares me," he said. "He always looks like he's up to something."

"Because he is." Ainsley grinned and shook her head. "You get kind of used to him after a while. He's mostly harmless."

"Mostly?"

Ainsley ignored him. "So where do you belong? You asked me, now it's your turn."

Townsley smiled down at her. "Right here, with you and your grandmother. It's where I've always belonged and where I always will. Besides, fellow humans just aren't as interesting as the fey. People all look so much alike. Faeries, though—" he shrugged "—you just can never tell which ones want to eat you and which ones only *look* like they want to eat you."

"That's a very important thing to be aware of," Ainsley said jokingly.

"Oh, yes, laugh now," he returned. "Laugh yourself right onto a goblin's campfire spit."

"There you guys are," Rowan's voice said from the doorway. "We were beginning to wonder if something had eaten you."

Ainsley and Townsley exchanged a glance and burst into laughter.

Rowan regarded them in confusion. "I was being serious," he said.

Ainsley paced up to him. "That's your problem, always so serious."

"I'll keep that in mind," he said, arching an eyebrow. "Now come on. Your subjects await you," he added, giving her a mocking bow before turning to leave.

She smiled at the thought. *Your subjects. My subjects,* she mused. *And my family too.*

"Rowan, wait up!" she called, running after him. She caught up to where he had stopped in the hallway and looped her arm around his.

He stared down at her. "What are you doing?"

Ainsley looked up at him with a smile. "I just found you guys. I don't plan on letting go for a while."

Rowan merely smiled back.

Made in the USA
Coppell, TX
22 December 2021

69802688R00193